A
BIRD
WILL SOAR

A BIRD WILL SOAR

ALISON GREEN MYERS

DUTTON CHILDREN'S BOOKS

Dutton Children's Books
An imprint of Penguin Random House LLC, New York

First published in the United States of America by Dutton Children's Books,
an imprint of Penguin Random House LLC, 2021

Visit us online at penguinrandomhouse.com.

Library of Congress Cataloging-in-Publication Data is available.

Printed in Canada

ISBN 9780593325674

1 3 5 7 9 10 8 6 4 2

FRI
Design by Anna Booth
Text set in Adobe Caslon Pro

To Will, who knows just what kinds of birds to favorite, and to Garry, who shares quiet thinking time with me.

CHAPTER ONE

Mysteries

The wonder of things—
of wings
of sky
of Mother Nature's secrets
packed inside
scattered seeds.

THE WORLD IS FILLED WITH MYSTERIES.

Clues, everywhere—cracked shells, forgotten feathers, deep prints left in soft soil.

Axel gathers clues wherever he goes. From the four walls of his bedroom to the rushing creek and deer-spotted trails tucked behind his house, he wanders and wonders.

Axel is never truly alone in the woods, even though he feels completely alone with his thoughts here. He brings with him a partner to gather clues. An exceptional partner, really.

Ray.

Ray, whose nose picks up things Axel's eyes can't see. Ray, whose ears perk to the sounds of songs invisible to Axel. Yes, Ray is an excellent partner for walking in the woods. And best of all, Ray doesn't talk. Doesn't try to interrupt the important observations or thinking time that the woods offer.

And the nest, of course, is a favorite place to stop and gather clues. To listen. To watch. To wait.

Today, Ray's whole body wiggles with excitement when the two approach the nest. Axel knows just how his best friend feels. His insides come alive at the sight, too. Five feet wide and four feet deep, raggedy with sticks and moss and lichen, the eagles' nest is squished into a crook in the branches of a massive pine located along the same creek that rushes past Axel's home. As though this tree was grown, in this very special way, just to host this family.

Listen! There's a rush of movement inside. An important clue. When a cry comes from high inside the nest, shrill and lightning quick, Ray bounces on his back legs. There is no response to the cry. No deeper, longer hush from an adult bird to its baby.

"I wonder where the parents are today," Axel whispers. Most days, after a cry, there is an adult eagle who responds. Axel knows that sound too. Some days, Axel and Ray are lucky to see an adult coming or going from the nest. Comes with food or goes for more, that is.

But not today. Today, it is just earth, and sky, and the cries from the nest.

Ray settles and Axel thinks. Thinks about the parents coming and going. Thinks about the baby or babies inside the nest. That's another mystery to solve: not just where are those parents . . .

But how many babies could there be?

Axel can't see into the nest. He can only hear—can only gather clues in this way from outside and down below. He has a guess about the number of babies—"Eaglets," he would say if asked. He's almost certain, even if he can't prove it just yet.

Ray leans into Axel, his short hair pressed soft against

Axel's leg. He stays quiet, though. He knows Axel likes thinking time and thinking spots. The woods being a favorite thinking place.

"Come," Axel says after a long while—after his listening, watching, and waiting for clues. Today's trip into the forest is a thinking day, not a solving day. Some mysteries can be solved quickly. Some mysteries go on for a long time. The best Axel can do is show up and wonder. The answers will come eventually.

Come, Ray says in his own way to Axel, bounding ahead of him, zigzagging through the woods on the paths that they've created, boy and best friend. He knows which knotty roots to leap over, where to turn, and where to pick up speed.

Axel likes to run too. This time for the fun of following his friend away from the thick green plant life, away from the nest and the missing eagle parents, across an imaginary line between forest and home.

Home. The farmhouse, the cottage, the barn, the fence.

Home. Where Ray finds his favorite people.

Home. Where Axel, just for a moment, wonders, *Where are those parents?* The question doesn't fill his brain long because, just as they emerge from the woods, there in the clearing, Axel sees Byrd in her flower garden.

Axel doesn't race to his mom the way Ray races to one of his favorite people.

It's okay to love someone so much that all you need to do

is think of them, not cover them in sloppy kisses the way the old pointer likes to cover the man who rescued him as a pup.

Ray's up on his hind legs, one brown paw on each of George's shoulders, placing stinky dog-breath licks onto George's white beard.

George doesn't correct him for jumping. Maybe because he knows that Ray won't listen? Or maybe because this is one of George's favorite parts of the day? The time when Axel and Ray first come from the woods. When Axel and Ray come home.

"If you have ever gone into the woods with me . . ." George says.

Words from one of George's poems. Actually, not a poem he wrote, just a poem he's gathered.

A fact about George: He loves to repeat poems. He loves to gather words the way Axel loves to gather clues, the way Ray loves to chase squirrels, the way Byrd loves her flowers, and Emmett loves his fancy foods.

George says you repeat the words so that the poem sticks. George says, that way, you always have the poem in your heart. But for Axel, hearing these words, George's words, is like comfort on repeat. He knows that George will show up when he and Ray cross from woods to clearing. He knows that George will say, *"If you have ever gone into the woods with me . . ."* He knows that Ray will cover George in kisses. He knows this because it isn't a mystery at all; it's the comfort of George.

George knows the best poems, like this one about thinking time in the woods, and others too, like the one about the golden eagle soaring above the mountains in the morning. Axel likes to imagine peeking underneath George's white hair, underneath the flesh and bone, and into the pulsing brain of George M. Flores.

How those words must snap along the synapses. *Go! Repeat! Words!*

We all have brains. The paths they make are as unique as feathers. Try to match any two, look up close, really closely, no two feathers are the same, and neither are two brains.

George's brain has always fascinated Axel. George's things include loving words, loving family, loving nature, and some stuff about being a lawyer. The last part is easy to forget when the other stuff matters most.

"Did you see the nest today?" George asks, like he does every day.

Axel sticks to the plan too. "Of course," he says. "Two cries. No adults."

Ray holds his gaze on the woods. Like he'd be happy to lead George back if he wants. Like he knows just where to find the nest, or any other clues his George needs to see.

"I think there are two babies this year," Axel says, the shrill calls still fresh in his mind. "Do you think there are two?"

"I suspect if I tell you, then you won't stay curious," George says. "And, really, who wants to spend time with someone uncurious?"

Axel doesn't have this fear for himself. He has other fears, but of being uncurious . . . impossible.

"I would still wonder about other things," Axel says, looking from the dense forest to his mom in the garden.

"Yes, but would you still go to the nest? Would you listen as intensely if I said how many babies I think there are?" George asks.

Axel is a good listener. Great, actually. George knows this; he's just testing, the way George does.

Axel claps his hands. "You just said 'babies,'" he says, presenting this clue back to George.

George smiles.

Axel's been observing the nest for many years. Back when George would walk him out to the water, then wait and watch for clues. Back when Axel's dad would too.

Axel has observed many pairs of eagle babies come from that nest. Once there were three, and Byrd said that was a miracle. One year there were no babies, and no one had to tell Axel what that was.

This year, though, Axel heard a hearty flutter of activity. He knows, deep in his bones, this year there are two. He wasn't certain before, but he is now. And, after all, George said "babies," didn't he? An important clue. A mystery solved.

Some mysteries can be solved like Ray's licks, quick and in your face.

Some mysteries are harder. Ones like missing parents.

The question comes back into Axel's mind. *Where are those parents?* It's stuck inside his brain, on repeat, the same loop. *Parents? Parent?* Like George's words or Ray's wags.

Axel can't solve this mystery today, not for the eaglets, and not for himself.

CHAPTER TWO

State Birds

The state bird of Pennsylvania is the ruffed grouse,
shaped like the splotch of white on Ray's brown chest,
a hardy bird made to survive deep winters.

The state bird of New York is the eastern bluebird,
a songbird unable to stick out deep colds,
the bird escapes south to feast.

(It should be noted, the eastern bluebird is among the first to
    return home each spring. Rushes the season, sometimes,
    arrives before the last of the snow melts. Races back,
    though it doesn't have the thick down of its neighbor, the
    well-armored talons of the grouse. It always comes back.)

It always comes back.

(Also of note, about ruffed grouse and eastern bluebird,
about Pennsylvania and New York,
Axel is in one,
his father feasts in the other.)

AFTER SCHOOL, and time with Ray, and George's poems, Axel makes his way to his favorite perch: the bay window that looks out over the twist of the creek.

Favorite perch.

Favorite book.

Favorite thinking spot in his whole house.

Everyone should have a favorite thinking spot. A place where thoughts flow like the creek outside Axel's window.

The window itself is an odd thing in the house, which makes it an even better thinking spot.

The window runs from the molding at the top all the way down to an inch from the wood floor. Made from a series of farmhouse windows, like his father got a whole house's worth of mismatched windows for free and decided to use them all in one place when he was building this home. All in one place. Here. This window, made of ten smaller windows, is the only place where Axel and Byrd can look outside from inside.

It's one of the many mysteries of his house that Axel wants to know more about. Why did Frank build it like this? Why, in a first floor that's only one big room, have only one place to look out? Why not one in each bedroom on the second floor? Is it even legal not to have windows in a bedroom? What if there were a fire? What if someone had to escape?

This is the kind of mystery that isn't easy to solve. The questions could go unanswered for days, years, forever.

Byrd doesn't seem bothered by the fact that only one wall has windows. She makes the most of what she has, filling the window nook with houseplants of all kinds, a bonsai weeping willow, a towering ficus with drooping fronds, a fiddle-leaf fig. There's a full staghorn fern that grows from the wall. It looks just like its name suggests, like a bright green buck has sprouted horns from the planter. Like the plant could come to life at any moment and wonder what he's doing in a place like this, stuck to a wall, near a boy reading about birds.

The fiddle fig presses against the other wall in the nook, just across from the fern. The fig is as tall as Axel, while some plants in the space are as tiny as eggs. Though, soon enough, Axel knows, with Byrd's attention, and the sunlight from the window, those nesting plants will grow up too.

In his thinking spot today, Axel bends his legs the way he likes, and leans full over his A. P. Brown's *Collection of North American Birds*. It isn't the first time he's read the book in this spot. Or even the hundredth. He lets the book take his mind on an alphabetic ride through bird names, bird songs, and bird predictability.

And then, almost as predictably as the book, Byrd bursts

through their front door. Maybe in a bigger house this blast would be mistakable. But not here, not in the cottage that Byrd and Axel call home.

Byrd isn't subtle in her movements. Not today, not ever. There are tears on good days and bad, kicked over clay pots, more times than Axel can count, and loud, loud laughter. She isn't afraid to let her whole body show just how her heart is feeling inside.

Though she is, even with all her out-loudness, at times, a complete mystery.

Today she rips her garden gloves from her hands, whips them at the kitchen island, and screams like she can't stand the very sight of them.

Byrd shifts from her naughty gloves to Axel in his thinking spot.

"Did you say something?" he asks. Sometimes his mind moves away from the sounds of Byrd so he can focus on the sights of her.

"There was a snake," Byrd says, her voice still high like a scream.

There's always a snake in Byrd's garden. Always.

In late spring, as the days grow longer and warmer, the snakes will all slither back to their thinking spots. They're creatures of habit, after all. They like what they like, and go where they know they can find food and warmth. So it isn't at all surprising, at least to Axel, that Byrd's flower beds filled with slugs and sunlight are happy spots for the garter snakes.

Axel appreciates the predictability of them. Byrd doesn't share this logic.

Though Byrd, too, is a creature of habit sometimes. Times like when a snake is in her garden and she acts surprised. Her habit, though flawed, is predictable.

"You should favorite roadrunners," Axel says.

"I don't have favorites," Byrd says. The panic settling out of her voice. "Except for you."

Caw. "Everyone has a favorite bird. Or at least they should," Axel reminds his mother. "And roadrunners kill snakes."

"I'll take it under advisement," Byrd says. She begins another one of her rituals, the garden-wear disrobing. Predictable in the order, but a mystery where things will end up.

Garden shoes off.

One here.

One there.

Hat on the back of that chair.

But the long-sleeve button-up, the one she always wears over her regular clothes. That one item hangs in the same spot, day-end to day-beginning.

It's the oversized one, a very light blue, almost like today's sky. The one with Frank's initials stitched onto the front chest pocket. She keeps it loose, unbuttoned. Sleeves rolled, though still long enough to protect her white arms from the sun.

Axel can smell the manure from her enriched soil as she takes it off. The shirt and the scent linger.

Byrd slips out of the shirt, lays the collar over the hook on the back of the door, and runs a hand down it.

With the last of Byrd's busy movements, Axel returns to his book. A real masterpiece, as thick as a brick and packed with noteworthy bird facts.

He's rereading the passage on kestrels and their perfect hunting groups when Byrd interrupts. "I've decided on my bird," she says. She waits for him to look away from the page. "The pigeon," she says, flopping down on the couch near him.

Caw. The scent that pops off of her is almost as putrid as her answer. "Pigeon?" Axel says in disgust.

Byrd's joked about this before. Axel's very own mother, a pigeon lover—or even liker . . . Absurd!

"Who would ever favorite a pigeon when there are arctic terns in the world . . . and great blue herons . . . and red-tailed hawks . . . and peregrine falcons . . . and golden eagles . . . and . . ."

"You . . . asked . . . about . . . my . . . favorite . . . bird," Byrd says slowly. Like there's a clue in these words. Like Axel better pay attention to a hidden message. Like there's a mystery to solve.

But Axel isn't up for a mystery right now; he'd rather point out that technically he did not "ask" about her favorite bird, he only *suggested* what her favorite bird should be. A roadrunner who kills snakes.

As though Byrd can read his very mind, she catches Axel, like snake to mouse, in her gaze. "Pigeons can always find home," she says. And before he can argue, adds, "Pigeons recognize kindness in others . . . Pigeons can do backflips."

Caw. Axel drops his head back to his book. Byrd knew not a wisp of those facts until he shared them with her. He does not see the point in bringing any of those pigeony things up when he could be reading more about kestrels. Finer birds, obviously.

"They taught themselves to ride the subway," Byrd continues. "They—"

"You know the only good thing about pigeons?" Axel interrupts this time. "Pigeons are a peregrine falcon's favorite meal."

Now, that's a juicy fact. But is it juicy enough to keep Byrd quiet? To let Axel get back to his own thoughts?

"What is it about those poor birds that makes you hate them so? You love all animals," Byrd says. "Even snakes. Why can't you love an animal that's mastered the art of adaptation?"

This is a test.

A Byrd mystery.

Axel wants no part. Byrd can solve it on her own.

Byrd presses flat palm to Axel's round shoulder. There's comfort to her touch. Byrd's not made of air-filled bones. Neither is Axel.

"I want you to have wings, Axel . . . I want you to soar."

"That's impossible," Axel says.

It's Byrd who looks away first, but it's Axel who feels her worry.

So he flips in his big, bird-filled book. The rush of pages fans against his thumb.

L-M-N-O—Osprey.

"What about an osprey?" he asks. "As your favorite? 'The osprey mom is the finest of all aves. Will protect her babies no matter the situation.'"

Byrd turns back to her son. Lets his words settle like the soil in her flower beds. Deep down and full of potential.

"Osprey, you say?"

Axel nods.

"Sounds like a lovely bird. But can she do backflips?"

CHAPTER THREE

Soaring

Rules for *soaring*
include *recognizing*
and *finding*
and *home*
and . . . *backflips?*

ON SATURDAYS Axel keeps his time much like on school days: there is still waking up, and a buttervore breakfast, and thinking time at his window, and walks with Ray, and dinner with Emmett and George and Aunt Nancy. And, best of all, every other Saturday is his time in the woods with Daniel Berrios.

Rain or shine. Daniel shows up.

Now, Byrd tried to make this a rule. She tried to make it a thing. She wanted to call it Friendship Club Saturday. But that's just ridiculous because Axel already has a Friendship Club at school, and the time with Daniel every other Saturday is not the same.

First, there is no Ms. Dale with her green hair and her games and the way she makes everyone say what they mean. Sometimes it's a good thing to take a break from all that, but it does get tricky when surrounded by people who don't always say what they mean.

Another key difference: it is just Daniel and Axel on Saturdays, not everyone else in Friendship Club. That's great, too. To be honest.

Friendship Club is part of Fairview's W.I.N. time. What I Need. The club isn't only for autistic kids or anxious kids or quiet kids. It is for anyone who needs Friendship Club and that makes it pretty great, too. To be honest.

During Friendship Club, Axel and Daniel, and the other students, play a lot of board games, and Ms. Dale repeats the rules, even if some kids say that they know them. She also makes sure they follow the rules, which is especially good because sometimes people say they know the rules of a game, but *knowing* them and *following* them are two very different things. Some of the games are like Apples to Apples and Shadows in the Forest. Both are excellent games. There are others that aren't board games—more like "Ms. Dale Stuff," where she asks big, mysterious questions, like "How do you find good friends?"

An answer: To find good friends, so much comes from what's inside. And that isn't as simple as peeking into someone's brain to see what's going on. More like looking at what actions can show about their insides from the outside. It's like trying to guess the temperature by looking out from the big window at Axel's house. The sun can be up, but that won't tell you what's really happening. Not like observing birds soaring, or the creek rushing, or clouds chasing. Actions speak louder than words, which is not a saying that George ever uses.

Axel can tell that Daniel is a good friend without ever peeking inside his brain. On the outside Daniel has brown skin, brown hair, hazel eyes, long fingers, bitten-down fingernails, and he's very short, and strong. He has one eyebrow that he can raise much higher than the other—much, much higher. Which is especially helpful when Daniel wants to make Axel laugh from across a quiet room.

On the outside, Daniel's got a mom and a dad and five sisters. *Five.*

And both his mom and his dad come to all the things that happen at school. Back-to-school night, and everything. Daniel also has a huge house, even bigger than Emmett and George's. At least six or seven times as big as Axel's house. Not that Axel's ever been inside it, but he drives past it on the way to school each morning with Byrd. Daniel's sisters are always outside on the front porch dancing or singing or playing whenever they go past.

This is all on the outside. Also on the outside, Daniel doesn't ever seem to worry about things.

But Daniel is Axel's friend, his real friend. So Axel knows that on the inside, Daniel is a lot like him. Daniel worries about all sorts of things, even though people can't always tell that from the outside.

On the outside and the inside, Daniel Berrios is a good friend, a great friend, actually—and not just because he checks all the boxes on Ms. Dale's friendship chart. Because he and Axel laugh together. Because he and Axel explore together. Because he and Axel imagine together. Because he and Axel can tell each other true things. Because he lets Axel be Axel. Because he says what he means. Because Daniel is fun.

So, yeah, every-other-Saturdays have become awesome because they are filled with Daniel Berrios time. It started back when Frank stopped coming on his every-other-Saturdays.

Daniel's mom drives Daniel out to Axel's house, away from the downtown, where they live, away from their busy street and their large house and all of those sisters. She pulls down Axel's long driveway, pulls all the way up to the gate in front of Axel's house. Daniel's mom stays. Sometimes Ms. Berrios and Byrd talk. Sometimes, when it is nice outside, she sits at the picnic table near the creek and reads. Sometimes Emmett will invite Ms. Berrios onto the porch for tea. Sometimes she sits in the car and stares at her phone.

The most important fact: Ms. Berrios doesn't leave. It can get awkward when it's time for someone to go and they can't because their ride isn't there. Not that this would happen with Daniel, because their time together, his and Axel's, seems to go so quickly. It is usually Ms. Berrios who says that it's time to go. Not any other way.

On those every-other-Saturdays, Axel and Daniel play Pokémon in the woods.

Not Pokémon cards or a Pokémon video game.

They play a game that they invented.

On this particular every-other-Saturday, Axel is already deep into imagining today's Pokémon game when he hears the rumble of tires on gravel, all the way down the driveway. Ray starts bouncing and barking up on his porch. It doesn't take long before a vehicle appears. But it isn't Ms. Berrios's shiny silver one. It's a blue truck.

Axel's insides tense, like someone has flipped a switch from off to on in the worry part of his brain.

Things settle down inside him when Daniel pops out of the truck. "Hey, Axel," he says. "This is my grandpa's truck. I get to ride in the front!"

Axel's brain is not on the truck, though; it is on the driver, who isn't Ms. Berrios. The questions build on each other with every step Daniel takes toward Axel. Every step he takes away from his grandpa's truck.

Axel wonders about Daniel's mom and where she is. He wonders about the day, and if this will be the first time in the history of their every-other-Saturdays that Axel gets bored of Daniel and Daniel's grandpa isn't around to drive Daniel away. Will Daniel still want to be friends if Axel leaves him outside alone?

As though Ray hears Axel's thoughts from across the driveway, he leaps off of Emmett and George's porch and comes to investigate. He sniffs at one of the truck's tires. Sniffs another. Then pees on a third before coming to rest at Axel's feet.

"Oh, gross," Daniel says. "Ray!"

But Ray pays no mind to Daniel. He presses his weight against Axel's bare leg.

Byrd has left her spot in the garden, already slipped off her gloves, and gone to Daniel's grandpa with hellos.

"You ready?" Daniel asks, but Axel is stuck in those rushing questions of how and where and when, so Axel doesn't hear his friend.

"Axel," Daniel says, kicking at one of the small rocks that make up Axel's long driveway.

Byrd crosses from one side of the truck to the other. Gives Daniel a quick hello, then presses a hand to Axel's shoulder. "Mr. Berrios is staying," she says. "I'm going to show him where the hammock is."

"Of course he's staying," Daniel says. "That's what Axel likes. Me too."

Daniel Berrios is an excellent friend.

Ray bolts after the plan is made. It seems at first that Ray might leave Axel and Daniel, help Byrd point out the hammock to Mr. Berrios, but no, that's not what he's up to, because after he zags one way, he zigs off to the right.

The left would take him past Byrd's garden shed, and the picnic table, and the tall, tall pines, and the hammock near the creek. But Ray goes right, which takes him past George and Emmett's house, through the wide open field, and to the woods.

"We better catch up," Daniel says. Daniel spreads his arms wide as he runs, like he might be a bird, a bird soaring in the sky, not a kid running across an open field.

Axel does the same, and it feels good. The wind dragging the whole way down his arms, across his open chest, over his face and into his hair. Axel is a good runner. It isn't hard for him to catch up to Daniel, but Ray is another story.

Sometimes Ray forgets to stay with his humans and goes off on unexpected adventures, leading to much worry.

"Come," Axel calls. "Come!" When he yells a third time and Ray doesn't listen, Axel kicks his running into high gear and goes into the woods after him. It feels like an entrance, going from open field to forest right here. The way the branches bend overhead and bright sunlight turns to pinpoint rays of light. The way the sound dampens from open space to tree-lined paths. From blue skies to golds and greens and browns.

By the time Daniel catches up, Axel and Ray are out of breath, but they are together in one bald patch of earth where the light beams inside the forest canopy. Where they can make a plan for today's game. Only Daniel's mind is not on Pokémon, not at all. "I think it's weird that you call your mom Byrd and that you act like this is your dog," Daniel says with his hands on his knees, his face scrunched up, looking at Ray.

"I just do," Axel says.

And the conversation could end there. Daniel said what he thinks. Axel said what he knows. Done.

But Ms. Dale's words must work their way into every-other-Saturdays, even if they aren't at Friendship Club. Ms. Dale would say to take the time to clarify, especially with friends. Ms. Dale loves the word *clarify*.

So Axel continues, "George and Emmett like that I take

Ray into the woods. We walk together every day. George and Emmett are old. And I know that Ray is not my dog, but he is my best friend."

"I thought I was your best friend," Daniel says, shooting up from his hunched-over stance. He makes himself as tall as he can, even waves his arms above his head. It's a funny thing to say out loud. And even funnier to say it the way Daniel says it now.

"I guess I am lucky to have two best friends," Axel says.

This makes Daniel's hand drop down but his eyebrow go way, way up. Which of course makes Axel laugh.

"Okay, so you've got two best friends. Me and this guy," Daniel says placing his hands on Ray's round head. "What about the Byrd thing? My mom wouldn't ever—and I mean ever—let me call her . . ." Daniel pauses, looks around the forest like just maybe his mom came today and could be listening. "Donna," he finally says in a whisper.

Axel tries to think back over the moments when Daniel arrived today. He can't remember saying a thing, not one thing to Byrd. "I didn't call her Byrd today," Axel says.

Daniel shakes his head like he can't believe his friend, his best friend, needs so much clarification. "What I meant was, why do you call her Byrd when you talk to her and not, you know, Mom?"

"I've just always called her Byrd. I didn't talk a lot when I was little. And I just never said Mom; I said Byrd, and Byrd is her name. Just like I never said Dad; I said Frank. Other people call him that, so I do too." It makes perfect sense all laid out this way.

But Daniel's eyes grow wide, and not in a funny way. "I didn't know you had a dad," Daniel says.

Sometimes you forget to tell best friends everything. Ray is the best friend who knows about Axel's dad and all of the things that happened before his dad left, and all of the times that his dad didn't show up. Daniel is the best friend who has only known Axel since Friendship Club started last year at school. And knows Axel for Pokémon battles in the woods, and playing games with Ms. Dale, and eating strawberry ice pops at the picnic table on hot days, and making silly faces, and being kind.

Not every best friend knows everything.

So Axel clarifies. "I do have a dad. He doesn't come around very much anymore. He likes trucks, and barns, and fishing." He doesn't tell Daniel other facts, like that Frank and Byrd stopped living together years ago. Or that he once found an index card in Byrd's potting shed that said *Terms of Separation*, like it was some kind of legal document George or Emmett once worked on when they were lawyers. It was not. This was a three-inch-by-five-inch index card holding four lines about how one family was ending.

Axel doesn't tell Daniel that he took the index card out of Byrd's shed and keeps it in his room, on the bookshelf next to his bed. That he looks at it sometimes, at Byrd's signature and Frank's signature. At the list of things that they said they wanted: To be good parents. To be good friends. To find our way back to each other. And how on the opposite side, the plain, white, unlined side, it said, "Visit Axel at least every other Saturday." And how the date at the bottom matched his own birthday.

He doesn't tell Daniel any of that. Just the fishing, and barns, and trucks, because those are facts he knows for certain.

"I bet he'd like my grandpa's truck," Daniel says. He picks up a stick and throws it for Ray.

Axel shrugs.

Then, out of nowhere, Daniel points to a tree in the distance. At first Axel thinks it might be where the stick landed, or that something is crawling on the tree's brown trunk, but that's not it at all.

Axel follows Daniel's gaze. "A Pikachu!" Daniel shouts.

And the game is finally on.

Time to find Pokémon in trees, on rocks. Time to use imaginary Poké Balls to capture as many as they can. Time to build their teams.

Axel sees the imaginary Pikachu too. It's hidden behind the eastern pine, its yellow tail popping out from behind the rough bark. Its tall ears camouflaged by rust-colored needles.

The game rages on, until Daniel stops near the creek. He puts his finger to his lips. "Listen," he says. Axel is so far into the game, when he listens, he hears a Purrloin purring. Turns out that Daniel hears something else. Daniel tucks his imaginary Poké Ball into his pocket. Takes a step closer to the tall tree with the nest tucked into its branches.

Axel should have recognized where the game had taken them. His favorite spot.

"I wish we could see them," Daniel says. There's another flutter today, only the cries are met by a deeper call.

"We have to wait for them to fly," Axel says, listening to the sounds coming from inside the nest.

"I wish we could take the nest down. Put it lower in the tree so that we could see inside," Daniel says. But Axel knows that they can't move the nest. He knows that eagles don't want to be disturbed. That's why they build nests so deep and so wide, so high into already-high trees. They want to protect their babies. They want to see enemies coming. These are important parenting instincts, Axel knows.

"We can't disturb them," Axel says. "We just have to wait."

Then, because Daniel is a great friend, he gets very quiet so that they can just watch and listen, and have thinking time. Axel too wishes for just a glimpse of the mom or dad, or a flutter above the lip of the nest. Something to give more clues about the mysteries inside.

"Okay," Daniel says after a while. "I'm done."

"Someday I'll see them," Axel says. Less to his friend than to the air itself. "They'll come out. They'll fly. It takes a while, but sometimes good things take a while." Isn't that what George says?

"Okay," Daniel says again. "I am ready to go."

Axel pays no attention to Daniel's words. He waits. He watches. There are clues to gather.

Daniel snaps a branch under his feet. He picks up another and cracks it in half in his hands. "Sorry," Daniel says when Axel turns at the sound.

"Why?" Axel asks.

"Because I'm bored," Daniel says.

"Oh," Axel says.

"Sorry," Daniel says again. He throws half the stick for Ray.

"Why are you sorry times two?" Axel asks.

"Because it's obvious that you don't want to go," Daniel says. "But I do."

"Oh," Axel says again.

"And I'm sorry I said the thing about Byrd, and Ray, and your dad," Daniel adds quickly.

Axel considers this. An apology from Daniel about being curious doesn't seem quite right. After all, who wants to hang around uncurious people?

"You don't have anything to be sorry for," Axel says. "Byrd is Byrd. Ray is Ray. And you didn't do anything to make my dad stay away. If I told you about him before and you forgot, then you could be sorry. But I don't really talk about him."

"Right," Daniel says.

And even though there is nothing to be sorry for, and even though the two friends just saw the most spectacular nest in the world, and even though they got to play their favorite Pokémon game on a beautiful Saturday afternoon, Axel has a flutter inside him when he mentions his dad. When he says these words about Frank out loud. It isn't Daniel's fault, of course; who's at fault is a mystery.

And even though Axel is getting used to the mystery of Frank being gone, his heart quivers now the same as it had the day he found the index card listing all those promises.

CHAPTER FOUR

Nests

They build up the sides.
They make it safe.
To protect babies inside.

So much care
in those raised walls
what happens
if one falls?

THE THING ABOUT AXEL'S HOME is that it isn't like the place Byrd grew up. It isn't like Daniel's house with its huge turrets and the attached garage for three cars. It isn't like the houses he passes when they drive to school or the raptor sanctuary. It definitely isn't anything like the apartment that Emmett and George lived in while they were working in New York City.

George's sister says Axel's house reminds her of the place she and George grew up, before George had to move away so he could fly like he was meant to fly, and love as he was meant to love. Except the big difference, according to Aunt Nancy, between their first home and their last, is that Pennsylvania hills "have got nothing on the Sangre de Cristo." Axel knows this is the mountain range running from Colorado through where they lived in New Mexico—with birds Axel would love to see up close, like golden eagles and maybe even an aplomado, if he was truly lucky.

Axel's home is nestled onto a plot of land that was a gift. When Emmett and George bought the property, his house didn't even exist. No stone walkway. No raised flower beds. No fence posts. Just a sloping field down to the creek. This gift from Emmett and George came at a time when Axel's parents were together. Frank built the house with help from Byrd, some friends from work, and George.

Emmett helped too, in his own way. Those builders never tasted such delicious food in all their lives as Emmett's pasta or fresh-baked sourdough. Maybe that was why they came back to help, even when Byrd and Frank couldn't pay them. Axel's home might be smaller than other homes, but it fits just right for him and Byrd. Everything they need in one open space downstairs, two bedrooms and a bathroom upstairs. And that's it. Perfect.

Axel wonders sometimes about this gift. The gift of a home. When someone does this, how can you ever thank them enough?

Back before Axel was born, Byrd green-scaped the whole property from the turn up the driveway to the big red barn. She cultivated wildflowers by the mailbox, relocated stones to form natural fencing. She respected the beauty of the land the way all humans are meant to. Frank must have cared for the land in his own way, too. Axel believes this, even if Aunt Nancy hasn't shared those stories yet.

George says the gifts that Axel and Byrd have given are priceless.

George says that he never expected to feel so loved in all his life. (Aunt Nancy ruffles when he says that. "What am I?" she says. "Chopped liver?")

And whenever George says that, and he says it a lot, Byrd always says she never expected to feel so loved either. It seems like an odd thing to say when her husband has left her, but she does. She feels so loved.

Aunt Nancy has things to say about that, too. About Frank leaving, not about Byrd feeling loved.

Aunt Nancy says that Frank doesn't have what it takes to be a family man. Maybe Axel isn't supposed to hear her say those things, but he does. He hears it, and he wonders why she's the only one who talks about him like that. Emmett just makes the sign of the cross over his heart. George says, "Ours is not to judge." And Byrd wraps herself up in her own arms, wraps her words up inside her, too.

It would be much more helpful if Byrd gave clues to the mystery of a disappearing dad. But she doesn't, so Axel must rely on things left behind. Things like the index card full of promises and Aunt Nancy's chatter. There must be answers there.

Aunt Nancy likes to say things. She's been known to yell her whole way through a six-word jumbler in the Sunday paper, like the whole thing is plotting against her. She likes to say she was never taught to hold her tongue. Whatever that means.

Axel appreciates this about Aunt Nancy. She, like Daniel Berrios, says what she means. And she means what she says. For instance, Axel knows that Nancy didn't really want to move to Pennsylvania. She's said many, many times, "I love where I'm from, but I love my brother more." Which explains a lot. She loves New Mexico, talks about her little piece of heaven on earth. But she loves George more, and so, when her own mother died—the mother that let George fly when he fell in love for the first time—Aunt Nancy came to find her brother. She brought him the round table with five chairs from the house where they grew up. She brought all of the memories with her too.

Both Aunt Nancy and George like to repeat things. Stories, poems, songs. Which is just fine by Axel. He likes to hear things again and again.

From what Aunt Nancy says, Emmett and George were some big-deal lawyers in the big-deal city, only coming out to the woods once a month to "get their nature on." Soon after Byrd started to care for the property, Aunt Nancy came to live in the house. Back before Frank had plans for a cottage. Back before Axel wandered the woods. Back to Byrd and Aunt Nancy, talking and sharing, and caring for the earth, well, that's when they figured out that you can grow a family from more than DNA. They grew it from place and time, and love, of course.

Like those eagles that come year after year to the same nest, in the same tall tree to bring new babies into the world. Time and place and love. They let those babies stay with them a good long time before pushing them out of the nest.

According to Aunt Nancy's stories, Byrd and Frank and

Axel and Emmett and George and even Ray were all "one big happy." That's how she says it:

"One big happy."

She never adds the word *family*, but that's what she means. One big happy family. George and Frank working on the barn, or Byrd making mint tea for everyone, or Axel learning to walk on George and Emmett's front porch. Aunt Nancy remembers all of these things. Axel does not.

He likes the way that Aunt Nancy gives clues about his past. If he gathers her words, maybe, like her word-jumbler in the Sunday paper, Axel can make sense of all the jumbles. Maybe he can make her clues tell a whole story? He can understand once and for all why Frank left.

More clues for many families, including Axel's, come by way of photos.

Like the pictures that show Axel and Byrd with Aunt Nancy, George, Emmett, and Ray on their special property, in these special woods in Pennsylvania. Pictures are a helpful clue, because people are frozen in the image. It is easy to observe something that is frozen in time, like a fossil or an image of smiling family members eating around a big round table, and a dog snoozing on the floor.

Axel doesn't always smile in pictures. But he definitely smiles at pictures—especially when the people he loves look so happy. And maybe, since everyone else is happy, it is okay that Frank isn't in the pictures anymore.

In George and Emmett's house, there are no pictures of

Frank. Not one in sight. Like they erased him, just because he no longer lived in the house next door. There are pictures of him in Byrd and Axel's house. Aunt Nancy doesn't comment on that because she doesn't go beyond the front path anymore, says her darn legs won't take her. But maybe there are other reasons she doesn't want to go inside.

Frank has come and gone from the house many times. Axel knows this fact. He knows that Frank would stay away for a few days, sometimes a week, then two. He knows that he would almost always come on the every-others, like the index card promised. But something changed five months and eight days ago. And since then, Axel would like the pictures in his house to disappear the way that the pictures in Emmett and George's house disappeared.

He's even considered ripping up the index card, letting it fall to the ground in a one-thousand-piece mess.

He wants Byrd to say more than "Frank can't make it again" or Aunt Nancy to say, "I remember when your daddy used to behave."

Axel needs more clues, more of Ms. Dale's favorite word: *clarify*. And who can Axel ask for that?

CHAPTER FIVE

Power

From A. P. Brown's *Collection of North American Birds*, page 661

BIRD OF PREY: any of the predatory birds: eagles, hawks, ospreys, falcons, owls, vultures; also known as a raptor

THE NEXT MORNING STARTS WELL ENOUGH, with the waking and the breakfast and getting to the car on time.

"There's no back seat," Byrd says as Axel reaches for the door behind the driver—his favorite spot in the car.

Caw.

"Sorry," Byrd says. But she's not *really* sorry. The word is one thing, but her shrugging shoulders say something else entirely.

"Things were going so well this morning," Axel says, still considering his options on the driver's side of the car.

"Well, sorry," Byrd repeats. "I have a plant pickup this morning." She tosses two empty trays into the rear of the car. Slams the hatchback.

"You didn't just take the seats out," Axel continues, the whole thing taking shape in his mind. "You must have done it before now. Maybe even last night? Why didn't you tell me when you did it, not wait until now?"

"Just get in the car," Byrd says.

"It seems like an easy thing to say," Axel says. *"By the way, I took the seat out,"* he says in his best Byrd voice.

"I can't this morning, Axel," Byrd says. She opens the driver's side door, plops inside the Forester, then slams the door even harder than she had the hatchback. Like when the wind picks up and all your strength is needed to shut the door before the storm erupts.

Only this morning there isn't a storm. It isn't windy at all.

Slamming the door does not motivate Axel to race around the car and jump inside; if anything, it leaves him frozen for a moment. And that's when Byrd does something wrong. There's no other way to put it.

She starts the car. A sharp sound. A metal on metal sound.

Even through the rattling start, the no back seat, the frozen moment, Axel starts to make his way around the back of the Forester. He holds his breath to clear the exhaust pipe. The smoke billowing out in a long plume on this cool spring morning.

Nearly ready to open up his mouth to the clean air on the other side of the smoke, Byrd does another wrong thing. She lays on the horn. One short beep, followed by a long wail.

If there wasn't a storm before, it feels like there is now, right inside Axel's tight chest. That horrible sound stuck and echoing inside him. He takes off, past the fence, through the field, the tall pines like open arms in front of him.

Go. Get away. His feet squish wet with morning dew. His lungs fill with fresh air, not like that exhaust. Not like back at the car with Byrd and her beeps.

The next thing Axel knows, he's joined by another runner.

A barking runner, who is more than happy to go on an early adventure in the woods with Axel. But just before they can, Axel hears another sound.

"Sorry!" Byrd shouts, a word she has said three times this morning.

She's about halfway through the field. This *sorry*, this third one, might be for Axel, for the horn and the no back seat, but it could very well be for George, who is out on his front porch, with his white, wild morning hair, and his tired body in sloppy pajamas.

"Come!" George calls, a sleepy rasp to his voice.

But Ray doesn't listen. Instead he turns his golden eyes to Axel. This is a plea too, and not like Byrd's "just get in the car"; more like "let's go!" Axel hates to disappoint Ray, but he knows what must be done.

"Come on, Ray," Axel says. "Let's go back."

They are almost to the front porch when George asks, "Everything all right?"

The question is nice enough, but Axel knows that George is feeling anything but nice. George is not happy to have a dog run off. Not happy to have to ask if everything is all right with a scowl tight on his face. Axel rarely sees George like this and doesn't care to see him like this now.

"We're fine," Byrd says. "Just mayhem on Monday."

"That's not true," Axel says, not wanting to feel the scowl on George's face but not wanting to lie to him either. Why lie when the truth is so much easier to tell? "Byrd removed my seat from her car. She started the car without me in it. I was surrounded by toxic exhaust fumes. She made the horn erupt into a horrible sound—"

"I gathered as much. Ray wasn't a fan of the horn either."

"Who would be?" Axel asks.

"Well," Byrd says. "Now we'll be late for school, and for once it isn't my fault."

"That's not true," Axel starts.

"Water is always only itself," George says, his face finally relaxing with the comfort of some favorite words. With no recognition, George clarifies, "We are who we are. Forget the morning and move on."

"I don't want to forget the morning," Axel says, feeling the wet of his shoes seeping into the wet of his socks and the wet of his feet.

"And so it goes," George adds. "Come on, Ray."

Ray would rather do just about anything than go inside the house. He would join Axel at school, even after Axel has told him about all the sounds and smells and the rules. The ones that help and the ones that don't make much sense. The thing about school is that there is just so much of it. But even in that, Ray would go there instead of inside, locked away with nothing new to explore.

"Ray," George says in a serious voice. "Come." Even Axel tightens at the sound. Ray leaves Axel's side with droopy ears and a low tail.

Axel feels the same when he turns for the car. Holds his

breath past the still-smoking exhaust and sits in the front seat, which is far too close to the windshield. He slips out of his too-wet shoes and socks.

"Let's try this again," Byrd says, handing Axel the Crocs from her own feet. This is one way to say sorry and mean it.

Axel doesn't need to respond to her kindness. He knows that she didn't mean to mess everything up and start the day in this way, especially after it was going so well.

Axel lets thoughts fill his mind. Important thinking can be done in the car when no one needs conversation and there's nothing to do but put the mind into high gear, just like the car's engine.

Of course he looks as they pass two important landmarks: Daniel Berrios's house with its huge front porch, and the exit ramp that he will take to the Delaware Valley Raptor Sanctuary this Friday. Just like every Friday. Fridays are for celebrations because it's the weekend and because the Delaware Valley Raptor Sanctuary is open to visitors.

"Still thinking?" Byrd asks.

This question is not enough to get a reaction from Axel. How could it be? His mind is flowing with thoughts about the Delaware Valley Raptor Sanctuary. Passing the exit ramp, how could his mind *not* be absorbed with thoughts of his favorite ornithologist? Which leads to thoughts of Maxwell, the golden eagle, his favorite bird to visit at the sanctuary until the eagle was set to the sky. He was rehabilitated. This was the plan. Dr. Taylor M. Martin knew just what to do.

She knew that a golden eagle struck by a truck needed to recover from the shock with quiet. Then softly spoken words, and a leather hood, and medication. She knew that when an X-ray shows no broken bones, it doesn't mean that more isn't broken, like forgetting how to fly. She knew that it would take four months and lots of frozen fish to motivate Maxwell to make his way to the sky again. She knew that he was only a visitor here in Pennsylvania, and he'd have to be set free in Canada, near chilly waters and plenty of marmots to snatch up!

Dr. Taylor M. Martin knew this because she asked questions, she observed Maxwell, she uncovered all the ways to make him better, and then she drove the 1,330 miles to take him home.

This was always Maxwell's plan for release, which is good. But it is also bad, at least a little, because this change means that Axel can no longer see Maxwell.

Caw.

That missing makes Axel's heart hurt all over again. Change, even good change, can cause so many new problems.

"Still thinking?" Byrd asks again. She clears her throat this time. Jiggles the steering wheel.

"Why are you doing that?" Axel says, ripped from his thoughts.

"Still thinking?" Byrd asks, like she didn't nearly drive them off the road.

"Can I just think now?" Axel asks instead of answering

her. He pulls his hood up. If Byrd needs a clue, this is the ultimate one to just leave Axel alone.

His mind wanders from the happy-sadness of Maxwell returning to Canada to the first time he ever met Dr. Taylor M. Martin, which, if there was ever any doubt, was the single greatest day of second grade, maybe in all of Fairview Elementary School history.

When she came to the gymnasium, a place that was too loud, and said, "You must be quiet. I can't bring my guests out unless you are quiet." And just like that, after giving that clarification, one by one she could take the guests from their cages. One by one. Bird by bird.

There was a great horned owl that had been sliced out of a tree and came into her rescue. She couldn't repair his wing, so he flew in circles. This would prevent him from surviving in the wild, so he stayed with Dr. Taylor M. Martin at the sanctuary. Now he can visit schools and teach kids about wildlife preservation.

By the time Dr. Martin pulled a bald eagle from a crate, inside that very quiet gymnasium, Axel was mesmerized.

There really isn't another way to say it.

He wouldn't be able to tell anything else about the world around him in that moment. All he saw was Dr. Taylor M. Martin and the bald eagle. The way it spun from the ornithologist's forearm. He nearly flew out of his seat. Then the bird settled back on Dr. Taylor M. Martin's glove and something inside him settled, too.

Dr. Taylor M. Martin talked about raptor rehabilitation. She talked about flight and instincts and power. She talked about kids like Axel finding ways to help.

Axel was hooked. He purchased his own membership to the raptor sanctuary that night, after a little convincing so Byrd would give him a credit card number. That was a good change, buying the membership card, but it took a whole year for Axel to use it. Though, since last spring, when he started going, he hadn't missed a Friday visit.

Dr. Taylor M. Martin is there every Friday, too.

CHAPTER SIX

Enemies I

Dark.

Bullies.

Pigeons.

Crowds.

Crashes.

Dogs that look friendly, but are not.
People who look friendly, but are not.

Storms.

Fire.

Blood.

Lies.

LATE TO SCHOOL MEANS FIVE THINGS:

1) Byrd must accompany Axel from the parking lot to the entrance of the building.

2) Byrd must tell the person on the other side of the intercom way too much about all the goings-on in Axel's home between waking up and the moment they step up to the school doors. (This list is not limited to actual things that happened. It could include traffic that wasn't on the road, construction that wasn't on the road, alarm malfunctions that weren't in the house, or last-minute work-related crises that just aren't true.)

3) Axel must remain still while the blinkie camera above the door judges whether he can enter school late. If the answer is yes, a long buzz will erupt from the intercom.

4) It is a mystery what happens if the answer is no.

5) Axel will walk through the door, through the school, and into his classroom where the day will have already started for everyone else. This is a worse buzz than the one at the front door.

Unfortunately, Axel knows this process well.

He has sixteen tardies this year alone. Byrd can blame a lot on made-up construction workers. Way back when Frank was responsible for driving Axel to school, they were always on time. Always. Frank never blamed a construction worker, perhaps because he was once one himself?

Today's entrance is a bit different from what Axel's come to expect. After Byrd's words and the blinkie-eyed camera, Ms. Dale's voice comes through the intercom.

"I went looking for you this morning, Axel," she says.

Ms. Dale isn't just the leader of Friendship Club; she's the guidance counselor for the whole school. She likes to go looking for people in the morning and afternoon. Axel has been her objective many times. For all the years he's known Ms. Dale—and he's known her through five different hair colors and four school years—he's never once seen her alone. Sure, she has IEPs and 504 plans that say "offer support," and other things, but Ms. Dale also finds her people because, well, they are her people and she likes spending time with them. That's a very true fact about her.

This morning when the annoying buzz erupts from the intercom, Ms. Dale holds open the door.

"We're late," Axel says, not wanting to wait through another Byrd-length explanation.

"It happens," Ms. Dale says. She nods toward Byrd. "Good morning, Mrs. Rastusak."

"Byrd," Byrd replies. "It has been a morning," she starts. "Actually, I was hoping we could . . ."

Axel has zero time to waste at the door with Byrd and Ms. Dale. His class has already started the day without him, and every minute he stands here letting Byrd fill the air with her chirps and chatter, his classmates get further ahead of him on the day's tasks.

He's not supposed to run in the halls. But, technically, Axel's already broken a school rule today by being late . . . so . . . he takes off.

He's nearly to the first stairwell when a screech startles him. Not an owl's call, a whistle. Like from someone's bare lips!

"Sorry," Ms. Dale says, lowering her fingers from her mouth.

Sorry. That word again. *Caw.*

"Haven't tried that in a while," Ms. Dale says. She adjusts her thick black-framed glasses over her very freckle-specked nose.

"I'm late," Axel says, ready to take on the steps.

"I know," Ms. Dale says. "I'll call Mr. Conner and let him know I need a few minutes of your time." And because Ms. Dale has also known Axel through her five shades of hair color and four years of school, she adds, "It's important. I want to go over a weather-related drill with you."

Suddenly the feeling of his classmates starting the day

without him is replaced by a new feeling, a mystery of sorts. "Did you say weather-related?"

Ms. Dale walks alongside Axel back to her office. "Axel," she says softly.

Axel pulls up his sweatshirt's hood, loops one thumb under each backpack strap. "Just let me think," he says.

Ms. Dale does.

Axel turns left the moment they enter the main office, splits off from the people talking to Ms. Dale, and goes straight for a seat at the round table in the back of her room.

Her office isn't always the easiest place to navigate. Sometimes papers are everywhere. Sometimes games are left out on the floor, with slippery cards on smooth linoleum. But it's nearly always quiet in the room.

Sometimes Ms. Dale has Axel visit her just to think. Other times she wants to talk. Sometimes he's with kids who need time and space for classwork. But this time, today, is to talk about weather-related drills. *Caw.*

"Axel, the school has a tornado drill this afternoon. This will be your first tornado drill at our school."

"Climate change," Axel says.

"Excuse me?" Ms. Dale says.

"Fairview is hotter now than it was. The hotter weather allows more instability in the atmosphere." Byrd might not talk about all of the changes in Fairview, but she can always find the words to share with Axel, or anyone else, facts about the environment. And even though Byrd isn't here right now, Axel can't help but share some of her facts.

"That's one thought," Ms. Dale says. "I just wanted to give you a heads-up on what to expect with the drill."

"Go on," Axel says. The words come out calmly, but his insides tighten.

He's been at home before when there's been a tornado warning. He doesn't love the smell of the tiny dugout basement under the cottage, but it keeps him and Byrd protected from high winds and bad storms. Schools don't have basements? Do they? And even if they do, how would five hundred kids fit into one basement?

And if they don't, the school is filled with glass. Nearly everywhere, every wall, every spot has sunlight coming from somewhere. This is usually a great thing for observing the outdoors, but with bad weather, windows turn into problems.

Axel gets out of his chair and moves away from his favorite seat in Ms. Dale's office, which happens to be near the only window in the small room, at the corner table, with the view of the hummingbird feeder and the tree-covered entrance to the building. Trees that earlier seemed to be standing still, now blowing around.

"You should probably know that we have these drills once a year," Ms. Dale says.

"Then why haven't I been in one?" Axel asks.

"Well, they're typically planned well in advance, and your mom has opted to keep you out of school on those days."

How about that? This is what makes mysteries with Byrd so hard to solve. She's always hiding one clue behind her back.

"Is that what she wanted to talk about this morning?" Axel says, piecing things together.

"I don't know," Ms. Dale says. "But I let her know about the drill before I caught up to you in the hall."

"When you whistled," Axel says.

"Yes," Ms. Dale says, and brings her fingers to her lips, like maybe the sound is coming again.

Axel pops his hood up.

"You've got this," she says, never making a screech. "Today is the perfect time to try."

Axel checks the zipper on the front of his sweatshirt. It cannot go any higher.

"We're in the middle of a tornado watch," Ms. Dale says. She pushes on her glasses, considers a new plan. "Here," she says. "Follow me."

They go back out into the main office, through the thick glass-that-could-shatter doors and into the hallway.

Ms. Dale kneels first, her knees facing the cinder-block wall. She drops her head so that her spiky green hair is just an inch away from the wall, her forehead resting on her knees. She wraps her hands over her head and freezes in place.

Axel lets his body bend the way Ms. Dale has shown. His

hood droops farther forward when he touches his forehead to his knees.

Eventually Axel and Ms. Dale sit back on their heels, side by side. "Very good, Axel," Ms. Dale says. "You should probably know there's an alarm that accompanies the entire drill from the time you leave your classroom through resting your head here."

"You mean there?" Axel says, pointing up toward the second floor.

"All students come to the first floor during the drill," Ms. Dale says. This is an important clarification. "I can play the alarm for you, if you'd like."

Caw.

"No," Axel says. Sirens suck.

"Very good, Axel," Ms. Dale says.

"You could always hang with me during the drill," Ms. Dale adds.

"No," Axel says without much consideration. If he has to be a pigeon while he's in school, it's better he just does what the pigeons do—put his head down and push through the terrible sound.

"Very good, Axel," Ms. Dale says. "Want me to walk you to class?"

"Did you know the fastest tornado in Fairview was three hundred and one miles per hour in 2016?" That was when the fence around his house had to be rebuilt. Industrial-strength style, as Aunt Nancy put it.

"I did not know that," Ms. Dale says. She presses up from the floor and offers a hand to Axel.

"Keep your friends close and enemies closer," Axel says.

"I don't know what you mean," Ms. Dale says.

It's one of George's quotes of course. He says this one so often, especially when it comes to Byrd and snakes. After all, if she'd keep this enemy close, by George's logic, she'd start to appreciate all that snakes do in her garden.

"George says that when you learn about things that make you uneasy, you know, 'enemies,' and it takes away some of their power. Like how he's always trying to get Byrd to learn about snakes. Like when he showed her the longest snake recorded in Fairview was in 2019 and was a northern copperhead. It was like eleven feet long."

"Well, that's terrifying," Ms. Dale says.

"Not really. It's better to just know, not have to guess, not make everything some big mystery," Axel says. "Like the tornado drill. What was Byrd protecting me from by not having me experience the drill? Does she think that I don't think about tornadoes at school just because she wouldn't let me do a drill? I think about tornadoes and fires and other enemies. I can't not think about them. But it is better that I know that there is a plan. We come into the hall, we kneel down, protect our heads, there's an alarm."

"Sometimes adults don't know quite what to do, so they make the best choice they can with the information that they have," Ms. Dale says.

"Well, that's stupid," Axel says.

Ms. Dale flinches at the word. This is a word that's not allowed in Friendship Club.

"I'm sorry," Axel says. "But Byrd's always making choices for me that don't make any sense, and I just have to go along with them. It isn't my choice to be late in the morning. It isn't my choice to ask people the questions she wants me to ask them, or say hello to strangers, or stay still when my body is telling me to go . . ."

"Why don't we head back to the office?" Ms. Dale says in a whispery voice. Axel knows that she wants him to be whispery too. After all, that's what a pigeon would do, but this isn't whispery stuff. This, the tornado drill, the being late to school, this is all just another example of the ways that Byrd keeps her mysteries. The way that Byrd keeps Axel from knowing the truth.

Caw.

"I want to go to class," Axel says. He doesn't wait for Ms. Dale to respond.

When Axel is called down to Ms. Dale's office just before lunch, he knows that drill is coming. Why else would she call him down again?

It must be that just like Byrd, Ms. Dale doesn't trust Axel to handle the drill well enough on his own. He needs to do it under her supervision or not at all.

It has been all he's thought about since they last spoke,

so they might as well do it together. By the time he turns left in the main area of the office, he's resolved to this. He's embraced the idea. The new plan. That's why, when he sees what's actually waiting for him in Ms. Dale's room, he turns right around and leaves.

No words. No *sorry*s. Just leaves.

Straight back up the hallway, past the kids singing in his old first-grade classroom, past the entrance to the gym, to the stairwell. That's when he hears George's words on repeat. *Enemies closer.* He stops to consider going back. Going back and saying the things he needs to say.

He turns just in time to see someone running out of the gymnasium.

By the back of his head, Axel knows. "Daniel!" he shouts, then runs to catch up to his friend.

When Daniel turns to face him, it looks like he's been playing monster dodgeball in gym, which sounds terrible, but is actually a lot of fun.

"Were you in gym?" Axel asks.

Daniel shakes his head. It looks like the words are stuck inside his tight jaw.

The next thing Axel knows, Principal Epstein is on her way toward them. "I heard you were coming," she says.

"Why?" Axel responds.

"I was talking to Mr. Berrios," Principal Epstein says.

"I know," Axel says.

"I believe Ms. Dale is waiting for you," she says. She puts an arm around Daniel's shoulder that he shrugs off immediately. Who wants to be touched like that? Especially without being asked.

Principal Epstein and Daniel go in one direction, and Axel goes in another. The door at Ms. Dale's office isn't closed, so he sees Byrd right away. "Why are you here?"

"I was thinking about the drill," Byrd says. She stands up the same as Ms. Dale. It's an awkward triangle, Byrd, Ms. Dale, and Axel. "I finished my pickup at the nursery and thought I'd come back to check in."

"That's not okay," Axel says.

"Axel," Byrd says, her face flushing pink. "They were talking about the storm at the nursery and then on the radio and I thought . . ."

"Maybe your mom wanted to be sure we all felt good about the plan," Ms. Dale says, and then adds, "Is that right, Ms. Rastusak?"

"Ms. Dale went over the drill. I know what I'm doing," Axel says, which feels great to say out loud. It is exactly what he needs to tell her. Exactly what she needs to hear. Axel turns to leave, since the conversation is over.

"Actually," Ms. Dale begins. "Can you step back in, Axel? Here," she says. "Come sit." She pulls one of the chairs with the hard backs away from the window. Axel sits, and Byrd pulls a chair over too.

Axel smells the plant pickup on her blue shirt. He wishes she had left that in the car. The car that still has no back seat, but definitely has her plants in it.

Byrd lays a hand on Axel's wrist. "This okay?" she asks. This is a thing. A clue that means *Listen up, this isn't going to be easy.*

And just before Byrd can get her first word out, a word that may or may not be 100 percent the truth, there's yelling in the main office.

"Daniel," Axel says. All his attention turns from Byrd on his wrist to Daniel outside Ms. Dale's door.

"Excuse me," Ms. Dale says as she rushes out.

The clues are mounting that this is maybe the worst day at school ever. With being late and the tornado drill that is coming any moment with the loud alarm, and Byrd being here when she shouldn't, and her not trusting Axel to be able to do anything on his own, and Daniel yelling, and Ms. Dale leaving Axel and Byrd alone in a room that doesn't belong to them. *Caw.*

Daniel's voice grows louder as the uneasy feelings start to spread from the center of Axel out into his limbs. Principal Epstein has a loud voice too. But without other clues, there's no way to know if she's trying to calm Daniel or yelling back at him.

"The tornado watch is in effect until six p.m.," Byrd says, like she has no clue that this fact is the least of Axel's worries right now. "There are eleven counties under the watch in Pennsylvania and just over the border in New York, too."

For a split second, Axel adds this fact to the growing list in his head. New York and Pennsylvania. Same storm, two places.

"I know how you feel about storms," Byrd says. "Enemies."

Thoughts spiral through Axel's brain. Thoughts Byrd can't see because she can't look under his hair, under his flesh, into his mind. She doesn't know everything about him, even if she thinks she does.

There are terrible thoughts about loud storms, louder alarms, lightning hitting trees, Frank being gone, Daniel yelling . . . And one more thought that bullies past the others. It's the kind of thing that links all the other pieces together, even the being late and the not knowing about drills in the past. "Don't treat me like a baby," Axel says.

"Axel, this isn't that," she says like she knows everything. "This is me supporting you."

Axel's eyes go to the window, to the leaves blowing around outside. No birds at the feeder. He isn't sure why, but this makes him even angrier. Blowing leaves, and missing birds, and Byrd at his school. "This is you thinking I can't handle it," Axel says, and not in a calm voice. In a voice that should tell Byrd exactly how this makes him feel. Isn't she the one who always says to listen to the *tone* of someone's words? "Ms. Dale got me ready for the drill. I can get through the tornado myself. If it's coming at all. Because Tornado *Watch* is not Tornado *Warning*," he says, like this fact, knowing this bit of information about his enemy is enough to make him brave. He doesn't tell Byrd that the not knowing only adds to the fear.

But Byrd doesn't need to know that right now. She doesn't need to know everything.

"I guess that's true," Byrd says.

"It is true. You should be able to tell the difference."

"Between a watch and a warning?"

Again, Axel's tone matches what he's feeling inside. His words are calm, his voice is calm, when he says, "No, Byrd, the difference between truth and lies."

At the word *lies*, Byrd flinches like a startled snake. She slips her hand from his wrist, slides it back into her own lap. With this, Axel feels free, and flies for the door.

"Axel," Byrd says like they haven't just come to the end of the conversation. "I—" she begins again.

Ms. Dale comes back into her office just then. She doesn't interrupt at first with words, but it is obvious she is on a new mission. "I'm walking our friend Daniel back to his home-room," Ms. Dale says. "Want to come?"

"He can get back to his homeroom," Axel says.

Ms. Dale smiles, leans against the doorframe. "I think Daniel could use a friend right now, and I would like it if you'd walk him back to class with me, and then I'll walk you back to your classroom, as long as you and your mom are finished."

"Oh, we're finished," Axel says, because they very much are.

He slips past Ms. Dale before she says, "Do you want to say goodbye to your mom?"

His answer should be obvious. If he wanted to say goodbye, he would have.

"Okay," Ms. Dale says at Axel's back. "I'll be back in a few minutes," she adds. Axel knows that this clarification isn't for him.

As soon as Axel sees Daniel in the chair outside Principal Epstein's office, he says, "Let's go."

Daniel smiles, raises his one eyebrow way up. "You hear about the tornado drill?" he asks.

"Yes," Axel says.

"Me too," he says. "I don't like it."

It is all so easy with Daniel. Axel holds the door open for him and then Daniel holds it for Ms. Dale. Axel feels like the whole day so far has been spent walking this long hallway. Back and forth. He's bored with it. Ready to stay in one place.

And because Daniel is a great friend, and because Daniel has a very imaginative mind, in the next moment, just as they hit the first stair, Daniel says, "So . . . I've been thinking about Rufflet."

This is not boring. "Interesting," Axel says.

The bird Pokémon. A favorite.

"Would be great to catch in the nest," Daniel says.

"What nest?" Ms. Dale asks.

Daniel and Axel don't have time to remind Ms. Dale about

the eagles' nest at George and Emmett's. There is strategizing to do.

"Why haven't we ever seen one in the woods?" Daniel asks.

"A nest?" Ms. Dale asks.

Caw.

"No," Daniel and Axel say at the same time.

"Rufflet," Daniel says, trying to include Ms. Dale just a little bit.

It isn't like Ms. Dale's questions are hard to answer, but Axel doesn't want to pull his thoughts from the planning with Daniel. The nest is a special thing to Axel, not an enemy at all. But if he lets his thoughts go from the imagination with Daniel to the very real nest, other very real memories might come too. And, after leaving Byrd in the office, he wants to leave those memories alone.

Thinking about the Rufflet is something his mind can do without worry, and right now, this is just what Axel needs.

CHAPTER SEVEN

Instincts

A voice inside—
poetry of direction
flowing forward,
setting paths—

human,
natural,
animal,

Go!

THE DRILL DOESN'T GO ACCORDING TO PLAN.

The pigeons do okay, at least from the outside. Alarm, hallway, kneel. But who can really tell just from the outside?

Axel's never considered himself a pigeon, even if they do backflips and other interesting things. Today is no different. He isn't a pigeon during the drill; he's a runner. Not like a gym-class monster-dodgeball runner, like flying away from an ear-piercing wail that rings through the classroom and hallways, vibrating the entire school and every inch of Axel's body.

"Tough one," Ms. Dale says. She's run with Axel in her way-high shoes, that match her spiky hair, but don't really seem like the best fit for running out to the flagpole.

Ms. Dale knows that running is in Axel's identity, like his eye color. She knows a little about his history, too. How running has brought him power in a way that others might not see.

Of course there was the one time, not at school, at a family reunion, back when Frank and Byrd and Axel were one big happy. Frank didn't want to go to the reunion. Axel didn't want to go to the reunion. But Byrd did a very Byrd thing and made them go. She said that it would be good, like just saying it means it's true.

It's like maybe she'd forgotten how special it was to be with Emmett, and George, and Aunt Nancy each day, where there was never a "reunion" because they were always together. All that Byrd could see then was that Frank's family tree was dropping branches and leaves, and that she needed to get Axel and Frank and herself to the reunion.

The day was hot, not unlike this afternoon. Frank parked the car near a string of other vehicles. Lots of trucks like theirs. Big tires, big beds.

This was just before Axel and Byrd had made the plan to fly to Frank's open truck bed when he wanted to get away from annoying things, scary things, unwanted things. And now it is clear—creek-water clear—that the family reunion, back when Axel was five, was the very reason to make this plan.

Back then, they exited the truck, Frank and Byrd in the lead, and entered a tent. Not a tent like Axel'd been in before camping with Byrd and Frank. A tent like the size of a house with a dance floor, tables, lights. A tent to shade lots of people in much fancier clothes than Axel or Byrd or Frank from the sweltering summer sun.

And then the people came. A thwack on Frank's back from a guy a full head taller than him, with a thick beard, a loud voice, and a face sunburned bright red just like Frank's.

"Thought you'd bail. I owe Dad fifty bucks now," he'd said. His laugh roared, and Axel could feel the words as they hit Frank. "And this must be your boy," the bearded man said. "You've got all the girls calling already, I bet."

What was Axel supposed to say to that?

"Like you, eh, Frank? Not really a talker," the bearded man said. "That's okay. Give your uncle Dennis a hug." The bearded man stepped too close. He wrapped his thick arms, like the thick heat, around Axel.

"You too," Uncle Dennis said turning to Byrd. "I haven't seen you since we finished the house. Still as pretty as ever, mama."

"Her name is Byrd," Axel said, loud enough to surprise even himself.

"He speaks!" Uncle Dennis said. "I know your mama's name, son. I've known her a long time, although she and your daddy like to forget that."

Axel grabbed for Byrd, but she was just out of reach.

"Dad," Uncle Dennis shouted, "get over here and catch these two before they fly away."

Another man started his way toward them. Frank took a step back, nearly knocking Axel to the ground. And so, with Byrd just out of reach, and Frank on the edge, Axel ran from these strangers. Out of the tent, past the trucks that looked a little like Frank's, but not just like Frank's, and back into the safety of his back seat. He buried himself down into the small space on the floor near Frank's toolbox and waited for Byrd and Frank to fly, too.

And it was a hot, hot day.

And Byrd was just out of reach.

And Axel didn't hear them yelling for him. Searching for him at this strange place with all of the strangers.

But now, on hot days like today, and other days too, Axel hears this story on repeat. This warning, not to go into a hot car on a hot day, no matter what. Byrd will say, "If you get uneasy, no hot cars."

And Axel will say, "Because that one time I passed out."

And Byrd will say, "Right, so let's find a safe place to land." This is the truth. Finding a safe place to land is important, not just for Axel, but for everyone.

Byrd sometimes tells things plainly. She sometimes tells important truths. She sometimes makes important plans. That's what makes it so hard to crack her mysteries. She remembers to talk honestly about hot cars and aisles at the grocery store and not going beyond where the big red barn can see Axel.

The problem is that Byrd doesn't trust Axel to remember her words, to know just how far he can fly.

Today Axel ran to the flagpole during the tornado drill. A safe place to land, just outside the school. Outside the buzzing alarm and the crowded hallways.

And now Ms. Dale walks with Axel back into the building, past the blinkie-camera and through the main doors. "Want to go back or come for a little quiet time?" she asks.

"I'll come with you," Axel says. He turns left when they

enter the main office. Ms. Dale closes the door behind them. And even though Axel was in her office just before lunch, the whole place looks different. Where once there was clean table by the window, it is now filled with game pieces. Where once there was a path to walk from this side of the room to that side, there are game boxes, like Ms. Dale decided to make her own Twister board with boxes. Axel hasn't moved from just inside the door when it flings open behind him.

"Daniel Berrios," Ms. Dale says, her voice lifting in delight.

"They said I could come down," Daniel says.

"This is great," Ms. Dale says. "We could use the help."

Daniel and Axel help Ms. Dale straighten up the office. They put away stray pieces of a board game, and Ms. Dale turns on her Echo. There are requests for all sorts of songs. Daniel asks for one about dragons. Axel loves theme songs and knows so many by heart. When they all know the words, they all sing.

When the beanbags are back where they belong and the table is clear and smells like the lemon spray Ms. Dale likes to use, she says, "Let's sit."

Axel goes to his chair by the window. The trees outside are calm.

Daniel plops down on a beanbag nearby. When his behind hits the center, the edges flap around him, sandwiching him into a tight hug. Ms. Dale takes a seat in the middle of the floor with no chair at all, like she's a kindergartner getting ready for story time. No adults ever sit this way, except Ms. Dale.

"I want to unpack the tornado drill," she says. Ms. Dale loves to unpack things, which is another important fact about her. She unpacks feelings and fears and what it means to be a good friend. "Instincts are a beautiful thing," Ms. Dale says.

"Definitely," Axel agrees. "Did you know bald eagles will perch for ninety-eight percent of the day during cold weather to conserve energy for a hunt? It's just something they know to do. To be quiet for hours upon hours, and not worry about anything but stillness."

"I didn't know that," Ms. Dale says.

"Or a mom can lift a car off her baby if she needs to," Daniel says.

"What? That can't be true," Axel says. Cars are far too heavy for the average human.

"It's true," Daniel says, a little sharpness coming into his voice. "My mom said so. She said she could do it for me with her one pinky."

"I believe your mom would and could," Ms. Dale says. She turns to Axel, and even though he doesn't expect it, or even know he wants it, when she says, "Your mom, too," Axel feels warmth spread through his whole body. It's nice to think of Byrd this way, rather than the way he felt earlier.

"Everyone is born with instincts," Ms. Dale says. "Birds, humans, slugs—every animal—because instincts come from within the brain and the heart. They are hardwired, not learned but programmed into you." She points to Daniel. She points to Axel. She touches her hand to her own heart. "You hear people say things like 'trust your gut.'"

"That's gross," Axel says. For some reason, picturing the smooth inside of someone's brain doesn't feel icky, but the inside of someone's guts . . .

"It means trust what your insides are telling you," Ms. Dale says. "And sometimes that can be hard because—"

"The world wants pigeons," Axel says, like this, too, is a fact.

"Pigeons?" Daniel repeats. "Pigeons!" he says, holding his gut. This gets him laughing like his eyebrow trick gets Axel going. Only Daniel laughs so hard about pigeons that he falls out of his beanbag's hug.

Axel doesn't see why this is so funny. It isn't funny. It's true. "Pigeons," he repeats, trying to get Daniel's attention back on the idea. "Pigeons somehow know just what to do. How to behave. Their instincts are to be just one thing, the same thing that all the other pigeons are. They adapt. If one pigeon does something, they all can learn how to do just that. If one pigeon says, 'Let's ride the subway,' eventually other pigeons know how to do that too."

Daniel shakes his head, looks up at Axel, like the words he said aren't adding up. Like subways and guts and pigeons don't belong together. He fluffs his beanbag before saying, "I don't get it, Axel." He slams back down on top of the beanbag, letting it swallow him.

"I think what Axel is saying is that he feels like many people have the same instincts. That they are like pigeons who seem to know what to do all the time. And can adapt easily to new situations because of these instincts. Is that right, Axel?"

If there was a way to peek inside Ms. Dale's brain, under this week's green spikes, Axel imagines it would be very clear, consistent, orderly; even if her desk and office get messy, her thoughts are always so clear.

Axel nods.

"Well then, I'm no pigeon," Daniel says. "I try. I do, but I feel like sometimes my insides are telling me what to do and it is definitely not what everyone else is doing."

"Like punching the wall during the drill," Ms. Dale says.

This is new information to Axel.

Daniel is the single nicest person at school, but even kind people sometimes have to get angry and let it out. One time at Axel's house, Daniel punched a tree. It wasn't to hurt the tree, Axel was sure of that; it was to let out his anger about having to leave, which actually made Axel feel good. Daniel wanted to stay so much, wanted to catch Pokémon longer, and run in the woods and be with him, that he got angry when his mom said it was time to go. It seems like wanting to spend more time with your friend would be a good thing, not a bad thing.

Daniel looks down at the ground, though, instead of nodding to show Ms. Dale she got things right.

Axel's friendship instincts zoom into action. "I don't always get it right, either," Axel says, because he wants his friend to know that it's okay. There are two of them—non-pigeons—

sitting here, and Axel is sure there are more, though on days like this it doesn't always feel that way.

"Hold on," Ms. Dale says. "I don't think words like *right* and *wrong* belong here. I think that both you and Daniel have strong instincts. Instincts that are wired into you to protect you. Axel, you run when you don't feel safe in a situation. Daniel, you push things and people away when you don't feel safe."

Ms. Dale can find so many right words, just like George. When they say the truth like this, it seems simple.

"It is okay to be afraid. That's a good instinct. It lets you know that something isn't right. And then you know that you need to do something. And if you have to run, Axel, can you? And if you have to hit something, Daniel, can you?"

"I only hit the wall," Daniel says in a small voice from the center of his smushed beanbag.

"You know what?" Ms. Dale says. "You only hit the wall."

"That's what he just said," Axel says.

"You didn't hit anyone," Ms. Dale clarifies.

"No. He hit a wall," Axel says.

"What I'm saying is, Daniel did make a choice. It's true that he hit something, and violence in the school is always scary," Ms. Dale pauses. She's talking so slowly. Like she's figuring things out as she goes. Like maybe she doesn't know all the answers, and she's willing to let that show on the outside.

"My mom has me punch a pillow at home," Daniel says. "I do. In the back of my closet. I do. But I don't have a closet or a pillow here. And . . ."

"Sometimes you need it," Ms. Dale says. She gets up from the floor, then gets busy scribbling something on a Post-it note on her newly clean desk.

"Sometimes I just need to find a quiet place to let my mind think," Axel adds.

Daniel spins the beanbag on the smooth floor. "You do like to think," he says.

"You could do that in here," Ms. Dale says. She writes something else on the Post-it on her desk.

Axel watches Daniel swirl on the floor, lets Ms. Dale's suggestion swirl in his mind. "But what if your office is on fire?" Axel asks. It seems obvious, but the question leaves Ms. Dale speechless.

Daniel starts laughing again. He has the best laugh.

"I think if my office is on fire, we'll come up with a plan B," she says. "Maybe the flagpole could be a plan B when there isn't the threat of storms, because avoiding tall metal poles is actually a good rule of thumb when lightning may be in the picture."

Axel hadn't thought of lightning.

"My mom likes to sing when she's stressed," Daniel says, like he can't help himself from adding ideas to Ms. Dale's list, or whatever it is she's writing on her desk. "She can really get going, and we all kind of give her space."

"Because her singing is kind of a clue that tells you she needs space," Ms. Dale says.

"My dad used to sing to me," Axel says, surprising himself

a little. It is weird when his brain dips into Frank memories. Sometimes he can't escape them. Like now, a song flutters into his brain. One that Frank used to sing to Axel. One about a bird. "I don't think that was for him, though. Not like Daniel's mom. I think he did it for me."

"Parents have great instincts," Ms. Dale says. She places her pen next to the Post-it.

"My mom could lift a car," Daniel repeats, like there is any way Axel or Ms. Dale could have forgotten.

Do all parents have great instincts? Like those eagle parents at the nest. Do all parents know what to do? Lift cars, build nests with high sides, and give warnings about tornado drills?

Axel's mind thinks of one parent in particular. One who will protect her baby, no matter what. "Have I ever told you about ospreys?" he asks.

Daniel stops spinning, looks up at his friend with one eyebrow raised way up. Daniel is ready for some new facts.

CHAPTER EIGHT

Facts

Most raptors look behind them,
as skilled hunters,
expert flyers,
divers,
capturers.

A last glance at the finish line to see if anyone has caught up.

But not the eagle.
Eagles don't need to look back,
they know that no one dare challenge them.
They know that man is the only thing
to bring them down.

Well, man,
and Mother
Nature.

WHEN BYRD PICKS AXEL UP FROM SCHOOL, she smells of manure and dirt. Frank's blue shirt is covered in plenty of soil, and her plants no longer take up the special spot behind the driver's seat.

"Seat's back," she says. Axel tosses his backpack across the seat, buckles into his spot.

He doesn't want to hang on to anger any more than he wants the terrible smell to hang on Byrd, but it is hard to let go of Byrd's visit to the school today. Of learning that she's kept him from experiencing something, even if it is a tornado drill, just because she doesn't believe in him. It was easier to let go of this when he was with Ms. Dale and Daniel. Easier when he wasn't sharing the same small space with Byrd.

"Want to tell me about the drill?" she asks. Before Axel can even think of answering, Byrd changes her mind. "Or do you want some thinking time?"

She's being kind. "Thinking," Axel says.

His mind swirls back over the day, over Ms. Dale's ideas about instincts and flight, and the way that Ms. Dale tells

Daniel and him about their world. It is *their* world, although sometimes it doesn't feel that way.

And if there was room for just those things, just those ideas to swirl, that would be one thing, but there's also the thoughts of the storm that may or may not be coming, and the mysteries of Byrd, and the disappearing dad, and so much more.

By the time they turn left at the mailbox, the one that reads RASTUSAK & CLARKEN-FLORES, the one that Emmett painted himself, Axel lands on a new idea.

Go to the place where the best thinking can happen. When all else fails you, go to nature, as George would say. More just-right words for a pretty weird day.

Emmett shoos Ray out the front door as soon as the Forester pulls up.

Ray chases after Axel, down the rock path, and into the cottage. The jingle-jangle of his tags makes a better alarm than the one Axel heard earlier. As soon as Axel drops his backpack, Ray and Axel race out of the house.

"Not too far," Byrd says. She looks up at the sky and shakes her head. "Better yet, why don't you and Ray just stick around the fence today? We're still in a watch; the weather could turn."

But Axel needs to think. He needs to walk with Ray and check on the nest. So he says the one thought out loud that he knows will show all this. "You don't trust me."

This cuts into Byrd like she's been ripped by a thorn. "That's not fair," she says.

"You're right," Axel says. "It isn't fair."

Byrd opens the door to her shed like maybe a response is hiding in there. Like maybe the words she needs to show that this is fair—or she is right—are tucked inside. Only, when she opens the shed doors, latches one back to the right, the other back to the left, the only word she finds is "Okay."

Axel knows that she's trying. He does. So he lets her in on an important reason for trusting him this afternoon, just in case she needs another. "I want to check the nest," he says.

Byrd rests a pot on her hip, wipes a canvas glove over her forehead. "Okay" is all she says.

Ray's instincts are fine-tuned, because as soon as Byrd gives the okay, he tears toward the woods. Axel runs too, just not as fast as Ray. He opens his arms like he and Daniel did on Saturday, lets the fresh air rush along him. There's something about the hush of air to skin that sets Axel's mind free of worry.

Axel catches Emmett out of the corner of his eye, waving a dish towel in his direction. The same red dish towel he leaves on his shoulder most of the day. To wipe his messy hands. From flour or butter, or whatever else he might be getting into in his kitchen. "Tell the girls we said hello," he calls from his front porch.

"The girls?" Axel shouts.

"The baby eagles," Emmett says.

"So there are two?" Axel calls back, then just because he wants Emmett to stay curious, he says, "And we don't know the gender!"

Emmett waves the towel again, not like he's trying to get Axel's attention, like he's cheering Axel on. "Don't let our Ray run off," he adds.

"He won't," Axel says. He trusts Ray to wait. Trusts him the way good friends can be trusted. Ray's at the edge of the red barn, nose to the ground, in pursuit of some scent. "Walk with me," Axel tells him, just like George would.

And that's just what happens. They walk together in the woods they know so well. Over snapping branches and soft patches of earth. Ray stops at a tree, bare in the back from deer rub, and sniffs, and sniffs, and sniffs. Axel smells the pine scent, too, but certainly not as strong as Ray. For Ray, this one scent is multiplied by one thousand. He smells the history of the tree, the visitors who have come and gone. Axel only smells the evergreen scent that reminds him of the cardboard cutout in Frank's old truck. The green one, the cutout, not the truck, that gave off that same musty scent. Only that was fake, and this is real.

Ray stares. Like if he looks hard enough, some squirrel will appear between the pine needles you can touch and the ones cast by pine shadows.

The squirrel doesn't come today. Not at this one tree, but there's hope. Someday Ray's wish might come true.

Someday Ray will find a tree full of squirrels, and Axel will see the eagles fly. Both of these hopes can come true.

"Walk with me," Axel reminds Ray again. They move from one fern-lined path to another. The paths made from years of walking the same ways, from Ray running the routes, back and forth. Back and forth. Axel can't help but think of the hallway he walked so many times today, how if those bright lights in the school were replaced by the dancing sunlight coming through the trees, that path would be anything but boring. That path would be like this. A place to think, and smell pine, and walk and walk.

When they arrive at the nest today, there is excitement inside. Not sad cries, or alarms like in the hallways at school. Ray and Axel get close enough to listen, but far enough to see it all. If they were too close to the tree, close enough to sniff it, they could only look up at the base of the nest. This way, from just a few feet back, Axel can take in the whole sight of it. Ray leans all of his dog weight against Axel's leg.

"Soon, Ray," Axel whispers. Soon enough those babies inside will try to fly. He feels this in his gut. Daniel might find this funny, but Axel doesn't care. Maybe it is funny, to feel something so strongly for another living thing. But he does. He knows that this is true.

Axel waits and listens. All of the worries of the day rise from him, and left behind is the hope for those babies in flight.

And then an unexpected gift comes to him, something he hadn't even thought to hope for. She appears at the rim of the nest. The mom. It must be the mom—big and proud, puffed up as round as an eagle can grow.

Her hooked beak turns down, like she's taking some thinking time, too. Axel knows that he can make the same face when he thinks. Emmett always points this out when he's driving Axel to the sanctuary. When he looks in the rearview mirror and sees Axel's thinking face.

It looks sad, but it isn't. Just thinking. Right now, Axel wonders what the mom is thinking. Does she know of storms? And drills? And tornados?

Her head nods in the direction of Axel and Ray. Instincts tell her to be cautious of them. And, as much as Axel might want to say, *We're friends*, he knows that's not what she needs to hear. She's a bird. A mighty bird. And she doesn't care much for what a kid like him has to say.

She doesn't need him as a friend. She only needs respect.

Axel says nothing. This is his way of showing her that she has his respect, and so much more. But maybe there's more magic to it all than Axel would ever admit, because even though she doesn't need to put on a show for Axel, and even though she doesn't know about the day he had, she gives something spectacular to Axel.

In one fluid movement, she lifts from the rim of the nest, wings expanding with the thinning tree cover to a full spread. She soars toward the clouds while Axel and Ray watch in absolute awe. Higher and higher she rises until the whole sky swallows her up. Gone.

"Holy crow," Axel says. Ray's pointer nose and wide eyes stay on the sky. "I can't wait to tell Daniel," Axel says.

And because Axel and Ray can be trusted to do just what

they set out to do, they head for home now. Back to George in the field, and kisses from Ray.

Axel doesn't stick around long with George and Ray. It's time for reading at the window, and besides, Byrd didn't want him to be gone long.

"I'm back," he says as he passes her shed, moves over the walkway, even the wobbly stones, with ease.

"Axel," she calls, but he doesn't stop.

It's time to read. Byrd will just have to wait.

Talking to her would rip the image that is resting in his mind.

A special image of that mother. That eagle soaring, knowing just how high she could fly.

CHAPTER NINE

Worries

No one worries about an eagle
in flight.
> Alone.

Soaring in solitude,
above rain clouds
one hundred miles or more.

Seeing the world
through sharp,
smart,
eagle eyes.

That's enough,
> until it's not.

When family calls,
the eagle focuses
sharp, smart
everything
on one thing
> the nest.

This is how an eagle soars.

FROM AXEL'S FAVORITE PERCH BY THE WINDOW, he can't fall into the pages of his book. This is an odd thing for Axel. He blames the day. From the way it started with a disappointment, to the way it grew to something great—the eagle soaring. And all of the moments in between disappointment and greatness. Somehow, all of these things together do not make Axel feel settled, and more than anything, Axel wants to feel settled when he cracks open a book.

Outside the window, the creek moves quickly, like his own mind. Which isn't so odd, because the clouds above rush their way through the sky, too. It was easy to forget about the weather in the shadows of the forest, in the presence of the eagle, but now Axel gathers clues.

Dark sky.

Thick clouds.

That odd feeling he knows to be a dip in air pressure.

Tree limbs that bend like Byrd when she does her yoga in the backyard. Bend all the way to one side, then back to the other. Clues that tighten inside Axel's gut, and this time, he knows for certain Daniel wouldn't find it funny. Not at all.

Just as the clues start to piece into something bigger, Byrd blows in from her garden. Wind and dirt slip in the door behind her. "They were wrong," she announces, throwing her gloves.

"Who?" Axel says. "The snakes?"

"Weather predictors," she says, no snakes on her mind today. "It's a warning, not a watch." Byrd swipes a banana from the counter, grabs a handful of other things. "Let's go," she says.

The demands of her voice have faded in Axel's mind. Instead, he gives one last long look out his window, his window framed, and framing sky, creek, tree. He leans against the cool of it then, presses his left cheek against it, trying his best to peer through the thick patch of trees that dot the creek, follow them up the bend in the creek to where the eagles' nest should be. He can't exactly see it, but he can picture it all the same.

"Did she make it home?" he wonders out loud.

Byrd knocks her hand against the basement doorframe. "Did you hear me? Warning, not watch," she repeats.

The words fall over each other in his mind the way the tree branches outside cross over one another. The clues snap in place then: sky, trees, creek, and warning. Like a bolt of lightning himself, he bolts for the door. Only it's the wrong door.

"Where are you going?" Byrd shouts from across the

room. "To the basement," she commands. And like a giant exclamation point on her words, the world lets loose a violent thunderclap.

Axel races across the room, flings open the basement door, all the while his stomach fills with woodpeckers all trying to hammer out of him.

He stumbles down the steps, which narrow to the dug-out basement. Byrd latches the door behind as Axel pulls the chain in the middle of the room for some light.

Frank's drawing table takes up most of the basement. Sloped on one side with Frank's papers left on top. A drawing of some barn somewhere. Like this barn stopped being a thing the moment Frank left it behind.

Maybe it's the storm, or today's drill, or the sound of thunder, but Axel can't stop himself from dragging a swift arm across the top of Frank's desk. Papers flutter to the ground, not the crash that Axel had hoped for. Uneasiness grows inside him.

"Come over here," Byrd says. She fights to work her hair into a pile on top of her head, like getting that locked down will replace the fact that they're stuffed into a tight space with Frank's old junk.

Axel leaves Frank's desk and the mess he's made behind. "It smells down here," he says.

"Damp has a way of getting on everything," Byrd says. She scans the rough floors and cement walls. She might be checking for snakes. She might be checking for water. Who knows? "We just have to ride out the storm for a little while, then everything will be back to normal."

"Yeah, right," Axel says. "My gag reflex is working his way up."

"Axel," Byrd says, her hair finally pulled tightly from her face. She rubs at the sides of her eyes, where she has deep wrinkles that never go away. Not when she smiles, and not when she cries. "Axel, we should talk," Byrd says. Her face twists in an ugly way.

"Let's not talk," Axel says. "I don't want to talk. I don't feel good." He holds a hand over his mouth. His queasy stomach fills with worry and the smell of the basement, and Frank's papers on the floor.

"I have a granola bar in here somewhere," Byrd says, pawing through her pockets. "Want half?" she offers.

Caw.

"It's not granola. It's fig. Do you want me to throw up?"

Axel isn't a fan of throwing up, but the thought of throw up makes him want to throw up. And now there is the bad smell and the thought of fig bars and the storm. Axel begins to pace in a space that isn't ideal for pacing. He may as well be climbing the walls.

Byrd's eyes move from Axel to the phantom snakes lurking in the dugout. She knows they're here somewhere, just waiting to strike.

That's when the first smack hits the house, like a bat to a ball. Another crack. Glass shatters. Wind howls. And Byrd grabs Axel by both hands. "This okay?" she asks. Axel lets her hold him.

The power goes next, lights out in the damp basement. Dark and rank, and too tight for two people who don't want to be there.

The smell battles into Axel's lungs. His tongue pushes to the back of his throat, ready to choke out the smell or push his lunch out into the angry world.

Byrd mumbles a song. Tries to be solid for Axel when her world has gone dark, too.

When the hammering ends, Byrd opens her phone, letting light pierce the dark room. The staircase comes sharply into view and Axel crawls toward it on hands and knees.

"Stay here," Byrd warns.

Axel holds like a statue, hands curled around the bottom step. Byrd slides past him. Next is the weight of her on each wooden step, until the door at the top of the staircase flashes open, light spilling into the basement.

"Oh no," Byrd cries. "My babies," she says.

Axel lets go of the step. He leaves the comfort of the quiet basement for the chaos of the world above.

CHAPTER TEN

After

Sometimes water washes,
sometimes she screams.

"**DON'T**," Byrd shouts when Axel bolts for the front door. "It's still raining," she adds, like any of that matters.

It's raining outside, yes, but it's also raining inside, where an eastern white pine has smashed through Axel's bay window. Where a tree sliced into the side of the house. The only side with windows. All those little windows that made the big window. Axel's favorite. Scattered. Smashed.

"The outside is already inside," Axel says before pulling wide the door. He looks to the sky above, which isn't angry at all. The blue coming back and chasing the gray clouds away.

"Don't leave the fence," Byrd calls after him. "If there's still a fence."

The last great storm, the one that Aunt Nancy called the Big One, took out the fence. Lifted it out of the earth and tossed it around. Axel doesn't remember this, of course. Frank was here then. Rebuilt the fence. Rebuilt George and Emmett's barn after that same storm. Had enough wood left over to make Byrd's potting shed. Even used a wood burner to etch those words: *Byrd's Potting Shed.*

And that all stands today. Everything Frank touched. George and Emmett's barn, Byrd's shed, the fence.

Byrd's raised flower beds survived. The flowers inside weren't as lucky. It's like one of those claw games from the arcade came and pinched nearly every box clean. Grabbed her flowers, maybe her snakes too, and just whipped the prizes into the air. Balls of roots and smashed stems tossed against the fence posts, against the cars, against the stone walkway.

Axel opens his clenched fists, palms to the sky, and lets the light rain tap against him. It's just rain, after all. The worst is over.

Ray's bark breaks the air around Axel.

"Everything okay?" George calls. He moves as quickly as he can, over downed limbs on his own walkway, to the fence. Ray slips under the fence, finds Axel.

Ray presses wet fur against Axel's bare leg. He doesn't smell quite like Ray, and doesn't feel quite like comfort.

"Everything okay?" George repeats. He grabs a limb from the hood of Byrd's car on his way past.

Axel opens and closes his hands, with the tickle of rain on the outside, then inside. Somehow he's calm, so calm, when he says, "There's a tree inside our house."

George moves more quickly than Axel has ever seen before, through the gate, down the walkway, even on the uneven stones, even over the slippery leaves on the ground. Ray leaves Axel's side to catch George. They both dash through the open door, out of the soft rain, and into the house.

Axel is too curious to go straight in, even though a knot inside his stomach starts to form. A knot that might be telling him outside isn't safe. But is inside any better?

From the outside, though, Axel sees the other half of the tree. The way it has tipped away from the creek, over the top of the picnic table, which it hasn't touched, and landed with only its top inside the house. More than 80 percent of the tree still outside. No longer a tall eastern white pine, instead a slanted one with all branches hanging like sad arms toward the ground.

The green still forest green, even inside his little white house. Even with rectangular pieces of roof hanging like ornaments from its needles.

It belongs straight up. Solid. Tall. Not hanging on to the side of the house.

If this tree has fallen, what about the others?

What about the trees outside Ms. Dale's office? What about Ms. Dale? What about Daniel and his house, and those trees near the front porch where his sisters sing and dance? What about everyone and everything?

The crash of all of this hurt and all this wondering pulls Axel from outside his house back inside, where Byrd sits on the floor, in a puddle of water and debris. Where Byrd sits with one small piece of glass pinched between her thumb and pointer finger. Just one. Even though there is glass all over the floor. This one piece, no bigger than a penny, has all of her attention. Are there clues in it?

"What are you doing?" Axel whispers, but Byrd doesn't say a thing. Axel doesn't get any closer than the kitchen island. He doesn't wander into the space that was once his living room, or to the puddle where Byrd sits that was once dry wood floor.

George drops from the bottom step back into the living room. "Upstairs isn't pretty," he says. "That tree might not be finished falling."

This is too important to ignore, and Byrd's mind is as clear as the glass in her hand. "Take Axel," she says. "I'll pack a bag."

Ray leaps for the front door, ready to lead his family outside. But Axel doesn't budge. How could he leave his house when it is hurt like this?

"Come on, Axel," George says. When Axel finally moves, he walks in the opposite direction of George and Ray. He goes closer to the tree, closer to the hole that was once his favorite perch. Ray can't help but follow Axel's lead.

Axel steps in Byrd's puddle, then on the soggy rug that was once dry. He can't place the scent at first, because he's never smelled it in his house. In the corners of the woods, yes. The fake version in Frank's truck, yes. But not right here. Right where his favorite thinking spot used to be. That musty nature smell. Fresh pine, right under his nose.

Ray sniffs at the tree too, like he wants to know its secrets.

"Axel," Byrd says.

Axel wants to know this tree's secrets too. Why did it enter this part of his world? Why his window? Why this storm?

Ray sniffs again, closer, still closer. It smells like the outside has come in. There's something about the way Ray sniffs it. The way it smells, really, really smells like something the inside is not supposed to smell like. All clues to let Axel know it is time to leave his home, to leave behind this mess. Time to make a plan for what happens next.

"Byrd rushes," Axel says. "I want to pack my own bag."

"No," George says. "Come to think of it, I don't want anyone to go back up those steps until you have an engineer out to check the structure. The steps look okay, but are they? Or am I just a lucky star who didn't fall from the sky?"

"What?" Axel says. He starts for the steps. He can pack his own bag.

And that's when Byrd whispers, "Frank."

And Axel stops.

And George says, "Any engineer, really. Anyone."

Byrd, frozen in the same spot on the wet floor, looks to George. "Frank," she repeats.

"He won't show up," Axel says. This is the same Frank who doesn't come on Saturdays, even though he made promises. Counting on Frank isn't a plan at all.

Byrd and George turn to Axel like he's said something surprising, which is weird because he didn't even say out loud everything he was feeling. And besides, they know Frank hasn't shown, so why would he now? Just because of a storm? Because of a fallen tree? Because he once loved this house? Because his kid can't go upstairs to his own room until he says that it is safe?

"Ray," George says sternly, snapping everyone's attention from one side of the room to the other. Axel turns just in time to see his best friend lift his leg on the indoor tree. "Leave it," George shouts. But it's too late.

Somehow a laugh curls from Byrd's lips, even though she's lost her fiddle-leaf fig, her ferns, and all the others. Somehow George smiles, even though his "leave it" sounded angry. Somehow Axel knows that it is okay to leave the house behind because at least he'll be with Ray and George and Emmett and Aunt Nancy. "Instincts," Axel says.

"Ray! Come," George says. And Ray does. He has left his mark on this outside tree that's fallen inside. Added a new scent that also doesn't belong in this little cottage.

"Let's go," Axel says, holding a hand over his nose.

George nods, then says to Byrd, "How about you call from our house?"

"I'll go outside and call," Byrd says. "Can you take Axel and tell Nance and Emmett?"

George nods again.

"I'll tell them about the pee," Axel says, already at the door.

"Fair enough," George says. "You tell them what a bad neighbor Ray's being."

"He's a great neighbor," Axel says. "He can't fight what his insides are telling him to do. Tree equals pee."

"That's true," Byrd says.

"Be careful," George tells her. There are other words not spoken just then, a look between George and Byrd.

Axel can't tell if the house is the only thing George wants Byrd to "be careful" about. So he adds, "Don't worry about the pee. It doesn't matter that there's pee in the house; there's already a tree in here."

"That's true," Byrd says again. She peels herself from the floor, follows Axel and George and Ray outside. The rain has ended, not even the soft spritz remains, just sky that is blue and a breeze that is soft.

"Walk with me," George says.

Axel knows that he's talking to Ray, but he walks with George just the same. Back down the stone walkway, through the sturdy gate, and away from his home.

CHAPTER ELEVEN

Cries

From A. P. Brown's *Collection of North American Birds*, page 661

BIODIVERSITY: the great abundance of life in an ecosystem

GEORGE SEES IT BEFORE RAY, before Axel.

Sees it and points.

Past the fence. Through the field that doesn't quite look like a field.

In all the hurt inside Axel's house.

In the worried way George rushed inside Axel's house.

They'd missed it. Missed a field with trees scattered all around. Missed a field that this morning was golden grasses and green shoots. Missed upended trees, roots facing sky not earth.

Axel has to squint. Has to try to sort out all of the things he shouldn't see, to find the one thing he must.

A nest.

"That's why she makes the sides so high," George says.

Ray runs. He whines his most worrying sound. His frantic race around the nest dizzying. George shouts, "Hush up," but it's no use. Ray can't stop himself from worry any more than Axel can. It isn't until George reaches Ray and grabs hold of his muzzle that another cry hits the air.

This one less fevered, low and painful. Unlike George, Axel doesn't need to get up close to the nest to know what's happening. Animals are far better at communicating their feelings, and this animal, this fallen bird, in a fallen nest, is communicating one thing: hurt.

"It's the eaglet," George says. It isn't like George to give away the answer to a mystery so quickly, but it is like him to pull Ray away, knowing what could come next.

"We need to move back," George says. "Everyone back."

He grabs Ray by the collar so that Ray has no escape, no way to race to the eaglet, no power to check on the fallen baby bird. George pulls at Axel too. And even though they are moving away from the nest, away from the eaglet's cries, somehow they feel louder, sharper, sadder.

"It isn't safe," George says, his eyes on the bent-over tree line, in parts looking like a giant lawn mower came across the earth, flattening trees in its path. "The standing trees could fall too."

But Axel's legs don't move just because George wishes they would. Nope. Axel, like his own fence, like Byrd's potting shed, like the flower boxes, like the remaining trees, is rooted to the ground.

"We need to let the bird rest in peace," George says. "We'll go see Nance and Emmett and wait for your mom."

"We need to help the eaglet," Axel says.

And because George can't manage both a wiggly dog and a determined boy, he lets go of Ray's collar. And naturally Ray bounds back toward the crying eaglet in the fallen nest.

"We need Dr. Martin," Axel says.

And even though George says, "Okay, okay, okay," he does not take out his phone.

Just like Byrd needs Frank for the house, the eaglet needs Dr. Martin to survive, so why isn't George calling?

"Axel, I saw the eaglet," George says slowly. "It won't survive."

"You don't know that," Axel says. "You aren't a veterinarian. You aren't an ornithologist. You aren't an expert on life and death."

"No one is an expert on life and death," George says. "But I saw the eaglet."

"Call Dr. Martin," Axel says. There is no need for "please" or "will you"; this is an emergency. Dr. Taylor M. Martin, bird rescuer, is what's needed to stop Ray from circling the nest, and to save the crying eaglet from death. "Call Dr. Martin," Axel repeats.

"*In death around thee—and their will / Shall overshadow thee: be still,*" George begins.

"No!" Axel snaps. "Not words. We need Dr. Martin."

Only action is needed. Action like calling Dr. Martin. Action like saving the eaglet. Axel's body shivers with the need to do something, anything, and yet he won't go back to the nest. He won't circle the bird the way Ray does. The image in his head is enough to tell him about the hurt. He doesn't need to see it with his own eyes.

He tears from his spot with George, through the field and

over branches, past the front porch, where Emmett stands calling out words that aren't strong enough to stop Axel. He snakes down the walkway, shouting for Byrd until he finds her, curled over a planter that is missing its plants.

"Call her," Axel pants.

"Him?" Byrd whispers, a swath of dirt across her face like she'd wiped at one thing, leaving behind another. "He didn't answer."

"Her . . . Dr. Martin," Axel says. He takes Byrd by the hands, pulls her tightly to him, like she does when the information is important. When the world needs to stop spinning. "Trees fell everywhere on the other side of the field. The tree with the nest must have fallen too—the nest flew. It landed in . . . It landed in the field with a baby inside . . . It's hurt. Call Dr. Martin."

"I'll call first thing tomorrow," Byrd says, still in her whisper voice. "Dr. Martin may have other—"

"No," Axel interrupts. How can Byrd be so wrong? This baby has been separated from its mom and dad, in a nest that has fallen from the tree that probably fell too, and George said it was bad. Maybe a broken wing, or sternum, or tail. That bird's whole world turned upside down during the storm.

"Call Dr. Martin," Axel demands again. He drops Byrd's hands, presses his own over his ears to shut out Byrd's response, to shut out the cries that he can still hear from all the way across the field, to shut out as much of the hurt as he can.

"You have to trust me," Axel says. He doesn't want to hear her say "wait" or "I do." He wants her really to trust him. To know that he knows what's best.

Byrd pulls her phone from her pocket.

She dials a number.

Her lips move.

And this is finally enough. Axel races back down the walkway, through the gate, over branches and debris, and to the front porch where George stands with Ray and Emmett.

"Help is coming," Axel says. He looks right at Ray. "Dr. Martin will know just what to do."

This is the truth.

Dr. Taylor M. Martin is an animal doctor, an ornithologist, a veterinary surgeon. An impressive list. She also gives presentations to kids, like at Axel's school. She's also the founder and president of the Delaware Valley Raptor Sanctuary. Dr. Taylor M. Martin is very important.

Axel knows the sanctuary. It is a place for raptors to rehabilitate. A place for eagles and owls, falcons and kestrels, hawks and vultures, ospreys and buzzards, too. A safe place for injured birds to heal, then return to the sky.

But how do the birds get to the sanctuary? That's another thing to add to Dr. Taylor M. Martin's very impressive list. She makes house calls.

Today it isn't as easy to get to the house who made the call, but after an hour or so, Dr. Martin's red pickup truck pulls its nose to Axel's fence.

Axel races from George and Emmett's porch, Ray at his side.

Ray's nubby tail wags so hard it seems like it could snap off and bounce down the gravel driveway. Ray starts to bounce, too, the moment Dr. Martin slips from the driver's side door.

"No dogs," she says.

"This is Ray," Axel says. He knows he's talked to Dr. Martin about Ray before. She must know that Ray belongs here.

"Dogs get in the way," Dr. Martin says.

Ray presses into Axel like if he anchors himself to his friend, there's no way he'll be taken from the rescue team. Emmett says, "Ray, come."

Ray leans harder.

George says, "Come," in his most serious voice. Axel feels Ray's body slump before turning toward the porch. "Come on, Ray," George says.

Poor Ray will miss the rescue. Axel can't help himself, he turns too, kneels down next to Ray. "I won't let anything happen to the baby," he whispers into Ray's floppy ear. "You can trust me."

As soon as Ray makes it to the porch and Emmett pulls him inside, Dr. Martin opens the back door of the truck. A little girl with bright yellow boots slides out.

Dr. Martin grabs a black bag from the floor of the truck. So does the little girl.

"This is my daughter," Dr. Martin says. "Lark."

After this brief introduction, Dr. Martin begins moving through the twilight toward the field. Perhaps Byrd gave very clear directions, though, more likely, Dr. Martin knows in her gut where the nest must be.

The whole pack follows her sure lead. Lark with her bag, George and now Emmett, and Axel. And even Byrd, who more than anything wants to fix her own house, not save another. But she's walking now, over sticks and clumps of soil, following Dr. Martin.

It isn't more than a minute before Dr. Martin shoots an arm behind her, her fingers spread out like a stop sign. Dr. Martin doesn't turn her body to the pack behind her; instead she nods her head in the direction of what's left of the tree line. "See the adults?" It's hard to focus on the remaining trees with all the destruction around them, harder still to squint into the dusk crawling in over the field. "They're too close for us to . . ."

Once Axel's eyes catch the unmistakable white heads, like two glowing circles in the tree, the rest of the world fades away. The parents came back for their baby.

Dr. Martin is lost for a moment, too. She never finishes her sentence; instead she looks from the parents, to the pack behind her, to George and Emmett's house, then to the nest.

She whispers something, far too softly for any of her fellow rescuers to hear.

A plan builds in the mind of this expert. An impressive plan, for sure. A plan that will require the entire pack to rescue one very important bird.

CHAPTER TWELVE

Plan

The compact brain
tight inside curved skull
light enough for flight

packs motor and senses,
reason
purpose,
and promise.

"CAN SOMEONE GET ME A SHEET?" Dr. Martin asks.

Emmett springs into action. "Anything in particular? Fitted? White?"

"A sheet," Dr. Martin says. Her fingers make imaginary calculations in the air before she calls after Emmett. "And a pot and spoon if you have them."

"Of course," Emmett says. Now, this he can really help with. "Wooden spoon, slotted, or . . ."

"A sheet. A pot. A spoon," Dr. Martin lists.

Emmett's kitchen has more pots and spoons than can fit in the cabinets. Copper pots hang from a wooden rack on the far side of the kitchen; big spoons and ladles are shoved into ceramic holders near the stove top. He must be thinking of all of the pot-spoon combinations he could make, because he waits for more clarification. Waits, though Dr. Martin says nothing more.

"I can help," George says, wrapping an arm around Emmett. "Check on Nance, too."

Dr. Martin gets binoculars out. Lark takes out a pair of

her own binoculars but doesn't peer through them the way her mother does. Instead she twirls the cord around her finger.

"What can I do?" Byrd asks. Dr. Martin has plans to make, Axel has eagles to watch in the tree, Lark digs through her own black bag; Byrd does not get a response. "Did you have any damage at your house?" Byrd asks Dr. Martin.

"We sure did," Lark answers for her mother. "The tree with my swing fell down."

"I'm sorry to hear that," Byrd says.

"I'll survive," Lark says, like maybe she's heard that phrase before.

"Sheet, spoon, and pot," George says, banging the top of the pot for emphasis.

"Shhhh" is the first thing Dr. Martin's said in a while. And even this she says, then returns to the binoculars with nothing more.

"I thought we were in a hurry," George whispers, more to Byrd than anyone, but Lark giggles.

"How's Nance?" Byrd asks.

"Emmett's making her some tea. You know storms really rattle her. Sometimes you think a person's seen everything, then you remember, once you've seen everything, you know what the fallout can be." George hands the pot to Byrd. "I can't imagine what this is for," he says. The pot looks entirely too fancy for a bird rescue, with its rolled copper edges and pristine silver handles. The spoon is wooden, stained after years of use, but thick and sturdy just the same.

George shakes free the sheet. It's from the guest room on the second floor, where Aunt Nancy used to stay before she couldn't do the steps any longer. Axel sometimes goes in there to think on evenings after dinners at George and Emmett's house. The sheet has tiny teacups covering it in all shades of blue.

Lark grabs at the end of the sheet and spins herself inside the teacups.

"It's for coverage," Dr. Martin says when she joins the group again. "The sheet," she clarifies. "The pot is for distraction."

"Oh," Byrd says.

"Distraction?" Axel asks.

"Yes," Dr. Martin says. "To distract the adults there or any other predator who might want to grab the prey."

"Predator? Prey?" Axel looks back at the adults. He looks to the nest. "No. Those are the baby's parents. They've come to make sure we're helping their baby, not eat the thing."

"You don't know that," Dr. Martin says. "They probably care more about the nest than the bird inside."

The words bite at Axel. This answer doesn't match with the other facts he knows about Dr. Martin: that she's a birder, that she heals injured animals, that she returns birds to the sky, to their families.

"I need to assess the injuries," Dr. Martin adds. These words make more sense. "See if the sanctuary is the best place for her. See if she can even be saved."

"We don't know that it's a girl," Axel says. If words matter to Dr. Martin, the way they matter to George, she should make note of such things.

"It's a girl, isn't it, Mommy?" Lark asks, peeking out from the sheet she's wrapped around her entire body, now only her yellow boots and round brown face are visible.

"We don't know. Axel's right. All we know is this bird is in distress," Dr. Martin says. Lark pulls the sheet back across her face.

"The eaglet isn't crying," Axel says, the silence only now upon him. The cries from earlier are gone, with the occasional shrill note coming from the adults in the tree.

"That's not a good sign," Dr. Martin says. "We need to get closer."

Dr. Martin tosses out orders to Byrd and George. One with a pot and the other a sheet.

George tries his best to gently unravel the sheet, to get busy with his part of the rescue, but Lark refuses to budge from her cocoon. Instead she murmurs, "I want to help, too."

Axel wants to be a part of the rescue. He promised Ray. And he was the one to bring Dr. Martin here in the first place. But the words don't come out quite the same as Lark's demand. He says, "I can take one side of George's sheet. Together we can spread out and hide the nest from the adults."

"Of course," Dr. Martin says. "And you," she says, putting a firm hand on Lark's covered head and freezing her wiggling daughter in place, "you can walk out wide with Axel's mom.

Stay clear of the trees, but in the eye of the adults. You can sing. Wave your arms. Bang the pot. Get their eyes on you."

Lark lowers the sheet, revealing a wide smile.

"Got it?" her mom asks.

"I can make noise," Lark says. She drops the sheet and grabs the wooden spoon, grabs Byrd's hand too.

"Go," Dr. Martin says, and Byrd and Lark skip and sing and hop as they head toward the big red barn.

Axel and George spread out before Dr. Martin, the teacup sheet stretching at least eight feet between the two. It hits the ground on Axel's side until he bunches it into his hands. "Higher," Dr. Martin says, and Axel reaches his arms as far as he can over his head. It looks like they might do a magic trick, Dr. Martin hidden behind the sheet with her black bag in her hands. It feels magical too, a rescue.

A rescue that Axel is very much a part of. His job is to focus on keeping the sheet high, keeping the nest concealed so that Dr. Martin can assess the situation. Only, as they near the nest, the cries that Axel thought hushed are suddenly audible. A ragged cry, but a cry just the same.

The nest is not meant to be his focus, nor the baby's cries, but with each step closer to the nest, he can't fight the urge to glimpse inside. To see what Ray circled around. To see who is making such a sad sound.

He and George lift the sheet over the back of the nest, let it drop down in front of the open side. George tall and focused, but Axel . . . not. As soon as his eyes catch the eaglet, he cannot look away. He cannot hold his arms high. He cannot do his job. Not at all.

He drops to his knees.

He drops beside the injured bird.

CHAPTER THIRTEEN

Rescue I

Gray puff of downy feathers,

Beak, a downward sigh,

Marble eyes set to the distance.

All a call for help.

DR. MARTIN'S SURE HAND covers the eaglet's gaze. The other hand moves feather soft across the rest of the bird's body.

"Axel," she says. "Open the bag."

Axel opens the black bag, wide like a hungry mouth. Dr. Martin cradles the bird and slowly lowers the eaglet inside. "Zip," she says.

She keeps her hands on the bird, all the while listening, watching, until the zipper closes in around her forearms. She releases her hold on the eaglet, slips her hands from the bag, and zips the last three inches. When she stands, the bag is not a bag any longer, at least not in Axel's eyes. This is a stretcher, a crate, a protective case to deliver this baby to the Delaware Valley Raptor Sanctuary.

"Go," Dr. Martin says.

And George and Axel, Dr. Martin, and now the baby, move swiftly through the field over fallen branches, past roots and leaves. When they reach the front porch, Dr. Martin and Lark disappear into the truck. The rescue goes on with them.

Ray's so happy to be out of the house his whole body

shakes. He jumps up, places front paws on George's chest with a huge lick to the face.

"Quite a night," Emmett says. "I don't know how Nancy fell asleep with all that commotion."

"Commotion?" Axel asks. "It was quiet. So quiet. Only the baby's soft cries."

"You missed the main event," Emmett says. "Byrd and that little girl were carrying on. Such a ruckus. What song was that?"

Byrd laughs. "Who knew a tree falling into the house wouldn't be the most exciting part of my day?"

"That wasn't the main event," Axel insists. "We saved the baby. Dr. Martin placed the eaglet in the bag so gently. We saved it."

"I guess the main event depends on where you were standing," George says. "I watched those adults take off at the sound of Byrd's crooning. That banging pot, too."

"That was Lark," Byrd says. "She's a character."

"I didn't hear the pot or your voice," Axel says. "I heard the cries. I heard Dr. Martin's directions."

"The story is in the eye of the beholder," George says.

"Is it too late to eat?" Byrd asks, taking the important story and mixing it with something else.

"Never," Emmett says. "I'll heat something up. Come in, come in."

The adults move from the porch, and Ray circles back.

"The main event was the baby," Axel says, running his hand down Ray's spine.

Ray moves for the steps, ready to circle back around the nest, ready to join Axel on any adventure he would like.

"Not tonight, Ray," Axel says. "We'll gather some clues tomorrow."

And even though that should be enough, the promise of tomorrow, Axel and Ray sit out on the porch a while longer. The day falling back piece by broken piece into view with school and the storm, the tree in the house. And the nest tossed like so many other things out of place.

Axel will have to sleep in the teacup room, without the teacup sheet, tonight. He'll have to wake up and see his house and the field in the morning light.

There are so many new mysteries to solve now, and none of them bigger than the baby's rescue.

None of them. Not even Frank.

CHAPTER FOURTEEN

Emails

FROM: Axel Rastusak
TO: Dr. Taylor M. Martin
SUBJECT: This is Axel

Dear Dr. Martin,

This is Axel.

I can't wait around for Byrd to call you. I want to know about the baby.

Use this email address to update me about the eaglet's rescue.

This is Axel Rastusak.

Sincerely,
Axel Rastusak

Dear Axel,

I'm happy to use this email address, and pleased to update you that the eaglet is alive.

This would be a much different email if that weren't the case.

He suffered some significant shock, and only today am I able to spend some more time with him in the exam room. He needs rest, though, not a human poking him. After today, however, if you want to see the eaglet, please come down. You don't need an appointment.

I've been thinking about the adults that we spotted last night. Eagles, like most raptors, are extremely attached to their nests. For some eagle pairs, that same nest might be used twenty times or more to lay, hatch, and nurture their offspring. They fly in, add to it a bit each year, really make something special. I didn't have much time to examine the nest last night, but do think it is possible that the adults were the former habitants of the nest and, therefore, the eaglet's parents.

Keep an eye on the nest, and on the woods. Don't go out there. Those trees aren't safe structures right now. Use your binoculars. See if they build a provisional nest nearby. Notice which trees they land in. Those are the safe trees.

As I said, please do come and visit the eaglet. You are, after all, the reason he is alive.

Sincerely,
Dr. Taylor M. Martin
Delaware Valley Raptor Sanctuary
VMD-PhD

P.S. Lark enjoyed the rescue so much she drew a picture. Maybe she can share it with you when you visit?

CHAPTER FIFTEEN

Frank

From A. P. Brown's *Collection of North American Birds*, page 491

"It should be noted the wild turkey (*Meleagris gallopavo*) is capable of flight.

The domestic turkey (*Meleagris gallopavo domesticus*) is bred to remain anchored to the earth.

AUNT NANCY, who gets all the good information first, says that a certain engineer does not deem Axel and Byrd's house livable.

It's a real mystery how Aunt Nancy is first to gather secrets and stories though she rarely leaves the house. Somehow her whole family feeds her with all the clues she needs to build a case against someone.

And she's not the lawyer of the family. But she certainly has a case against Frank.

She's a storyteller.

Fitting that both she and her brother love words so much they have to share them. George with his poems, and Aunt Nancy with her storytelling. She used to tell stories during catechism at the church in New Mexico, but when she moved here, she stopped going out, even to church. She still prays. All the time. Everywhere.

But not inside a church.

After praying over her meal, Aunt Nancy starts gossiping

at the table with Emmett about what Frank said. Axel starts to pace. He goes the length of the front room. Over the hardwood floors and the thick braided rug. All the while Aunt Nancy uses that term "certain engineer." Why doesn't she just say his name? Everyone knows who she's gossiping about.

"Byrd just letting him back in that house," she says. "Like he can come and go whenever he wants."

"Nance," Emmett says. It might sound like a warning, like the way George might correct her for gossiping, but the way it comes from Emmett means *tell me more.*

So she does.

"Said that whole second floor could come down if they don't shore up the crossbeam. Said he had to go fetch the plans. Why did he hang on to those plans, anyway? Isn't the house yours?"

Axel stops.

This is new information. This house, the farmhouse with the big round table and chef's kitchen, belongs to Emmett and George. But that home, the one across the stone path, on the other side of the fence, that was a gift to Byrd, wasn't it?

"And why's she hanging around over there with him? She doesn't know anything about rebuilding a house," Aunt Nancy adds. "He's not even there. She's just waiting for him to come back, like she waited all those times before . . . And did he come back?"

These really aren't questions to answer. They are questions to shout. Questions to shout at a certain engineer and a certain gardener. They are the only two who know the answers to these mysteries.

"George is over there playing referee," Emmett says. "A splendid job for a man with so many opinions."

"That's the truth," Aunt Nancy says.

The truth.

Truth and mysteries crash into each other in Axel's mind. Until a rumble in the driveway stirs Ray from the floor. Ray bounces and his collar jingles wildly. His bark comes next, ready to alert people for miles and miles about the truck approaching.

It's Frank's shiny new white truck with FDRemodeling, Rebuilding, Renovations on the door in red and yellow lettering. If this truck were a bird, it'd be a peacock. A male peacock. All *look at me, look at me.*

Caw.

"Your mom will find out what happens next," Emmett says, coming to stand behind Axel and Ray at the front window. Like Axel hadn't heard all the things Aunt Nancy just said.

"Next?" Axel says, but this isn't a question, really. Axel wants to believe he knows what happens next. "Next they fix the house," he says.

"Humph," Aunt Nancy says from the dining room. "I can tell you what's going to happen next."

"Nance," Emmett says. This time it does sound like a warning.

"I'm just saying, that girl gives away forgiveness like it's candy, then she comes over here licking her wounds when things don't work out the way she wants. If it were me, I'd . . ."

Outside the window, away from what Aunt Nancy would do, Frank exits his truck. He has a laptop in his hand and a long roll of paper tucked up under his arm.

Plans. Frank and Byrd are making plans, looking over plans, plans for a house. A house that, until a few minutes ago, Axel believed was his—his and Byrd's, and Frank's. But he's the only one not in on the plans.

Byrd and George and Frank are hunched over the same long white papers that rest atop one of Byrd's unflowered flower beds. The plans supported by plenty of dirt. And maybe even a snake. Or two.

Axel would love for a snake to come slithering out now. What exactly would Byrd do then? *Caw.*

Axel wishes that his mind didn't think those things. That his heart weren't so heavy with thoughts of the two of them out there making plans without him. If his heart weren't so heavy, his mind wouldn't think about snakes that way. He tries to clear the mean thought, replace it with another. "How long do you think it will be?" Axel asks.

"I don't know, maybe two weeks," Emmett says, looking at the same scene outside.

"A lifetime," Aunt Nancy calls. She slaps the bell on her rollator like she's said the most remarkable thing.

Axel looks back at Aunt Nancy. "I mean, how long will they need to do that?" he says pointing out the window.

"What?" Aunt Nancy says. The curiosity too much, she pushes up from her seat, unclenches the brakes on her rollator, and makes her way into the living room. She throws open the front door to get a better look at the goings-on outside. Sits right down on the cushion attached to the rollator.

It is a better view, so Axel goes to stand at her side. "I hope it isn't long," Axel says. "He doesn't even like it here." Axel reaches for Ray, even though Ray is nowhere to be found.

"Axel, what on earth would make you say that?" Emmett says.

"What wouldn't?" Aunt Nancy says to Emmett. "Listen, kid, your dad . . ."

But Axel's moved on to his next thought. He interrupts Aunt Nancy midsentence. "He either doesn't like the house or he doesn't like me," Axel says. This is one of the mysteries of a disappearing dad.

Aunt Nancy slaps at her knee. "You want to know the truth? I'll tell you the truth," Aunt Nancy says.

"Nanette Marie Flores," Emmett says. This is the ultimate warning, and Aunt Nancy hears it loud and clear. At least for the moment. "Let's just close this door," he says, moving Aunt Nancy, rollator and all, from the open door. "Axel, this is a freebie day. No school with the power out. A late night with the rescue. This calls for chocolate chip cookie pizza on the stove top!"

As though he could have any morsel of the treat, Ray bounces at the excitement in Emmett's voice.

"Come on," he says. "I need someone to mix."

But Axel isn't distracted by the cookie, or Emmett's warning to Aunt Nancy. If Aunt Nancy knows something, if she has the truth, if she has all the clues, he needs to know.

If it were Daniel or Ms. Dale or Dr. Martin, they would just say what they meant. They wouldn't try to hide anything. They wouldn't try to protect him like some baby.

Why is it so easy for some people to tell the truth and so very hard for others?

He turns to Aunt Nancy, takes a deep breath for courage, and readies his mouth to say the words, to ask the question that needs asking. He's ready for the truth.

But in the very next moment, in the very next deep, bravery-making breath, Ray starts barking from outside. Axel throws back open the front door in time to see Dr. Martin's truck stirring up dust when it pulls behind Frank's in the driveway. A stray rock kicks out from Dr. Martin's tire and tings Frank's gleaming white beast of a truck.

If he can't have the truth, at least he has this. "Over here," Axel calls, racing out onto the porch.

"Right," Dr. Martin says. She approaches the porch until Ray leaps at her. This is a friendly hello, but Dr. Martin turns and runs right back to her truck.

Emmett grabs Ray by the collar. "Sorry," he shouts, then

coaxes Ray inside the house. Ray joins Aunt Nancy at the window.

"Ray's friendly," Axel says when Dr. Martin approaches again.

"He's too much," Dr. Martin says.

"Oh," Axel says. "Where's the girl with yellow boots?"

"Lark," Dr. Martin clarifies. "She's at school."

"There's no school today," Axel says. "Storm damage. Power outages." It's hard to miss with the fields covered in fallen trees and the hum of generators running at the house.

"Lark goes to the Quaker school in Narrowsburg. No storm damage there."

Axel looks at his own front yard, where just behind the fence, among the fallen branches, Byrd, Frank, and George are so wrapped up in planning that they haven't turned to see Dr. Martin. "My dad lives in Narrowsburg, New York, now," Axel says.

Either this does not interest Dr. Martin, or it isn't news; either way, Dr. Martin holds up one hand. "Binoculars," she says. "I came to look at the forest in daylight."

"Is it safe?" Emmett says.

"We'll stay a safe distance," she replies, then turns to Axel. "Do you have a pair?"

As any birder would, Axel has two pairs. One that he started with, and one that he saved for. Unfortunately, both of them are in the house that he is not allowed to go into because Frank says so.

"I do," Axel says.

"Grab them," Dr. Martin says. "Let's see if we can find those adults. Get a closer look at the nest too."

"I can't," Axel says.

But before he can offer clarification, Dr. Martin says, "Look!"

She points toward the tree line, where a thick wall of trees used to be at the edge of Emmett and George's field. Now only few dot the space.

"There, in the tree to the left," she says.

And there, in a tall tree, a tree that withstood the strong winds, is one gray fluffy baby and one adult eagle. The baby isn't perched the way the adult is. It rests in the crook of the tree on a smattering of sticks no bigger than a bowl of pasta.

Dr. Martin passes her binoculars to Axel. "I wondered," she says. "Kept thinking about it after I sent you that email this morning. Would they come back?"

Through the lens Axel watches the adult preen the baby, touching it with his beak. The baby leans into his parent, leans into the feel of being cared for.

"Is that the father?" Axel wonders.

"I wonder if one is off looking for a new nest?" Dr. Martin answers Axel's question with her own. "Do they want this nest?"

"Does he wonder about the other baby?" Axel asks. He's certain that this is the father, the way he looks out to the fallen nest, and the way he cares for the baby that was spared. "Does he want to help his other baby? Did he come back to see if it was okay?"

The wondering could go on forever between Axel and Dr. Martin. Each questioning the scene before them, what is told and what is not. There aren't many answers to these questions, though. For a moment, Axel takes his eyes off the father eagle and baby bird.

He turns instead to the big white truck in his driveway.

FDRemodeling, Rebuilding, Renovations.

Maybe he has a few answers after all?

CHAPTER SIXTEEN

Questions

Do birds dream?
    Some scientists spout
    speculation, theory.

    Yet, ask the kestrel,
    the crow, the hawk,
    do theories matter if they can't talk?

BYRD PULLS THE COVERS TO HER SIDE OF THE BED.

"Now we need to start over," Axel says. They rise from bed, reposition the blankets so that there is some fairness in the matter. After all, sharing a bed isn't tops on either person's list. Being without his weighted blanket and the glow-in-the-dark hawk eyes in his bedroom do make a certain list for Axel. One titled *Caw!*

Another item for that list: Byrd not being available to drive Axel to the sanctuary tomorrow thanks to her other priorities.

"I have to go," Axel says, tucking the seam of the quilt under the mattress.

"We need to be here," Byrd says. "I already told you that."

"Right, you told me that, but you weren't being honest. *We* don't need to be here . . . *You* want to be here. You don't know how to fix a house."

"Tell me how you really feel," Byrd says, flopping back into the bed. Staying with George and Emmett does have its comforts; a king-sized bed in the guest bedroom is one such thing. If they are going to share, at least they can spread out.

"I need to be here; I just do."

"You said 'we.' Now it is just 'you.'"

"Axel, let's go to sleep," Byrd says, turning out the bedside lamp.

"It's too dark in here," Axel says.

Byrd turns back on the light.

"That's not what I meant," Axel says. "Turn it off."

Byrd huffs, then snaps off the light.

Axel returns her huff with his own. "I just don't get why you need to be here. Why can't you take me to the sanctuary? I have information about the nest. Dr. Martin asked me to keep watch, and that adult keeps coming back."

"Well, that's awfully sweet," Byrd says. "One big happy family."

Axel can't tell if she's doing that thing where she's only acting like she's telling the truth, not actually telling the truth. Because it is true that a parent with its babies could make a happy family, and she should know that. But she sounds like she thinks it's a joke.

"I need to go, and you need to take me," Axel says.

"Just send her an email," Byrd says. She yanks on the covers again, pulling the edge from the bottom of the bed. "Good night."

Well, that's just not good enough. Axel sits up, turns on his own bedside light. "You have to tell me why you need to be here."

"Don't you want to get back into our house? Into your

room?" Byrd says, like her questions answer the one he asked. They do not.

"Of course I do," Axel says. "But why do you have to be here?"

"Listen, your dad can fix the house at cost. He knows this house better than anyone else. He loves this house. He loves—"

"That's him," Axel says. "That's not you."

"We built this house together, Axel," Byrd says. "Before there was you. Before there was this storm, there was Frank and me and the dream of this house. It's the place we made our family."

Axel considers this fact. A place where a family is made. It's *still* where her family is made! Maybe smaller in size, the family, not the house, but still a family lives there. And even when they are in George and Emmett's house, even now, even tonight, aren't they still a family? With or without Frank. With or without the walls that he built.

"You might need to be with him, but I need to be at the sanctuary," Axel says. "Dr. Martin said I am the reason the baby is alive. That's just as important as saving the house that you and Frank built."

Byrd closes her eyes, not like she's falling asleep, more like she's giving up on her side of the fight. She runs her hand along the quilt, smoothing the space between herself and Axel.

"I'm sure George or Emmett could drive you, as long as the roads are okay," Byrd says. "We can ask them in the morning."

"And if they say no?" Axel presses.

"They won't," Byrd says.

"Maybe we should go ask them now?" Axel says.

Byrd takes Axel's hand. Squeezes once, then again. "Take a deep breath," she says. "We have a plan. We'll ask them in the morning. Save your worries for another time. Turn out the light. It's time for sleep." She says it all very slowly, like she's said the same five steps at least one hundred times before.

Axel turns off the light. He closes his eyes, trying to picture the glowing hawk eyes from his bedroom walls. The way the green glowing circles make his own eyes feel heavy and make his other worries feel light.

He takes a deep breath, just the way Byrd said.

If Byrd wants to stay at the house—that's fine. Axel has Emmett and George.

Emmett and George can take him to the sanctuary. Emmett and George will help him tell Dr. Taylor M. Martin his ideas.

She needs to know that the baby and the adult that she saw earlier today are the injured baby's family. And that they kept coming back. That they are waiting for the missing piece of their family to come back to them.

Axel has a plan. Yes. He'll tell Dr. Martin, and she'll find a way to bring the baby back here, back home, safe and healed, and back with his family.

––––

Axel waits all morning for George and Emmett to load up their SUV for a shopping trip. The shopping trip will coincide with dropping Axel at the Delaware Valley Raptor Sanctuary for one hour.

Emmett will get to shop at the gourmet grocer in Milford, which is only thirty minutes from Fairview, but a world away in excellent ingredients. George will sit and read at the bookshop while he waits for Emmett, while they both wait for Axel. It is an excellent plan.

Leaving their driveway, the roads are dotted with trucks servicing electrical lines, no birds in sight. It isn't until they reach downtown, just before the exit ramp to the highway, that Axel spots a few crows gathered on a phone wire. The crows and Axel have found their way to safety. Even if it's busy downtown streets and an exit ramp, it's not the damage from miles behind them.

In the car, George and Emmett sing show tunes along with channel 72, which, as Aunt Nancy likes to put it, is just another reason the two of them were destined to fall in love. She means Broadway shows. They both do love theater. They also have lovely singing voices, Emmett's very high and George's very low. And together, they make a pleasant song.

This is all well and good, especially because, with the two of them singing, Axel can listen to his own thoughts in the back seat. No one asking about little, unimportant things. Or ridiculous things, like people who ask about girlfriends or future occupations. Axel would much prefer to think about the eagle and the nest, and bringing the family back together.

And also, thoughts about visiting the raptor sanctuary on a Wednesday, which is such a special thing. The raptor sanctuary only hosts member hours on Friday afternoon and Saturday morning. The rest of time it is dedicated to helping birds, which is a very good thing to do. Axel usually goes on Fridays after school, but with no school, this trip is even more wonderful.

Only, when the noise of the radio softens and Emmett's and George's voices strain, Axel can't help but dip in and out of their words instead of his own good thoughts.

"He's getting awfully comfortable," George says. "Not that it's any of our business. She made that perfectly clear."

"What do you expect?" Emmett says. "It's his house. His family. You know he needs to be needed."

"Needs to be needed?" George huffs. He peers over his shoulder into the back seat, like what's about to come out of his mouth is the kind of truth that sometimes stays hidden, especially from Axel. Axel must look busy enough in his own thoughts, because George doesn't wait any longer to say, "He thinks that there is only one way to be a man."

"You've met his father. Can you blame him?" Emmett says, his voice falling to a whisper.

"I *can* blame him. He's made choices," George says. "I hope that Byrd can stick to her choices, too."

Emmett touches the top of George's hand. "She's our girl," he says. "She's got this."

George nods. "I should've stayed behind. Do you really think Nance is going to be helpful?"

"We all needed this," Emmett says. "Favorite places, time away, and tonight a feast. Besides, Nance has a way of getting things done, even from inside the house. If she wants something, she'll make it happen. If he gets out of line, she'll know."

George slips his hand out from under Emmett's and turns the volume up. They fall into a song about a window, and someone on the outside looking in. When Emmett laughs, something in the air settles, and the ride snaps back to the plan of before. Time to sing, and to think, and to breathe.

Emmett pulls the car to a stop. "Pick you up in an hour," he says.

"Need us to go in with you?" George asks, but of course they know the answer.

Axel gets his membership card out from his pocket.

"Have a good time," Emmett says.

No need for goodbyes when you know everyone will be back together in exactly one hour.

The building itself looks unexceptional. Painted pale green with shuttered windows and a very small sign. Someone passing by on the highway would never, ever know the wonders that are healed inside this space.

Inside, there is an educational room where Dr. Martin puts

on programs to teach people about raptors and rehabilitation. Axel hasn't missed one of those programs in over a year, and even though the words are the same, going all the way back to the day he first met Dr. Martin, it doesn't matter. Each time feels special and important.

Inside the center there are also operating rooms and veterinary spaces. Places Axel has never seen and tries his best not to picture. He has no interest in seeing animals in pain or their blood. He keeps to the educational room, and the outside cages and paths.

The cages are behind the building, tucked into pine trees and landscaping. They're set apart from one another, a path connecting them all. Places where injured birds can still be near the sky, but not become prey while they're healing. There are even benches scattered throughout. Perfect places to sit and think. Perfect places to observe and listen and learn.

Axel rests his membership card on the front desk as soon as he steps inside the building.

"Hey, Axel," Molly, the receptionist, says. Of course she knows Axel from his visits on Fridays, and that one Saturday. She takes his card and pins it to the member board. "Special day, huh?" she asks with a smile.

"Do you mean because we still don't have school? Or that Byrd didn't drive me and wait here? Or that Frank came back this morning and still didn't ask to see me? Or that Emmett is getting supplies for the Pasta-palooza? Or . . ."

Molly clears her throat. "You're here on a workday, not a member day," she says. "Dr. Martin is expecting you."

"She's the one who invited me." Axel paces in front of the reception desk. Lets his feet stomp along the shiny floor.

Molly lifts the phone to her ear. "Dr. Martin, Axel Rastusak is here for you."

Once Molly rests the phone back into the cradle, Axel stops. A thought just popping into his head. "Is Lark here?"

"Lark?" Molly looks confused. "Dr. Martin's daughter?"

Now it's Axel's turn to be confused. "I don't know another Lark."

"No, Axel, Dr. Martin is at work," Molly says.

This is beyond obvious.

Axel is at the Delaware Valley Raptor Sanctuary on a workday, not a member day. "I know that," Axel says.

"Lark isn't here," Molly repeats. "Why don't you wait for Dr. Martin in the educational room?"

Axel is happy to move into one of the single greatest places in the entire world. The educational room, where birds hang in staged flight. Red-tailed hawks, barred owls, a ruffed grouse, an osprey with brown wings the color of Byrd's eyes, and even a male wild turkey, fluffed and frozen in time.

The plaque below the turkey states a very important fact: *Wild male turkeys leave the moms behind to care for the young while they go on with their lives. Young turkeys will follow their moms anywhere, from field to field and even in front of oncoming cars.* Dr. Taylor M. Martin is always quick to point out,

"Drivers should stop and let them pass. Let them stay together. Don't honk . . . Would you want someone to honk at you?"

Definitely not.

Back at Axel's first sanctuary visit, during a Saturday member meet-and-greet, Byrd was excited for him to meet other bird enthusiasts, only to find that Axel was the youngest member at the center, by thirty years, if not more. They'd spent the first half of the meet-and-greet outside, while the other members were inside, and then inside, while the other members were outside.

Axel didn't care. That visit was also the first time he entered the educational room, the first time he marveled at every staged bird, read every plaque. All plaques hold important facts, like the wild turkey sign, not only about the animal in flight, but about conservation efforts to help them. During that meet-and-greet, Axel read and reread each sign. The membership cost was worth it just for this room.

When he saw the plaque under the peregrine falcon, the one that was just plain wrong, the day took on a different tone. What had it said originally? *No known bird can match the speed of a peregrine falcon in flight.*

This simply isn't true. At level flight, the peregrine falcon is unremarkable.

Axel took Byrd's phone and voiced variations of a correction into her notes app:

"No bird on earth can match the speed of a peregrine falcon's stoop."

"No matter how hard it tries, no bird in a dive comes close to a peregrine falcon."

"The peregrine falcon is the world's fastest animal when it's in its hunting stoop. It can dive at speeds near two hundred miles per hour."

When he showed her the note, Dr. Martin took it all very seriously. She thanked Axel for finding the error and picked his third statement because, "It gives important details that the other statement was missing."

The plaque today lists this very fact, and Axel's name, and his age, at the time, nine.

Axel is reading his plaque when Dr. Taylor M. Martin comes into the room. She's wearing a white lab coat, baby blue scrubs, and a tight cap over her head. Dr. Taylor M. Martin has little fuss to her look, on this workday and on member days. No paint on her lips or nails, her brown hair cut very short. Axel likes this about her, the way she looks today will be the way she looks tomorrow.

"Nice to see you, Axel," Dr. Martin says.

Axel feels the same about seeing her and he can tell that Dr. Martin really is happy to see him. It isn't just her words, but that he knows she tells the truth. Just like Daniel and Ms. Dale, Dr. Martin says what she means.

Axel would like to believe that he is the same, telling the truth and saying what he means. He'd like to be like Dr. Martin in that way, and in so many other ways too.

CHAPTER SEVENTEEN

Enemies II

Dark.

Bullies.

Pigeons.

Crowds.

Crashes.

Dogs that look friendly, but are not.
People who look friendly, but are not.

Storms.

Fire.

Blood.

Lies.

WHEN DR. MARTIN LIFTS THE THIN SHEET covering the eaglet, his body stirs. His head is covered with a leather hood, and his movements seem slow for such a magnificent living thing. The makeshift nest that Dr. Martin has created has pieces of shredded cloth, not twigs, and is no bigger than a shoe box, even though his real home was the size of a dining room table.

There's dried blood on the curve of the bird's shoulder. While his shoulders are not firm like a human's, the bones do press out from his back, making him even more angular than what Axel remembers from the night of the rescue.

"Is he okay?" Axel asks. The baby cries, and the sound is different from the low tones of a few days ago.

"Those are food vocalizations," Dr. Martin explains. "He can tell someone is approaching, but doesn't know the difference between you or his father right now. Either way, he's asking for food."

The baby's beak searches the air.

"Will you feed him?" Axel asks.

"We will," Dr. Martin says. "Together."

She hands Axel a pair of latex gloves and slides into her own. When she lifts the eaglet to her chest, the crying stops. The eaglet's head rests on Dr. Martin's chest, his breath steadies.

"Would you like to hold him?" Dr. Martin asks.

An answer forms in Axel's mind too slowly. It's an answer with lots of shredded parts to it, just like the baby's new nest. Of course there's the "yes, more than anything" answer. But there's also the "no, that's too much" and the "no, I won't do it right."

Dr. Martin is already handing him off, though, moving him from her safe chest out into the open space between her and Axel. The unsafe space between them. Axel's eyes fall against Dr. Martin's white lab coat, where the eaglet had rested contently just moments ago.

And there he sees it . . . rose red blood. Not dried a rusty brown like on his shoulder, but fresh. Blood.

Axel looks down, but it's too late, the image of the fresh blood on Dr. Martin's white coat is already imprinted in his mind. His hands push away from his body, he wants Dr. Martin to stop moving the baby into the unsafe space between them. Wants her to stop sending the bleeding baby in his direction.

But Dr. Martin confuses the clues. Somehow she confuses the clues, thinks that his hands reach out for a different reason, not to say *no*, but to say *yes*.

The eaglet's life with all of its hurt crashes into Axel's mind next, sending the blood from the lab coat into a storm of other thoughts: the fallen nest, the missing parents, the leaving home, this strange place with its strange smells and very bright, buzzing lights.

Suddenly Axel's hands don't work. They don't push, they don't pull, they only drop, and so does the baby bird between Dr. Martin's hands and the ones she was trying to place him into.

Already bleeding, already missing his home and his family, the baby bird falls.

Axel doesn't stay for this rescue, he flies from the room with the suffocating glossy lights, and away from the injured bird.

The outdoor path only goes so far—past twenty cages and a storage building—until it ends abruptly at a black iron fence. The kind of fence that keeps some people out and some people in. The kind of fence that won't blow over in a storm, and won't let Axel continue his run.

"I'm here," Dr. Martin says. "The eaglet is okay."

Axel wraps each hand around the fence bars. He holds tightly to Dr. Martin's words.

"He's stronger than he looks. He fell into the blankets. I kept him over the blankets. He's okay," she says.

Axel drops one hand from the fence, then the other. He turns, rests his back against the smooth metal.

"You're okay, too," Dr. Martin says. "You're stronger than you know."

Axel swallows hard, forcing all of his *sorry*s back into his throat, then into his hammering chest.

"Let's go back," Dr. Martin says. She doesn't take his hand or guide him from his firm shoulders; instead she waits. Waits until Axel is ready to move. Then walks in front of Axel, past the old owl who isn't calling out, past the turkey vulture eating from a steel tray, past the pair of kestrels resting in the sun.

"Drink," she says when they get to her office. She hands Axel a paper cup filled with water.

The cool water hits the back of his throat, sending other words farther down into his stomach.

"Those are hard," Dr. Martin says. "We all have them," she adds. "You're not special, and you're certainly not alone."

Dr. Martin rests against the edge of her desk, removes her cap, then runs a hand over her head. "When I was younger, I was a runner," she says. "Still can be. When things crowd in, my whole body wants to get away. One time I ended up running in front of a truck; I ended up in the hospital more banged up than our little eagle."

Try as he might, Axel can't picture Dr. Taylor M. Martin as younger. She is only Dr. Martin: bird expert, veterinarian, rescuer of falcons and eaglets. Not like Lark, in her little yellow boots, spun around in the teacup sheet. He doesn't want to picture her like that, or hurt from a truck.

Dr. Martin takes Axel's cup, fills it again. "Drink," she says.

She makes her way to the chair next to Axel. Sits slowly. "My mom was a great mom. I mean, the greatest. She always wanted to let me be me. It was hard then, for so many reasons, to have me running off. But she knew that my body was telling me to go, get out, fly away, and there was nothing my brain could do to make it stand still. You know what I mean?"

Axel nods. He does know what Dr. Martin means. Exactly.

"She knew that I wanted to move away from harsh lights, and loud noises, and pressure, and smells." She looks out her office door, across the hallway to where the eaglet rests. "She'd say, 'Be safe, be free, I'll be with you.'"

"I'll be with you," Axel whispers.

"Sometimes people want us to be one thing, and we need to be something else," she says. "My mom didn't expect me to be . . ." Dr. Martin pauses, searching for her next word.

"A pigeon," Axel says.

"A pigeon?" Dr. Martin smiles. "A pigeon. Sure. My mom didn't expect that, and I realize what a gift that was. Even though she didn't know what it felt like to be inside my body, she knew enough to trust that I did. I do. I know what I need. For me, flight is as natural as breathing. Flight is an instinct. I move away from one place so I can get my thinking straight . . . I think you might do that, too."

"Byrd knows that I need thinking places, too. But Byrd's not here," Axel says.

"Axel, it's great that Byrd knows that you need thinking

places," Dr. Martin says. "But you can't count on Byrd to tell everyone what you need. Byrd doesn't know what it means to be autistic, she only knows what it means to be your mom. You have to tell her what you need."

Asking for help, saying what he needs, Dr. Taylor M. Martin sounds like Ms. Dale. And that fills Axel with bravery. "I don't want to be treated like a baby," Axel says.

Dr. Martin waves her hand at him, not like she's waving away his words, more like she knows they're true. "Of course you don't," Dr. Martin says. "Who wants that, except, you know, a baby!"

She's right. More bravery rushes into Axel's chest. "I did want to hold the eaglet, but I was scared," he says.

"I wish you had told me that you were scared," Dr. Martin says. "I can't read minds."

Who can read minds? No one can open the top of a head, peer inside, and see exactly what is happening inside another person. Everyone's just looking for clues.

"Ms. Dale says that we have to trust our guts," Axel says. He figures that Dr. Martin may appreciate some of Ms. Dale's words, since what she said before sounded so much the same. He clarifies, too. "It sounds gross, but she means we need to do what feels right, and say what we mean."

Dr. Martin nods. "I like that. So . . . what's your gut telling you now?"

Axel takes a deep breath. "I don't want to go back in there today," he says.

Dr. Martin fills the cup with ice cold water, one last time. "I understand," she says. "But I do want to go back. Okay?"

Axel finishes the last drip of water. He crushes the cup in his hand. "Okay," he says.

Dr. Martin opens her office door, the sign on the front now visible. DR. TAYLOR M. MARTIN, VMD-PHD. "Keep an eye out for those adults," she says, slipping her baby blue cap over her head.

Axel stands, drops the crumpled paper cup into the garbage basket. "Dr. Martin?" Axel asks.

"Yeah," she says, tying a bow at the back of her cap.

"My gut tells me that those adults are the parents," Axel says. "They are coming back to look for their baby." Those were the things he really, really wanted to say today.

Dr. Martin crosses her arms over her chest. "It's possible, Axel." She doesn't say much more, even though Axel knows that she must have more ideas. Maybe she's a little like Ms. Dale, but maybe she's also a little like George and wants Axel to stay curious. "Need to call your mom to pick you up?" she asks.

"No," Axel says. "Emmett and George will be here soon. I can wait for them out front."

"You sure? I can wait with you, or Molly?"

"No," Axel says. "I can do it on my own."

Axel walks out of the office first. Dr. Martin closes the door behind them. And even though she doesn't wait with him outside, she does walk Axel to the front desk. She does get his card from the member board. She does open the front door, stays at the door while Axel sits. The visit didn't exactly go as planned, but it was special all the same.

"Can I just say one more thing?" Dr. Martin asks. She props the door open with her foot, leans outside in Axel's direction. "It's okay to have things that make us uneasy. I do. I've never met anyone who doesn't. But we can't let those things, those scary, hard things, keep us from doing what we love."

"Like holding the eagle?" Axel says.

Dr. Martin nods. "Exactly. Or standing up for yourself, or telling someone what you need," she says. "I'm glad you came today, even if we didn't get to do too much with the eaglet. This will make it easier the next time you visit. You'll know what to expect, and I'll know what you need."

"Next time?" Axel asks.

"Of course. I can't rehabilitate this eagle without you," she says. "Promise me we can try this again soon."

Axel gives his word before Dr. Martin leaves him alone with his thoughts on the bench outside the Delaware Valley Raptor Sanctuary.

When Emmett's navy blue SUV pulls up, Axel slides into the back seat.

The car smells like Emmett and George ate their favorite spicy beef jerky. They didn't forget a treat for Axel. He finds a peanut butter cluster ball covered in shiny silver wrapping.

"Did you have fun?" Emmett asks, looking to Axel with a hopeful smile.

"No," Axel says.

"Oh . . . Is . . ." Emmett starts, but now it's George's turn to put a hand over Emmett's hand.

George turns to Axel now, too. "Ready for the Pasta-palooza?" he asks.

"Yes," Axel says, unwrapping his treat. This is just what he needs.

CHAPTER EIGHTEEN

The Truth

In the car
    on the ride
        in the quiet

There are thoughts
    A plan:
        Tell Byrd,
        About the eaglet
        About Dr. Martin's words
        About Frank.

There are thoughts
    A plan:
        Clarify.
        Give   Truth.
        Expect   Truth.

At home,
the tree is gone,
Frank is not.

      Axel's thoughts
      Axel's plans
          Fly away.

BYRD STAYED FOR OTHER REASONS, this Axel knows. He leaves her at the fence, goes right past her. Goes over branches and roots to what was the open field. A place where he felt open before the storm.

When Byrd comes, she doesn't even say, "Is this okay?" The fact that she's here. Or the fact that she followed him when clearly he needs thinking time. All she says is "It's a good thing." And then "Emmett and George invited him to stay." These words, coming from Byrd, cannot be the truth.

They simply can't.

Axel heard Emmett and George in the car. They did not say anything about wanting Frank to stay for the meal. Besides, when would they have invited him to their Pastapalooza? When?

At the grocer?

In the driveway?

Caw.

It isn't possible.

And Byrd? Byrd seems downright pleased with the whole thing. She's all smiles about it. "It's a good thing," she keeps saying. A good thing.

"Why?" Axel asks. A simple question, not the whole big mountain of whys: *Why hasn't he asked to see me? Why hasn't he come to see me in months? Why is him being here a good thing? Why are you so happy about it now when you are so sad in his shirt, in his office, in his goneness?*

"Him being here is good," Byrd says. "He's better." She says all this in a rush, like maybe she'll actually tell some truth. Tell some of the things she kept from him for herself.

Words like *good* and *better*? What do they even mean? "Was he sick?" Axel asks, because this is something he definitely didn't know.

"He," Byrd begins. "We," she starts again.

Without realizing it, Axel has followed Byrd from the field back to the fence, back to Frank.

"Hey, Axe," he says. "I heard about your bird."

At first a response won't come, since words like *better* and *sick* are still stuck in his head, but eventually, Axel is able to say four words. "It's not my bird."

"Oh," Frank begins; the hurt hanging on this one word feels heavy, like a fallen tree. Axel doesn't wait around for the rest. He goes to a place that makes sense, Emmett and George's house, then to a friend that is as loyal as they come, Ray.

Axel doesn't need to say a word to him. Instead, he curls up under the dining room table with his best friend. The table above them is set, five spots. That is until George grumbles in with a chair. "And where am I supposed to put this thing?"

"I'll tell you where," Aunt Nancy says. The wheels of her rollator stop at the circumference of the table. If Axel wanted to, he could reach out from under the table, from under the table cloth and run his hand over a smooth wheel. But he doesn't. He leans into Ray, closes his eyes. Pictures George trying to shove a sixth chair into the perfectly set round table above.

"Didn't you hear me?" Aunt Nancy says. "Shove that chair—"

"Nance," Emmett hollers from the kitchen.

"I'm not pleased about this either," George whispers to his sister.

The floor creaks when Emmett's loafers rush into the room. "Put it right there," he says. Then gasps. Axel doesn't know why until Emmett says, "The wine. Give me the wine."

"Oh, for Pete's sake," Aunt Nancy says. "Leave it there. We'll see how much he's really changed."

"Nance." This time it's George cautioning his sister.

Axel can't put together these clues without seeing, so he crawls out from under the table. When he stands it's like he's on display in one of Emmett's fancy grocers. Their eyes, all of them, wide on Axel. Their mouths, all of them wide.

"Where . . . ? How much . . . ?" But just like Axel's mountain of questions before, George's questions don't all come out. If they would, maybe Axel would get more information. Maybe he'd get more of the truth.

"Did you invite Frank to stay?" Axel asks.

George looks to Emmett. Their eyes saying a whole lot more than their mouths.

"You know I didn't," Aunt Nancy says.

"Nance," George says.

"Ack," Aunt Nancy says. She waves a hand in the air like she's given up. Pushes her rollator back through the kitchen and into her room at the back of the house. Slams her bedroom door. "Happy?" comes a muffled shout.

But in the dining room, no one says a thing.

Emmett clutches an open wine bottle to his chest.

George scratches at his old man beard.

And Axel waits for someone to tell him the truth.

"Well," Emmett finally says. "This pasta isn't going to cook itself." He takes one step toward the kitchen, then turns back to face Axel. "Byrd said he's doing a lot better. Let's all keep an open mind." He doesn't wait for Axel to ask any questions. Maybe that is a good thing, because what would those questions even be?

"Keep an open mind," George says under his breath. "I need another plate," he says a little louder. "Can you grab one?"

Axel likes the way that George sets the table. Pasta bowls, bread plates, glasses, two forks, two spoons, and a butter knife. A very important knife. But he doesn't like the way things look today, too tight.

"Was Frank sick?" Axel asks for the second time this evening.

"That's a big question," George says. "As Mary Oliver would say, that is *the white fire of a great mystery.*"

Caw. Axel can't add those words to the even greater mystery in his head. So he tries again, this time with more facts, more clarity. "Why hasn't he come to see me since January?"

George reaches for a plate, slides silverware around the table. "He wasn't doing too well," George says. "Byrd thought it best . . . I thought . . . We all thought that . . ." George pauses. For a man with all the words—words borrowed and words of his own—it is odd to see him without the right word. He's more concerned with the placement of a butter knife than giving Axel the truth.

"He's here now, but where was he before?" Axel asks. Ray slips out from under the table just in time to stand next to his friend. Axel rests a hand on Ray's round skull. Bony and comforting to the touch.

George comes from around the other side of the table. He rests a hand on Axel's shoulder now, comforting to the touch. "He hasn't come inside this house since the divorce," George says. "So, three years, four?"

"Four," Emmett calls from the kitchen, because at least this is a question he knows the answer to.

Axel shakes his head. They're wrong. They don't have the facts. "They're not divorced," he says. "They're separated. I have an index card."

"Separated." George says the word like it tastes bitter, spitting it from his lips.

Ray's head turns to the front door before the knob even jiggles. In the next moment, this new conversation has ended because Frank and Byrd step into the living room.

"Hello," Emmett shouts from the kitchen in a tone that doesn't match the one he used before.

Byrd pushes her sleeves to her elbows. "I'm coming to help you," she calls back.

Both of these actions are perfectly normal. Emmett giving a hello to family, Byrd ready and willing to help. But Frank standing alone in the living room of a house that he hasn't entered in four years is not. He looks like a bird on a basketball, definitely not normal.

George rushes across the room, reaches out his hand. "Frank," he says. "Thanks for coming."

The two men, long legged and thick chested, could be father and son. They are not. Both of them lost their fathers, not like the eaglet lost his. Axel doesn't know the mysteries of those lost dads, and Aunt Nancy hasn't said a thing.

Frank takes a seat on one end of the couch, crosses his right foot over his left knee; George sits at the other end, crosses a left leg over his right. No one asks Axel to sit. That's fine. He pulls the ottoman from the center of the room into the corner. Sits with one eye on the men on the couch, one ear on Byrd in the kitchen.

"I didn't get to ask yesterday with the tree removal, but I was wondering about your business. Are you doing well?" George asks.

Ray leaves his post in the dining room. He'll return when the pasta arrives. That way, if a stray meatball plummets to its death, he'll be right there to catch it. For now, he wags his way across the living room. He gets right up into Frank's face, front paws lifted off the ground and crawling into his lap.

Now, Ray's too big to technically be a lapdog, at least seventy pounds, but that doesn't stop him from trying. Usually, however, these tries are reserved for family.

"Ray," George warns. "I'm sorry," he says to Frank.

"He's fine," Frank says. "You know I love my Ray." He scratches behind Ray's floppy ears.

Axel pulls both feet up onto the ottoman.

"I'll tell you, George. We're up to our noses in barns. I mean, none like yours, but some good ones along the river, down near the lake, too. When we got that blizzard last winter, we must have reconstructed ten, fifteen iron horses and gambles. Your barn was fine?"

"Still standing," George says.

"We've gotten a few calls since Monday about cleanup, but I'll have my whole team here so we can expedite things. I might regret it when there's no money coming my way, but I just want to get Byrd back home."

Frank turns all of his attention to petting Ray. And George just lets the words hang in the air between them. George doesn't say anything about "money not making the man" like he normally would, or about the fact that Byrd isn't the only one who needs to get back home. Axel lets the words hang too. Words like *money* and *expedite*, and *Byrd back home*.

It isn't until Axel hears the sound of round wheels on wooden floors that he takes a deep breath. "Who the heck is this?" Aunt Nancy says to Axel, shooting her thumb toward Frank.

"You know Frank," George says loudly. He always gets loud when he thinks his sister needs a warning, or when he thinks she's forgotten something she shouldn't. This isn't one of those times. George knows that his sister is being brassy. He goes on. "Of course you remember Frank. Byrd's husband. Used to live next door. Built the house. You remember him, don't you?"

Nancy stares at Frank like she can unlock every one of his secrets. She bites her wrinkled lip.

"Nancy, I'm Frank," Frank says slowly like he's talking to a baby. What was it that Dr. Martin said? No one wants to be treated like a baby, except, of course, a baby. Aunt Nancy is no baby.

She lifts one hand from the grips of her rollator, lets it dance around in the air like something important is coming to her. "Frank," she says, matching Frank's slow speech. "Never heard of him." She twists her whole rollator, turns it back toward the corner of the room, lets her eyebrows do all the talking she needs to do to Axel. This reminds him of Daniel. Which is a very nice thing.

"Having some thinking time?" she says to Axel in a whisper.

He nods.

"You keep right on thinking," she says. "I'll do all the talking."

Nancy pushes across the living room and over the braided rug and sandwiches herself between Frank and George on the couch. She isn't graceful when she lets go of her rollator and flops down, but she looks pleased, just the same.

"I always had my heart set on a dog like Ray," Frank says, like maybe he didn't hear Aunt Nancy's words before. Like Aunt Nancy pretending not to know him doesn't deserve a response.

"Then you should've stayed put," Aunt Nancy says. "Ray lives here. Doesn't go wandering off in the middle of the night and leave his family for a barstool."

"Nanette Marie," George says. First and middle names, but no last. This is a moderate warning. The kind of warning George believes he should give, not the kind he really feels.

And Frank? Frank says nothing but "Maybe I should go see if I can help in the kitchen?" He pushes Ray from his lap, jogs out of the living room and through the dining room.

Axel doesn't wait another second; he leaves the ottoman for Frank's warm spot on the couch, lets Ray jump right back up into his lap. Ray's eyes close as Axel runs his hands from his head to his shoulders. Aunt Nancy starts humming a song until George reaches over and throws his arm around her.

"We're lucky you're on our team," he says.

"That's very true," Aunt Nancy says. "I just don't understand why she lets him come and go."

George shakes his head. "I've said my piece," he says. "*There was a new voice which you slowly recognize as your own . . .*"

Aunt Nancy holds up her hand, not like earlier with a flourish, more like a stop sign. "None of your poetry crap," she says. "Just tell us what you mean, for Pete's sake." Aunt Nancy doesn't always use the nicest words.

"Poetry crap! That's Mary Oliver," George says. He can't be mad, though, not after what Aunt Nancy just did. "I mean, she needs to recognize her own voice. Trust her gut."

Trust her gut. As Ms. Dale would say, listen to those instincts. Maybe Byrd's instincts are telling her that it's okay for Frank to be here now? Maybe her instincts are saying that things are "better"? Whatever that means.

But if it's okay for Byrd to listen to her instincts, then maybe Axel should listen to his own? Listen to the way his insides quiver at the sound of Byrd's and Frank's voices mixing together in the kitchen. Listen to the way the truth and secrets mix to tell him something isn't quite right.

Listen to the facts. Like the fact that Frank was sick before, and for some reason, no one ever thought to tell Axel.

CHAPTER NINETEEN

Pasta-palooza

What it is:

    Elbow macaroni.

    Gluten-free fettuccini.

    Angel hair.

    Rigatoni.

    Fusilli.

    Marinara.

    Alfredo.

    Butter.

    Pesto.

    Meatballs.

What it's not:

    A place for Frank.

EMMETT AND BYRD FLUTTER IN from the kitchen, each with steaming bowls of pasta in their hands. Gluten-free for Byrd, and angel hair for Aunt Nancy, who doesn't like thick pasta. Who says, "If I wanted something thick, I'd eat paste."

The last bowl to come to the table is for Axel. Elbow macaroni with heaps of butter and salt. It is in a red bowl, also Axel's favorite. Leave it to Emmett to make things special for Axel.

Axel waits for Byrd to say, "And for our buttervore," like she usually does when the elbows come to the table, but tonight she's more interested in fluffing the napkin on her lap. Frank reaches for the bowl. For Axel's special bowl of pasta, and digs the serving spoon deep into the middle of the bowl. It's only then that Byrd leans over to whisper to Frank.

Axel hopes that when Byrd leans close, placing her hand on Frank's wrist, she will say, "No, Frank, those are for my buttervore." Instead, when she's at Frank's ear, she says, "Pasta-palooza now includes trivia."

Now includes?

Now? When has Frank D. Rastusak ever been to a Pasta-palooza? Weren't they started after he left for the first time? After he decided to live in his own cabin along the Delaware River. The cabin that has only one bed, in the middle of only one room. Not a place for any visitors.

Wasn't the first Pasta-palooza then?

For Axel and Byrd to have special dinners with their special friends?

And hadn't they added trivia just last year in Aunt Nancy's effort to stop George from talking through dinner with his poems?

Now includes?

Now?

"Sorry, Frankie," Aunt Nancy says. "Only five categories."

"Five things," Axel adds. "Five areas of expertise. Five people in the game." Axel swipes the bowl of elbows from in front of Frank to dish out his own mound of noodles, even though Frank probably got all the best ones that were the exact right slick of butter and salt from the top.

"There's always room for one more," Byrd says, leaning forward like she might leap across the table at Aunt Nancy. But Aunt Nancy doesn't flinch.

"Always room for one more," she says. "Sounds like you're talking about bottles of beer, isn't that right, Frank?"

"Nance," Emmett warns. He pulls a sauce-speckled dish towel from his shoulder. "I'm waving the mercy flag," he says. "Let's just eat."

George clears his throat. "Let's give thanks, then eat." He

dips his head, so he doesn't see that some people at the table aren't in the mood to give thanks. He starts his prayer anyway, says the words that should make everyone grateful. Only the words don't work this time. The words aren't telling the truth. We aren't all "thankful" for the guest at the table.

The prayer does press the reset button on Nancy, at least for a few minutes. She twirls her pasta, dabs the corners of her wrinkly mouth with a red napkin.

"Who's ready for question number one?" Emmett asks, reaching into his pocket for his phone.

"I'm the expert in babes," Aunt Nancy says. "I bet there isn't a dame in history you can stump me on." She's talking to Frank again, even though Emmett is in charge of starting the questions. He starts, then passes the phone to the next person. Aunt Nancy knows this. She hasn't missed a Pasta-palooza.

She knows the routine. But she sticks out her chin all the same, says, "Try me" to Frank like she's ready for a real challenge, like she's a barn swallow going after a hawk. You wouldn't think a swallow could stand up to a hawk. Stand back and watch. If a swallow's territory is in peril . . . the hawk's luck might run out.

"Okay," Frank says. "A dame? A woman in history?" He pauses.

"Stop," Axel says. "You don't know how to play. You don't know what we do. You don't belong here."

"Axel," Byrd says, like she isn't the reason this is all happening. "We can try it this way. Go on, Frank, ask a question."

"No," Axel says.

"Enough." Byrd's voice goes low.

Change always leads to trouble. Should they really try it Frank's way today, then what, at the next Pasta-palooza go back to the right way, then what, have Frank come back again and do whatever he wants? Then what, he leaves? Six people one week, five another. Then what, four the next time?

"No," Axel says again, much louder this time.

"I should go," Frank says.

"Yep," Aunt Nancy says.

"Nance," Emmett says.

"Don't," Byrd says, putting her hand back on Frank's wrist, like she cares about calming him. Like he's all she cares about.

That's when the mystery gets solved: Frank doesn't need to leave, Axel does.

He pushes back from the table, his chair knocking backward to the ground. Ray leaps up too, follows hot on Axel's heels. They run into the living room, they run through the front door, slamming it shut, they rush out onto the wide open porch. Axel tips his head back like he's drinking the fresh air the same way he drank the water in Dr. Taylor M. Martin's office. Big, full gulps.

If Dr. Martin were here, or Daniel, or Ms. Dale, they would tell the truth. They would play trivia the right way. They wouldn't give thanks for a person who wasn't even supposed to be at the table.

Axel breathes in the cool night air. He feels all of Ray's

weight leaned up against his leg. By the time the front door opens again, the balloon around Axel's heart has popped.

It isn't tight.

It isn't too full.

Byrd and Frank stumble out, nearly falling over Ray and Axel.

"You didn't run away," Frank says, like the very sight of Axel on the porch is a surprise, not the other way around. He takes one step back from Axel, then another. "I'll come back tomorrow after things settle down."

"We didn't even eat," Byrd says as she steps over Ray's tail. Walks down the two steps to Frank.

"Tonight's not the night," Frank says, shaking his head. He pulls a crumpled baseball cap from his back pocket, slides it down until his forehead is gone.

Like the baseball cap brought on a new idea, Frank takes a step back in Axel's direction. "Maybe you want to see the new plans for the house?" he asks.

New plans. Axel doesn't want new anything. He wants things to go back to before Frank came here. When Pasta-palooza was just the five of them, and everyone knew the rules for playing trivia, and Axel got the first big spoonful of the elbows with butter, and Byrd called him her buttervore. That's what Axel wants, not new plans. "I like it the way it is," Axel says.

"Oh, really?" Byrd says in a jokey voice. "With a tree-sized hole in the side and wrapped in plastic?" She tries to laugh, but it comes out more like a sigh. Her joke wasn't funny, and she knows the tree-sized hole isn't what Axel meant.

Frank takes one more step in Axel's direction. "Good night, Axe," he says. But he doesn't wait around like he used to, doesn't say, "You need to say good night back to me, Axe, or else I can't fall asleep." Instead, he and Byrd wander side by side toward his peacock truck.

Yes, Axel would prefer things to be left just like they are, tree-sized hole and all.

CHAPTER TWENTY

Aunt Nancy

For hollow bones
there's a heaviness to her,
hardy in her humerus.

She bends in the wind,
but won't break.

"YOU GOT ROOM ON THIS PORCH for an old lady's back-side?" Aunt Nancy asks.

She wheels her rollator out onto the porch and tries to use Ray as a crutch to lower herself down. She tries once. She tries twice. She tries a third time. "Son of a biscuit, my knees don't go that way."

Axel stands, offers his arm to Aunt Nancy.

"Well, aren't you the nicest kid around?" she says.

"I'm the only kid around," Axel says.

"Yeah, but you're still the nicest," Aunt Nancy says. "Think you can help me get out to that nest that you and the boys were talking so much about?"

"I could try," Axel says.

"Yes, Axel, we can always try."

She waits until they are on the first step, until Axel is solely concentrated on not letting things end up an Aunt Nancy–Axel–Ray sandwich on the steps, before saying, "Got yourself into a little steam back there, huh?"

Axel can't answer, what with Aunt Nancy's life in his hands.

"I mean, Frank visiting has got you hot like me. Hot as a frying pan." They make it to the next step, the last step before rocky ground. "I don't like seeing him either. It was me who took all those pictures of him out of this house the day he moved to that cabin. You know that, right? Just went and cut, cut, cut. Does he think he's part of this family? Like he has some right to come and go? He. Does. Not."

It feels like a real triumph to be on the first stone of the walkway. To have Aunt Nancy back to her rollator. To get moving toward the nest, no matter how far away it is or the debris in the way.

And then the words do all come rushing, like a rain cloud just opened up overhead. The *steam* and *hot* and *cut, cut, cut* and *does he think he's part of this family*.

"We're not family," Axel reminds Aunt Nancy. "I mean you and me. Frank is my dad. I am his son. But you aren't my anything."

"Am I not your Aunt Nancy?" Aunt Nancy tests.

"That's your name," Axel says.

"My name is Nanette Marie Flores, thank you very much. That's Aunt Nancy to you and any other sweet soul that lives in these parts . . . Even Ray." At his name, Ray bolts off like he's finally been dismissed. Every few steps, Aunt Nancy pulls on the brakes of her rollator, stops to look up, look around. "What a night," she says.

Axel can't tell if she is talking about the literal night, the way the twilight is crawling in around them like it did the night of the rescue, with the sun still pink on one side of the field and the first stars on the other.

Maybe she means "what a night" with Frank and the not eating dinner, and she doesn't even know about the new plans for the house, or the problems with the eaglet. Or anything that Dr. Taylor M. Martin shared.

But Aunt Nancy is the kind of person who will say what she means. All Axel has to do is be brave enough to ask. "Aunt Nancy," Axel says after a few more slow steps. "Was Frank sick?"

"Where'd you get that intel?"

"Byrd said he was 'better,' Emmett said 'a lot better.'" Axel shares the only clues he has to this mystery.

"It's like she has two babies, not one, if you ask me."

"I did ask you," Axel says. "So, does that mean he was sick?"

"Ack. I shouldn't have said that," Aunt Nancy says. "As my brother has said, this is not my place."

"But," Axel starts, letting more pieces fall into place, "if you are my family, Aunt Nancy, then why isn't it your place to tell me the truth?"

Aunt Nancy stops the rollator. Puts the brakes on and drops her butt into the chair that rests on top. "You aren't just the nicest kid in these parts, you are the smartest, you know that?"

Axel shakes his head. "I'm the only kid," he reminds her.

"Listen, your daddy was a real masterpiece at one time. I joked in there that I couldn't remember him," she says, pointing back at the house. "But of course I remember your daddy. He helped move me into the house. He put the rails up in the bathroom when I needed them, and moved all of my stuff from the upstairs room to the downstairs room when I needed it. He was . . . Well, he was part of our pack. Our team. Our . . ."

"Family," Axel says. Even though Axel's memories can be sort of fuzzy sometimes, when Aunt Nancy shares stories, when they do look at pictures, when a spark lights up the past, Axel can remember Frank being here too.

"So was he sick? Is that why he moved to the cabin? Is that why he stopped wanting to see me?"

"Oh, Axel, he'd have to be some kind of fool not to want to be with you. You, the nicest and smartest kid in town. You, with your jet-black hair, your big brown eyes, your pointy nose. Heck, you look just like him."

"You can just tell me the truth," Axel says. "You don't have to say nice things because that's what you think I want you to say. I don't need to know those things. I need to know if he was sick. I need to know why he left."

"There you go with those smarts again," Aunt Nancy says.

Almost every inch of night has fallen now. The solar lights along Axel's fence cast a glow around his house. The moon over the big red barn illuminates the open field. It's the kind of light that can unlock a mystery, shine a light on the truth.

"I remember the first time they brought you home. Walked you up the path to George and Emmett's before even walking you into the cottage. They just had to show you off, your proud mommy and daddy. You had those tiny fingers, reaching out to the sky for answers, always reaching. Couldn't keep you tucked in a blanket to save their lives. To save our lives. It was just what they needed after, well, after the disappointments with the pregnancies and of course your dad's family. Ack. I won't go there."

Aunt Nancy raises up from her seat, turns back to grip the handles like she's just remembered they were on their way to the nest, but not like she remembers the real question. She still hasn't said anything about being sick.

Axel already knows that he should have had a little sister. Willow. That Frank and Byrd lost her before she could come home. He already knows about Frank's mom and dad, and his too-loud uncle. He knows these mysteries. He doesn't know the other one.

"My stars, though," Aunt Nancy says. "You would cry." She rubs at her ear like she can still hear it. "Me and George and Emmett, we'd try to help Byrd. Rock you in your car seat, walk you around the field, but no hushing or rocking would do. Then, of course Frank would pull up in that old truck, the one from that construction company, you know, before he went out on his own. It was like you could hear it, that rusty, bumbling truck, and you'd start really wailing. He wouldn't even get his work shirt off before he'd have you in his arms. He'd start singing." She hums a little. Not enough to make out the song, but just enough to get in Axel's memory. He knows that song too.

"You'd quiet up. Little eyes on Frank's face. That's why we all sing to you, sang to you. It started with Frank. No one could do it like him."

"Byrd likes to sing," Axel says. "Emmett, too." This is a fact.

"Byrd hums. Emmett pretends he's on Broadway. But for you, they wished they could sing like Frank. We always wish the hardest and work the darnedest for our family," she says. "I mean, family sticks together. Look at my brother giving me a home. I bet there are times when he wishes it were just him and Emmett living like lovebirds, but family is family, you stay together."

"Frank didn't stick around," Axel says. "But I don't think about that too much. I mean, sometimes. But more because he stopped coming back on Saturdays, like he's supposed to. Like the index card says."

Aunt Nancy shakes her head. "I don't know anything about an index card. I do know that Byrd's calling the shots over at your place, so you need to talk to her. Tell her what you're feeling. Ask her what's going on with your daddy. I love to put my nose in your business, but I also know when to keep my caboose out." She looks back out over the moon-soaked field. "This stuff is between you and Byrd and that flighty daddy of yours . . ."

If another bit of advice was coming, it stops. Stops right there in Aunt Nancy's wide open mouth. "Sweet jellyfish and marigolds, that's some bird." Aunt Nancy jams a finger toward the nest glowing in the moonlight.

There, perched just a few yards away, is the eagle. Axel feels it in his bones: this is the dad. This is the eagle from the tree the night of the rescue, from the branch the next day. His bright white head moves like he's scanning the nest, trying to figure out the mystery of his family's home.

"He's missing his baby," Aunt Nancy says.

And even though this is what Axel feels inside his whole swelling heart, he says, "They don't do that." That's the fact. The fact that Dr. Martin knows. The fact in A. P. Brown's *Collection of North American Birds*. "Eagles don't return for fallen young."

"Well, that guy didn't get the memo," Aunt Nancy says. "He wants his kid."

Before Axel can agree or disagree, or even share the words from Dr. Martin's email, Ray comes out of nowhere, hurtling toward the nest. The eagle leaps to flight. His wings open as wide as the nest. He lifts into the sky, silently rising higher and higher into the darkness.

Aunt Nancy is left without words. Even Ray follows the shadow without a peep.

And Axel? Axel watches too. Only, his mind takes flight along with the bird, thinking maybe, just this once, A. P. Brown's *Collection of North American Birds* is wrong. Maybe Dr. Martin, too?

Maybe this dad came back for his baby?

Maybe this family, this beautiful bird family, is the kind that sticks together?

CHAPTER TWENTY-ONE

Byrd's Words

Stopping by the water's edge
its sloping neck surprised them.
    "You shouldn't be here," they called.
    The crane's reply? "Honk,
    honk,
    honk,
    honk,

    honk."

WHEN AXEL WAS YOUNGER, he would find his way into Byrd and Frank's bedroom nearly every night. He was never a great sleeper. Still isn't, but now he has his things, his sleep things, the hawk eyes and his weighted blanket and the sound of the clock that hangs on the wall. These are all things he needs to sleep now, and they are all in his bedroom. They are all in a room that he isn't in, so they can't help him fall asleep.

Not until Frank fixes the house. Not until Frank uses his new plans to fix the old house.

And that would be a good thing. Frank fixing the house. Right?

Only, the question on Axel's mind tonight, without the ticking clock, without the hawk eyes, is about the other side. What if, after Frank fixes the house, what if that means he's gone for good?

In the teacup room tonight, Byrd doesn't mess the blankets, and the house is fine and quiet. But Axel's mind is not. And, as though she can hear the questions stirring inside him, Byrd whispers across the dark, "Take a deep breath. Go to sleep."

He knows that he should talk to Byrd. He should tell her what's keeping him awake, but he's just not sure what it means to send those words out into the air. What it means to say it all at once.

When he was little and he couldn't sleep, he'd pad across the hallway from his bedroom to Byrd and Frank's. He'd always go to Byrd's bedside, the one closest to the door. Stand near her, until, like those eagle instincts, her eyes would flutter open. She just knew he was standing there.

"Want to crawl in?" she'd say, and he didn't have to reply. Come to think of it, sometimes she didn't even ask; she'd just raise the corner of the blanket, and he'd crawl in. And there he'd sleep.

When he'd wake up, he'd come face-to-face with the picture on Byrd's bedside table. It was a picture like so many others in the house, with three people inside a thick frame. Byrd and Frank and Axel. It was the three of them along the bank of the pond at the cabin. The cabin where Frank lives now. The cabin that has water all around, so it has birds all around. Birds, after all, are opportunists. They go where the food leads them. And the cabin, with its own pond to the back, and the river down the bank out front, was special. Is special for birding.

The little family would go and fish and sit and listen. In the picture Axel's looking to the pond, maybe wishing for a sandhill crane to visit. Byrd's on the dock behind Axel, her tan pants rolled to her knees, a huge hat hiding all but the smile on her face. And Frank? Frank's closest in the frame, zoomed in and blurry, with his hat lifted enough to see his thick eyebrows and squinting eyes. The picture, almost like a selfie of Frank, only, the point wasn't ever to capture his smile, it was to capture his Byrd and his Axel in the place he loved most of all.

It was, perhaps, the last great day that Axel can remember as the three of them. Maybe this is because it was captured in a photograph, or maybe because of the way that Frank's smile went all the way up to his eyes, or maybe because they actually did see the sandhill crane and Frank fell into the water trying to get a closer look?

So many maybes.

Tonight, in the guest bedroom in Emmett and George's fine house, Axel thinks of Byrd and Frank's bed, of the old photograph, and then, of course, of the time at the cabin with the sandhill crane.

Byrd pulls lightly on the cover they share. She takes one of her full belly breaths. The kind she encourages Axel to take when the world swirls inside and outside him.

Maybe it's the sound of this breath that makes him take his own, or maybe it's the image of the crane in his head, but something inside him lets him ask.

Ask one more time for what he needs. "Was Frank sick?"

He says it into the night air without the ticking clock or the hawk's eyes. When she doesn't answer, Axel thinks that maybe she's fallen asleep. That maybe she was able to picture the image in her room that helps her feel comforted. Is it the photo by her bed? On the day with the sandhill crane?

The crane's head is special and reminds Axel now of a Poké Ball, white and red with its circular eye in the middle. He can remember its long legs looked like the stems of the cattails all around the pond. Axel remembers the way Byrd loved the crane's dancing, the way Frank wished for the bird to make its trumpeting sound, and how he watched and listened for both. "I bet if I get too close, it will—" Frank said, just before tumbling down the soggy side of the pond and into the muck.

The sandhill opened its beak and its wings. Its call less like the trumpet Frank wished for and more like a jackhammer. And when it disappeared, Frank, wet and muddy, hugged Byrd. "How about that?" he'd said.

Axel feels a jackhammer now in his heart. It hurts sometimes to think of the time before Frank went to live alone at the cabin. Did the crane come visit him there again? And it hurt even more to think that Byrd knows why, and hasn't told him.

Sometimes when the hurt piles up, Axel can't do anything but feel every tap, tap, tap of it. Only tonight it feels more like a jab, jab, jab.

He doesn't know when it starts, but it does, humming. A song. It's Byrd, awake, like before when she'd ask, "Want to crawl in?" But she doesn't ask that. She reaches across the bed, takes Axel by the hand. Hums a low song about a bird with broken wings who learns to fly. She doesn't really pull Axel, but what she does pulls him from the jabbing in his heart, into the comfort of Emmett and George's fine house.

And so he asks again. "Was Frank sick?" He's calm now, not like before.

She's calm now too, and ready to tell the truth.

"Even when two people really, really love each other, like your dad and me, sometimes life gets in the way."

Axel closes his eyes, sees that soggy hug again between Frank and Byrd. Sees, right behind his eyelids, like a movie, that kind of love.

"When your dad lost his job—" Byrd says.

"What?" Axel interrupts. His eyes flash open to this fact.

But Byrd doesn't stop; perhaps she's afraid if she does, the truth will never get out. "We didn't know if we could keep the house or the cabin, and he called his dad for some money, I mean, we couldn't ask Emmett and George for one more thing . . . And he got so angry . . . Not your grandfather, your dad. Well, you remember. You remember how we'd fight," Byrd says. "Money can be such an ugly thing."

These are not facts that Axel knows, big fights or a lost job. He wants to find the image of Byrd and Frank hugging on the dock at the pond on the last great day, but he can't. It has disappeared like that crane into the sky with its jack-hammer cries. "What?" is all he can say.

"He was so sad, depressed, really. I mean, I know it was depression now, but then . . ." Byrd pauses. One more deep breath. "Do you know how hard it is to see someone you love in such a dark place?"

Axel wants the image of Byrd and Frank, but he can't find it in his mind, even with his eyes closed tightly again. He can't open up his brain and look inside. He can't get to that picture, as much as he wishes he could.

"I mean, the last time we . . . he . . . Well, you know about our Willow," Byrd says.

Axel knows about Willow, because that's the kind of sad that a mom can't hide, not like she was able to hide all this. They celebrated what would have been Willow's tenth birthday once. A candle. A prayer. And then Byrd and Frank told Axel the truth about a baby that never got to come home.

Sometimes when there is so much hurt, Axel can't help but think about it all at once. And now, now he can't find the good picture of Byrd and Frank, but can find them crying at the picnic table, over a birthday cake for a ten-year-old that wasn't at the table.

But Byrd doesn't stop to feel it. She gets louder. She gets further away from humming and helping. "His drinking, and his moods . . . When he was good, he was so good, but when he was careless, I couldn't have him at the house, I couldn't," she says. "It was supposed to be temporary. I always thought he'd come back to us, but then when his dad died, and he— well, you remember that night with the snowstorm."

She doesn't stop to check if Axel remembers. She doesn't

grab for his hand to hold him to her. She just keeps telling him things that she kept hidden before. Dark things. Murky things.

"And I wouldn't let him drive you in that old truck. He came for your Saturday, your every-other-Saturday, but I couldn't let him drive you. Not like that."

"What?"

"You remember the fight," she says.

What fights? What snowstorm?

"I needed him to think about what he was doing, how he was getting farther away from us, not closer. That's when I told him to stay away. Leave me alone to figure out when and if he could come back. I couldn't take the worry. You didn't deserve the fighting, the worry. And I needed time to figure things out. And that was the end of it."

She says "the end of it" like that really is the end of things. Like she can close the book on this bedtime story, in this bed that doesn't belong to them. Axel starts to form a new picture in his mind; this isn't Byrd and Frank hugging by the pond, or crying at the picnic table, this is Byrd standing in the cold, sending Frank, a sad and lonely Frank, out into a snowstorm. This is a picture of Byrd closing the book on their family without ever giving Axel a chance to know why.

His bones pulse under his skin. His feet shake. Axel leaps from the bed unable to keep his legs from moving. He paces the long boards of the wooden floor.

"Shhh," Byrd says. "You'll wake George and Emmett." Like that matters, like everyone shouldn't be awake to hear what Byrd did.

Or worse, that they should all be awake to tell Axel that they knew. They knew about the lost job and the sadness and the snowstorm. They knew all this, and they hid it, like Byrd hid it.

Could that be another part of the truth?

"Shhh," Byrd says again.

But Axel doesn't want to stop pacing. He doesn't want to take a deep breath and save his worries for another day. He wants to think, and there is only one way to do that. So in George and Emmett's fine, quiet house, with all of Byrd's secrets out in the open, Axel slams the bedroom door, closing her inside. He doesn't care who he wakes up.

CHAPTER TWENTY-TWO

Feathers

Worry has no wings
Not light
Not air
Not feathers.

Worry is made of stone.

AXEL RACES DOWN THE STAIRS, across the creaky wooden floor, out the front door. This door he leaves wide open to the night air. Wide open to all the secrets that people keep trying to shut away.

He runs through the darkness as words swirl in his mind, and buzzing, like one hundred buzzards, fills his ears. He runs like being chased through the field by raptors. Like the worries are predator, and he is their prey.

Like those raptors, he can taste something on his tongue. For him, it's a word; for them, it's blood.

Axel hates blood. But he hates this word on his tongue even more. *Anger.*

It makes him want to throw up, like cooked carrots or bananas or figs. Or the smell of moldy basements. Or the feel of Byrd's betrayal.

All along, Byrd had secrets locked away beneath her blue shirt, under her canvas hat and gloves, tucked into her cold, stone bones. Frank had a secret, too. A secret that made him too sick to be with Axel.

Why had they kept these truths from him? Was it that he didn't deserve to know, or that they didn't think he could handle it? Who wants to be treated like a baby? Not him.

The anger boils from his insides and out his throat in long, loud screams. If he wakes up the world, or Emmett or George or Aunt Nancy, he doesn't care, because if they knew and didn't tell him, they deserve to wake to anger.

The moon from earlier has gone behind thick clouds. Darkness fills his field, not the light from before. From when he'd seen the eagle dad on the nest. There's no eagle dad, no moon-soaked field, nothing but night and anger.

It isn't until he crashes into the nest that he knows where in the field he's run. Not until the slice of sticks on his skin that he realizes he's lost his way.

Ray's bark breaks into Axel's pain, followed by Emmett's voice.

"You're okay . . . You're okay," Emmett says. He takes Axel into his thick arms, pulls him into his soft, round belly. "Shhh . . . shhh," he says. Emmett starts to sing a gentle song about a bird in the dead of night. Ray licks at Axel's leg.

"The nest," Axel says, like Emmett can't tell that's where they are. But it isn't location that Axel calls to, it's more pain. "She made me break the nest."

Ray turns and barks at the shadows moving through the field.

"Axel," Byrd says. She reaches for her son.

"Don't," Axel says. He pushes himself to his own two feet. He can do that all on his own.

"Axel." Byrd tries again.

George turns the light of his phone on them. On Emmett still on the ground near the nest, on Ray licking at Axel's hurt leg, on Byrd's pleading, on Axel standing on his own two feet.

"I'm not a baby," Axel says sharply, the taste of anger still on his tongue.

"I know," Byrd says. "I know."

Emmett rises, touches Byrd on her shoulder. "Let me," he says to her. "Let's go inside, get cleaned up," he says to Axel. "You're bleeding."

Axel hates blood, but he hates secrets even more.

"I don't need help," Axel says. Not just to Byrd. "I can get cleaned up myself."

And where does he want to go? He wants to go home. To the comfort of his own house, with his own room, and the hawk's eyes on his walls, and the ticking clock.

But he's not home, and nothing about this night is comfortable. He leaves all of the adults outside. Byrd can tell them about letting out the secrets. Byrd can tell them that now Axel knows the truth.

And Axel? Axel goes inside, looks down at his scraped-up legs, and makes a new plan.

CHAPTER TWENTY-THREE

Dear Frank

Ostrich
Penguin
Steamer duck.

Kiwi
Emu

Wounded, cut.

IT ISN'T AS EASY to stop the blood on his own, what with it making him want to throw up. So Axel has to let one person help. Aunt Nancy is his choice, but she's already taken something to help her sleep. So Emmett is next in line. And it goes okay, because at least Emmett doesn't try to talk about anything.

Emmett does his job. He puts the Band-Aids on and stops the leaking blood. He makes a cup of hot chocolate with extra mini marshmallows. And he gets a comfortable blanket for Axel on the couch.

"Come up if you need anything," Emmett says.

Axel won't need anything. "Thank you," he says, because Emmett really did help.

Axel takes his iPad to the corner of the couch, lets Ray curl up next to him in the now-quiet house.

There are two emails to send. Both of them the truth. One to Dr. Martin. One to Frank.

As he always does, he rushes the email to Dr. Martin. It pours from him easily, black letters on white screen.

The next email is harder to write. Harder still to send.

So he doesn't.

He leaves the words on the white screen, unsaid.

Maybe it is harder to tell the truth than Axel had ever realized?

Or maybe he just needs the light of day to help him hit the arrow icon that will send his question off to Frank.

So he goes from his email to the Cornell Lab of Ornithology online library. Lets the birdsong fill his corner in the otherwise sleepy house. Lets Ray's ears perk to the sound of a sandhill crane's cries.

Lets himself linger over the facts about eagle instincts. There's a line, "instincts don't rule out learning." A fact that no one has shared with Axel before, not Ms. Dale or Dr. Martin, not Emmett or even A. P. Brown's *Collection of North American Birds*.

An eagle can learn to swim before it flies.

Eaglets learn to play before they hunt.

Telling the difference between instincts and learning isn't all that easy—especially when it comes to learning how to navigate secrets and lies. Byrd thinks that they are meant to protect, but that doesn't seem quite right. How could a lie be better than the truth? If Axel expects Byrd to tell the truth, to speak up, to keep promises, then he must do the same. It won't be easy, but that hasn't stopped Axel before.

FROM: Axel Rastusak
TO: Dr. Taylor M. Martin
SUBJECT: This is Axel

Dear Dr. Martin,

This is Axel.

I ran into the nest. I ran and hit the nest with my human scent. And Ray was there, too.

What if the dad won't come back? What if he smells me, smells Ray, and leaves the nest for good?

You should know that the nest is still standing. It did more damage to me than I did to it, at least on the outside. At least from what I could see.

Do you think he was looking for his baby?
And now he'll give up on him?

Sincerely,
Axel Rastusak

DRAFT

FROM: Axel Rastusak
TO: Franklin D. Rastusak
SUBJECT: This is Axel

Dear Frank,

This is Axel.

Byrd told me everything.

Why didn't you come see me anyway?

Sincerely,
Axel Rastusak

CHAPTER TWENTY-FOUR

Dear Axel

FROM: Dr. Taylor M. Martin
TO: Axel Rastusak
SUBJECT: Re: This is Axel

Dear Axel,

It is a common misconception that birds abandon their babies because of scent. Really only turkey vultures could pick up the scent of a human. And we aren't talking turkey vultures here. I asked you to steer clear of the nest because the birds won't fly to it if they see you—not smell, but actually see you near it.

If they assess that they can't return to that nest, then they will either steal or build another.

I don't know about the adult. Most adults abandon fallen or missing babies for one reason: HOPE. They hope that their baby made it. That he left the nest to learn to fly. That he's started a life on his own. They trust that nature will do its thing. Instincts are powerful.

The eaglet's adults are more worried about their nest than their baby, but to answer your question: Anything is possible.

Maybe the dad did come back to the nest, once all the human activity was away, to see if his baby was okay. Maybe, Axel, maybe.

The fledgling is starting to move a lot more. Are you still off school? Come for a visit soon.

Sincerely,
Dr. Taylor M. Martin
Delaware Valley Raptor Sanctuary
VMD-PhD

P.S. Lark wanted me to tell you that she says "Hi."

CHAPTER TWENTY-FIVE

Sway

Water returns to river
because it never left.

RAY'S COLLAR JINGLES; his quick bark wakes Axel from his spot on the couch. He wipes his eyes, pulls the curtain from the window, and feels bravery fill his bones.

Both Ray and Axel run out the front door, across the porch, down the steps, but this time, Axel doesn't turn to run across the field. This time he greets Frank's truck in the driveway.

"Axel," Frank says, dropping from the cab of his truck. "About yesterday." He's almost as breathless as Axel, wanting to get the right words to come out this morning.

"Byrd told me," Axel says.

Frank shakes his head like he couldn't have heard what he just did. He looks at his son, from the Band-Aids on his legs to his sleep-messed hair.

And because words don't come to Frank and Axel still has all of the bravery he needs, he says, "I could've handled it. You should've told me. And even though she said not to come, you should have come anyway. That's what family does. They stick together. They come back for each other. That's what you should have done, no matter how sick you were."

Frank takes his big, wide hands and places them over his face, like he's hiding from the truth. Axel doesn't want to hide anymore.

"I don't even like this new truck. And I have a friend named Daniel who comes to visit me on Saturdays now. Every other Saturday, just like your stupid index card said. Daniel shows up. I can count on him."

And even though Axel isn't quite sure that Daniel will be able to show up soon, because of the storm, and the no school, he knows one thing: Telling Frank all that stuff made him feel better.

Trucks start up the driveway then, four or five of them. Many of the workers in the trucks wear ball caps with FDReMODELING, REBUILDING, RENOVATIONS in the same flashy letters that are on Frank's truck. Axel leaves Frank to talk to his team, that is, if Frank can find the words, because right now, he has none.

"Come on, Ray," Axel says. He passes one truck, then another, keeps walking in one direction, like he knows where he's going. He's trusting his gut. Ms. Dale and Daniel and Dr. Martin would be proud. It isn't until he reaches the mailbox all the way at the end of the road, the one mailbox for two houses, that Axel hears his name.

"Axel," Byrd calls. "Stop."

"I'm not going to run into the road," he says, because he knows that she thinks she knows what he'll do next. She doesn't know.

"Where are you going?" she asks. "What happened?"

"I just need to walk, okay? Ray and I can't go into the woods because of the trees. I can't go to school. I can't go into my bedroom because Frank isn't finished with the house. And I can't be up there with you."

"Oh, Axel," Byrd says. Her pink lips start to tremble, and suddenly she's crying.

And even with the anger and the secrets, Axel can't handle seeing Byrd hurt. He knows that she needs him to say that he's fine. That things are okay. But he won't lie. The only thing he can do is tell the truth.

"I'm angry you kept this from me. That you were treating me like a baby who couldn't handle something big. That you didn't think I deserved to know."

She steps closer to Axel, rests a heavy hand on his round shoulder. "When your dad lost his job, lost his dad, then he lost us, I didn't know how to help him, and I didn't know what to tell you. It was complicated."

"But I needed to know the truth. If there's more, you have to tell me. I can handle it."

And maybe it is the new day? Or the road, still dusty from all of those huge work trucks, but something in the air feels different, like by telling a few secrets last night, Byrd might become brave enough to tell a few more. Axel leans against the mailbox. He runs his hand along the names and waits for Byrd to find her words.

"There was the drinking at first," she says. "Well, honestly, always, but then after his dad, he just got reckless. Drinking more, and driving when he shouldn't. That truck," she says, then pauses to point down the long driveway toward the memory of Frank's truck. "That truck replaced the one that he rammed into a telephone pole. You could have been in that truck with him, Axel. I just couldn't. I couldn't let him be with you."

Axel pictures the snowstorm, and the fight. The fight that he forgot before. The last time he saw the old truck. The last time he saw his dad before the tree that fell through his house, before the eaglet fell from the nest. Before the storm.

Her face twists then, like the last secret is wrestling its way out of her. "I couldn't tell you, Axel. I mean, what would I have said? He's your dad. He didn't want to be doing the things he was doing."

Axel wants to hear all the words now. Every last one of them. As scary as they all sound, he needs to hear them. They are the truth he's been missing.

So he asks one more thing, one more important question to help solve the mystery. Now he knows about being sick, and he knows about why he stopped coming. There's just one thing left to ask. "But why didn't he want to come see me? Even when he came back this time, he didn't come to see me."

"Oh, Axel," Byrd says again. "Of course he wanted to see you. He wants to see you."

Axel plays back the days that Frank's been here now. How

the house changes day to day, and how Frank and Byrd find time to talk, but Frank hasn't come to him. Frank hasn't sat with him, or walked with him.

"I don't think that's true," Axel says.

Byrd crosses her arms over her chest. Holds herself in a hug. "You know, Axel. Frank may need to know that you want him to come see you, talk to you."

"That's ridiculous," Axel says. "He's my dad."

Byrd nods her head, her loose morning curls hug her face. "Even dads need to know what you need."

For some reason, Axel thinks about the nest, and not his own dad. He thinks about the eagle, the one that he and Aunt Nancy saw, dipping his head from one side of the fallen nest to the other, like he was trying to figure out a mystery about his own baby.

And how would the dad know? How could he without the baby there to show him? Without the baby coming back right here when he's healthy and taking to the sky to show his dad, "I'm okay. I'm okay."

Without cluing in Byrd or even Ray, Axel starts back up the driveway.

"Where are you going?" Byrd yells.

Ray races to his side. "I have to go see the eaglet," Axel says first to Ray, then loudly to his mom.

"But I have to be here," she says, trying to catch up.

"I know you do," Axel says. "I'll ask Emmett."

Emmett is not awake.

Aunt Nancy is not awake, and neither is George. But that's okay.

He sends a message to Dr. Martin to let her know he's coming. He sends a quick email to Daniel to let him know that he's hoping they can see each other soon, and that he hopes Daniel's house is okay and that his sisters are making funny videos for him to watch, and that Axel told Frank about him.

And after the emails are sent, Emmett is awake, and Axel tells Emmett just what he needs.

They haven't been in the car long when Axel asks, "Do you like to sing?"

"You know I do," Emmett says. He sings along to the song on the Broadway station. A song about breathing and some girl named Emma.

Axel listens for a few moments, then asks, "But do you like to sing now? Or have you always liked to sing?"

"Axel, where's this coming from? You know I like to sing. I love to cook. I love spending time with you and George and Byrd, and Nance. And I know that you like the back seat in the car, and learning facts about birds, and walking with Ray, and—"

"Yes, you know me and I know you, but what I mean is, did you like to sing before Frank?" Axel says.

Emmett turns down the volume, hushes the upbeat song. "I did. Yes," he says, but he drags out his answer like it is a question all its own.

"Aunt Nancy said that you all learned to sing because of Frank. That he could do it in a way that was special, and you all had to learn, too."

"That Nance has a lot of opinions, doesn't she?" Emmett sighs. "Frank sang to you in a special way when you were little. He'd get so close to your ear, like there couldn't be any air between the words and your brain, and he'd sing in this whisper." Emmett hums.

The song plays again in Axel's mind. He knows just how it sounds.

"It helped," Emmett says. "Like nothing else. And when you got too big to hold in our arms, we'd pull you close, sing right into your ear, until, well, you just didn't need the song anymore."

Axel does the whisper singing. He hears the words. He feels them, too.

"Just like that," Emmett says. "Back then, you were growing so fast. I just couldn't stand to go back to the city after a weekend with you. George either. And of course, your mom and dad weren't just looking after you, they were helping Nancy too. We just kept growing our country time as you grew, and before we knew it, the city wasn't our home anymore. You were our home." Emmett's voice drops off.

Axel wonders if these are the kinds of things that Emmett

shares because Axel asks, or if everyone knows all of this information and it's something Axel's missed. Like missing out because he didn't know to ask, or because they didn't think to tell. Like how Axel never thought to tell Frank it was okay to come talk to him. He didn't even know that was something he could do.

"Thinking about your dad a lot now, huh?" Emmett asks.

"I'm just trying to fit it all together," Axel says. "Like how my dad knew how to sing to me when I was a baby, but he doesn't know how to talk to me now."

Emmett turns the radio off completely. "It's like babies need us one hundred percent of the time, so everything we do feels like the right thing, somehow," he says. "But when you get older, and you start having your own thoughts and your own way of doing things, well, it gets harder. And your dad, he wasn't around all the time to see who you've grown up to be."

"I'm not all grown up," Axel says. He knows this sounds funny, especially when he keeps telling Byrd not to treat him like a baby, but there's a big difference between being a baby and being all the way grown up. "Sometimes I miss the song," Axel says.

Emmett reaches back behind the driver's headrest, taps it with his hand, like that is the same as tapping Axel. "We all miss his song," Emmett says. "We all miss Frank."

"Not Aunt Nancy," Axel says.

"Oh, don't let Nancy fool you, she's an old softy. Your dad

was a big help around the house. He was always doing things for Nancy. Byrd and I would sit on the porch swing with you. We'd watch Aunt Nancy boss your daddy around, and he'd do everything she asked. And we'd just swing and laugh, swing and laugh."

In all the things that Emmett's sharing in the car ride today, this is the first to stop Axel, because he just can't picture it. "I don't remember a porch swing," he says.

"Fell down years ago. I miss it so. We keep saying we'll hang another, but we don't. Too hard to hang a new one alone."

The car's been stopped for a while now, in the parking lot outside the sanctuary, but Axel can't pull himself from the back seat, no matter how much he wants to see the eaglet.

He wants Emmett to say one more thing. One more thing that will make him feel warm inside. Something about how even when things change, like when a dad is reckless, or a mom forgets to tell the truth, or even when a porch swing falls, it doesn't mean that everything else has to fall too. It doesn't mean that there can't be good things, too.

Emmett doesn't say those things, and he doesn't get a chance, because suddenly there is flapping outside Axel's window. Lark's curly hair is all that Axel can see before she slaps the glass. "You coming?" she shouts.

"I'll be back in an hour," Emmett says.

"I know," Axel tells him. Emmett always comes back.

Axel slips from the back seat, and Lark starts to fill the air between them with chatter. About the eaglet, about being off today from school, and her damaged swing set. The words rush past Axel, whose mind is already so full of things.

And like he's forgotten something important, Axel leaves Lark at the thick wooden door, races back through the parking lot, back to Emmett's SUV. Where Emmett sits with tears streaming down his pink cheeks.

Axel slaps the window, just like Lark did a moment ago, open palmed. He opens the door before Emmett has the chance, leans all the way into Emmett's ear.

"What is it, Axel?" Emmett asks.

"You're not alone," Axel says. He'd meant to say it before, with the swing, but he didn't. "You have me," he says.

"Of course," Emmett says. "And you have me."

These are facts.

Emmett likes to sing. Emmett loves food, and spending time with George. And Emmett is not alone. He has Axel. And Axel has him.

CHAPTER TWENTY-SIX

"Braviary"

Egg
    hatchling
        eaglet
            fledgling
                juvenile
                    immature
                        adult
                    egg
                hatchling
              eaglet
            fledgling
        juvenile
      immature
Adult

"SMELL THAT POOP," Lark says when they enter the back room of the sanctuary. "That means his insides are working. I got to feed him. You hold the fish in tweezers and let it hang. It was so stinky. Worse than the poop. But he ate it up, one, two, three." Lark finally takes a breath.

Dr. Martin reaches inside the crate, pulls a plastic bin from the inside, and the air stops being overrun with Lark's words and fills with the little cries of the eaglet. Dr. Martin slides the makeshift nest from the crate.

"Is he still bleeding?" Axel asks, too afraid to look himself.

"No," Lark says. "Mom told me what you did. You have to be careful holding the babies, or you're not allowed to hold them, right, Mom?"

"I don't want to hold him," Axel says, which is definitely the truth. At least at first. Because after he sees the eaglet in Lark's arms, he's not so sure. He's bigger, and darker in just a few days. He's no longer wearing the mask over his eyes.

"We should keep him," Lark says, nuzzling her chin

against the eaglet's head. "Forever. We could name him and take him to schools."

"No," Axel says. "He needs to fly with his family. Right, Dr. Martin?"

"Right, Axel," Dr. Martin says. "He's not the kind of bird you keep; he's the kind you set free. We only keep the ones that can't go back, Lark. You know that."

Lark pulls the eaglet closer to her, as if there was any space left between them before. "I'm going to call you Braviary," she whispers into him.

The name excites Axel at first. "Like the Pokémon?" Axel asks.

Lark looks down at the eagle. "It's the perfect name. He's a flying type and valiant Pokémon. That means brave, right Mom?"

Axel doesn't need to wait for Dr. Martin to answer. "Yes, that's true. Valiant type. And brave." But when Axel considers it, really thinks about giving a Pokémon name to this eagle, he isn't so sure it's the right fit. "The eaglet is unique. Shouldn't he get his own name and not someone else's?"

The fact is, if Daniel were here, they could talk for hours about Pokémon. They could think of all the reasons that this would, or would not, make a great name for this bird. But, right now, in the bright examination room, he isn't so sure.

And even so, even if he's not sure, he can hear Lark whispering, "Braviary, Braviary, Braviary," right into the eaglet's side.

Dr. Martin brings a tray from across the room with gloves and tweezers. The tweezers are long, beaklike, not at all like the ones Axel's seen before. "We're going to encourage the eaglet—"

"Braviary," Lark interrupts her mother with the reminder.

Dr. Martin nods. "We're going to encourage Braviary to do a little branching today, Axel. I'm glad you could be here to help."

"I already know how to do it," Lark says. "I helped with Lizzy and with Hoothoot, remember, Mom?"

Dr. Martin pulls two trays from the refrigerator. "Yes, Lark, of course I remember."

Lark lays the eaglet back into the box. "If you want to hold him, now's the time. Mom's going to make him work after this."

The sharp scent of fish hits the room. Axel's stomach churns, and the eaglet starts to cry.

"Pee-ew," Lark says, pinching her nose.

Axel can feel his gag reflex jumping in the back of his throat. "That smells really bad," he says.

"Once we get outside, it won't be as strong," Dr. Martin says. She passes Lark a small cube of fish clamped between long tweezers. "You can give him a taste. Then he'll be motivated to work for more."

Lark does just that. She squeals when Braviary takes the fish.

Dr. Martin covers the plastic bin while the eaglet calls for more food. There's a handle on the cover, and she passes the whole thing to Axel.

"Don't drop it," Lark says.

He isn't 100 percent sure that he won't, so he says nothing, just concentrates on holding the bin. He slides one hand under it, holds the handle in the other. It feels light as air, really. Not like there is something so powerful inside.

Axel follows Dr. Taylor M. Martin through the back door. The birds in outdoor cages jostle, and Lark calls them all by name as they pass. "Hi, Lizzy! Hi, Bill! Hi, Stephanie!" One after the other, after the other.

Dr. Martin unlatches a cage near the back gate. There's a play set inside, two long logs that look like they could've come from the fallen trees at Axel's own house, and a bunch of smaller stumps.

"Is this yours?" Axel asks Lark.

Lark flops across one of the swings, her belly to the ground. She lifts her arms and feet like she's flying. "No," she manages. "This is for the birds."

"This is one of the training areas. We try for mostly organic materials, but this wooden set was donated, and it works; sometimes that's the best we can do," Dr. Martin says. "There are plenty of heights here for Braviary to practice branching."

"Yeah," Lark says. "See?" She jumps from a wooden step, then climbs up an angled piece of lumber and jumps again.

"Once we get him branching, it won't be long before he's ready to fly," Dr. Martin says. She takes the bin from Axel's hands. Carefully rests it on the ground. She removes the lid but doesn't touch the baby inside.

"So, once he flies, you'll set him free?" Axel asks.

"Oh, we might even be able to do it before then. We just need to know he can get himself around, that everything's in working order, then we can let nature take its course. Birds that can be rehabbed, especially eagles, should spend the least time possible in captivity. We don't want him to get used to fish cubes and cut-up baby blankets when he's meant to hunt and soar."

Dr. Taylor M. Martin reaches into the bin, gently takes out the eaglet, and places him on the ground. "Maybe they were already branching? Do you remember seeing any gray feathers on the ground near the nest?"

Axel tries to think back to the days and weeks they visited this spring. Tries to remember the strong, straight tree with the nest in its arms among the other tall trees. He can't remember a gray feather clue, and back then, he didn't know to look.

"I don't know," Axel says. He's mesmerized by the eaglet making little hops across the mulch-filled cage. The curiosity in his sharp eyes. Axel thinks it's random at first. But the eaglet soon finds the container holding the cubes of fish. "I think he's hungry."

"He's always hungry," Lark says, walking a fallen log like a balance beam.

The eaglet flaps his wings, cries out. Hops around and cries some more.

"I think he needs help," Axel says.

"Learning to fly takes grit," Dr. Martin says. "Curiosity, too." Dr. Martin moves across the cage, sits on the swing where Lark once flew.

"But he can't do it," Axel says. "Look." He points to the frustrated eaglet, wriggling in front of the container of food.

"If he doesn't work for it, he won't make it in the wild," Dr. Martin says. "Only forty percent of birds live long enough to fly; eagles are slightly better at fifty percent. Only half. Only half in the best conditions. It's hard. It's nature. Some can't do it, and if we give him the food, if we don't even let him try, if we don't even let him struggle, he'll definitely be in the dead group."

This fact is hard to hear. Axel was so sure that nature was where the eagle was meant to be, that returning to the sky and to his parents was all that mattered, but now he isn't so sure. Is it better to be safe here, in a cage with a swing set and cubes of frozen fish? "Maybe Lark was right," Axel says. "Maybe we should just keep him here?"

Lark stops her twirling to listen to this. "Was I right, Mom?"

Dr. Martin pumps high on the swing. She makes it look easy. "I already told you, Axel, when it comes to flight, the most important word that we can have, the one that bird moms know by heart." She pauses, waits to see if Axel knows. Soars out and back on the swing. "Do you remember?" she shouts from the highest point.

Axel does remember. He remembers reading it in the email from Dr. Taylor M. Martin. It was in all capital letters.

"I remember," he says.

Hope.

CHAPTER TWENTY-SEVEN

Pigeons

Wild pigeons keep babies close
longer than most
in nests built for two.

Fathers make their own milk—
crop milk—
inside their bodies after
babies are born so they can
care for their young
no matter
Mother Nature's plans.

They find their way home,
from distant locations.
Even when the landscape has changed.
Due to flooding, fires, or

                    storms.

SOMETHING INSIDE AXEL has shifted by the time he and Emmett pull up to his fence. It isn't that Emmett and Axel talked and talked the whole way home, because that didn't happen. The most that was said was "Want one?" from Emmett and "No," from Axel. It isn't that the eaglet ever made it to the box of food either; he didn't, try as he might. Or that Lark showed him the video of her cockatoo dancing to a theme song he knows by heart. Nope. It happens— the shift, the warm feeling—when he sees Frank sitting on the fence and all the other FDR trucks gone. It happens when he opens the car door before Emmett even turns off the engine—something Axel never, ever does—and he sees Frank look up.

Frank with his baseball hat and his thick beard. Frank with his dirty clothes from a day of work on fixing their house. Frank with a slight wave and the smile only he can make where one side of his face draws up and both eyes grow very wide.

It isn't the kind of smile that would make it onto a card that says "Happy" in the caption. Or the kind of face that would make Axel laugh from across a quiet room. But it's Frank's happy, and that's good enough to make Axel feel different than he had earlier in the day.

They don't say anything at first, Frank on the fence and Axel on the ground. Until Axel climbs the fence and sits just like his dad, feet looped behind the middle beam.

This is an invitation. Like when Axel stood beside the bed in the middle of the night with no words. And somehow, without saying "talk to me," Frank picks up on this clue.

"What should we do with the nest?" he asks, pointing out over the field.

The nest on its side, the trees all around it.

"We leave it," Axel says. This feels obvious. How else can the eagles stay in the area? What else would they do with it?

"George said that they might have made a new nest somewhere," Frank says. "I guess we could push it into the burn pile when we clear the other brush. I wonder if George called a forester yet? I wonder what it's all worth? All that wood back there."

"You can't burn the nest," Axel says. This stops Frank from all of his out-loud wondering.

That nest belongs to the eagles, not to any of them, and certainly not Frank.

Axel unloops his feet and jumps from the fence.

"Axel, I'm sorry," Frank says. "I didn't mean that's what I wanted to do; I was just talking."

Axel looks out over the field now, to the fallen nest and the fallen trees. "You just need to finish the house."

"I don't know why I said that," Frank says. He jumps too. Stands close to Axel. "I'm not sure what to say."

There is so much to say, much more than plans to burn the nest or make money cleaning up the fallen trees. There are plans about their house, and telling Axel the truth about staying away so long. There's the way they left things this morning. Now Frank knows that Axel knows, so why, why is he only talking about the fallen nest and the fallen trees?

And because Axel knows about hope, and bravery, because he's seen it in a tiny eaglet no bigger than Frank's baseball cap, he asks, "Are you still sick?" The question so heavy on his heart comes out in a rush, the words all falling on top of one another.

"Sick?" Frank asks, like that couldn't possibly be the word he heard.

"Byrd said you were making bad choices. She said you were reckless. She said that you smashed your old truck, the red truck, the one that you drove me to school in, the one that we used to pick up mulch for Byrd, the one that had the ceiling with fabric that fluttered in the wind, the one with the pine tree air freshener, the one that ran into a telephone pole because you were sick."

Axel says all this, and his mind plays like a movie, like one he's already seen a hundred times. The fluttering fabric of the ceiling in the truck, his hand out the back window gliding on the wind as his dad, his Frank, drove them over belly-dropping little hills, over rumbly gravel roads, until the part that he didn't see comes into view. A smashed truck and sirens and blood. He didn't see it, but he can picture it, he can feel it just the same.

"She said that she told you to stay away," Axel says while his whole body tries to shake away the image of Frank's old truck. "She said 'stay away,' and you listened."

Frank reaches out for his son, puts a firm hand on his round shoulder. His jaw tightens under the pressure of his strong bite. Axel wishes that he could open up his dad's mind, go under the red baseball cap, under his thick black hair, under his scalp and into his brain, just to see all the words that Frank is holding back. To see the clues and secrets and truths that he's locking away behind his tight jaw. But Axel can't see inside Frank's mind, and he doesn't know what words come next.

Until Frank opens his mouth, lets a long breath escape into the spring air. "Axel, your mom is the strongest person I've ever met. She's braver than anyone should have to be."

"Not with snakes," Axel says.

Frank tucks both hands into his pockets and smiles. "I think if a snake came along, even an anaconda, and you were in harm's way, that snake wouldn't stand a chance."

"My friend Daniel says his mom could lift a car off him if she needed to."

"Your mom would do that too, with one pinky, while fighting off that anaconda with her other hand. To protect you, she'd do just about anything."

"Would you?" Axel asks.

Frank presses his hands down into his pockets, like he might find the answers in there. "I am doing better. I want to be better for you and your mom," Frank says. He rocks up onto his toes, then back onto his heels like Axel does sometimes. It helps, that feeling of your feet on firm ground; it helps sometimes when you need to find the right words.

Axel feels the next words coming, like when Ray hears the cars coming up the driveway before anyone else in the house. He knows what they will be without peeking inside Frank's brain because he feels them all over his body. So he waits, very still, while Frank rocks back and forth.

"I love you, buddy," Frank finally says. "More than you could ever know."

"I need you to tell me the truth," Axel says, because this is the moment to say what he needs. "I need you to promise me."

Frank clears his throat. "Okay," he says.

Axel shakes his head, because "okay" is not good enough. "Not just 'okay' but 'I promise.' You and Byrd have to tell me the truth. I can handle it. I can."

"Okay," Frank repeats, and like the mistake knocked him in the head, he takes off his baseball cap, holds it over his heart. His hair is matted down from sweat and work on the house. Without the hat, Axel can see his dad's whole face when he says, "I promise."

"And don't burn the nest . . . Promise me," Axel adds, because now is the time to make promises.

"I promise," Frank says again.

CHAPTER TWENTY-EIGHT

Dear Dr. Martin

From: Axel Rastusak
To: Dr. Taylor M. Martin
Subject: Re: Re: This is Axel

Dear Dr. Martin,

This is Axel.

They started working on our woods, clearing leaning trees.
George doesn't think the eagles will come back with all this
noise.

Do you think that this is true?
Do you think it is still okay to HOPE?

I go back to school on Monday.

I look forward to your reply.

Sincerely,
Axel Rastusak

Dear Axel,

Have fun in school tomorrow.

The eagles will be fine.
They adapt.

Braviary fluttered around today. It won't be long. We'll release him in the same location we found him. (And we will need your neighbors to keep that dog inside.)

It is always okay to HOPE.

More soon.

Sincerely,
Dr. Taylor M. Martin
Delaware Valley Raptor Sanctuary
VMD-PhD

P.S. Lark wanted me to ask if you like the name yet?

Axel!
Thanks for writing me.
My sisters made like a thousand dance videos since we've
been off school.
And they built me a fort. We finally got power back at our
house. It was getting BORING.
Is it still bad at your house? Is your dad still there? Will I see
you at school tomorrow?

That's bananas about the nest. We'll still find all the
Pokémon when I come back.

I promise.

From,
Daniel

CHAPTER TWENTY-NINE

Conversations

Purrt
> cluck, cluck
> caw.

Skree
> gobble
> hoot.

Titter
> ta-ha
> ti-whoop.

> ka
> killy-killy
> coo.

Whoo
> Who-cooks-for-you?

BETWEEN BEING BACK AT SCHOOL, with so many school things all at once, and the way the house changes every single day, the week starts to fly.

On Monday Axel gets to catch up Ms. Dale and Daniel on the eaglet and his parents, and Daniel gets to catch Ms. Dale and Axel up on the fact that his sisters have 1,500 followers on their YouTube channel.

The woods behind the house aren't filled with mysteries anymore; they're barely filled with trees either. They've cleared a path all the way up to the creek. It looks like a tree stump graveyard.

Axel doesn't love it, but at least it's a safe enough space for him and Ray to walk. And they do, each day after school.

On Thursday, Axel's pencil won't keep up with the thoughts in his mind during ELA and he goes to Ms. Dale's office to finish his WHAT I DID ON MY BREAK report. Which is such a ridiculous title. It's not like it was a vacation or anything, certainly not for Axel. Yes, he had the week off school, but there was the rescue and sleeping at Emmett and George's and Frank coming back and so much more.

A break would obviously include lots of walks with Ray, and thinking time in his thinking spot—which was smashed by a tree, so that's out. It would be a successful Pasta-palooza with his family.

Last week was definitely not a "break."

Ms. Dale doesn't care to hear Axel's reasons for not writing the report based on this technicality. However true it may be. Axel tries a different approach. "Maybe we should clean your office first?" Axel says.

"No way. No delay. Get typing," Ms. Dale says. She shoves a pile of papers to the floor to make space for Axel's laptop.

"Your hair is blue," Axel says.

"That's what I did on my break, but Mr. Conner wants to know what you did," Ms. Dale says, opening the laptop.

"Maybe I should finish writing it in pencil like everyone else?" Axel says.

"Maybe you should start typing?" Ms. Dale says.

Ms. Dale frowns. A big frown that makes her look like an ostrich. "We can play Uno after you finish," she offers.

"Fine," Axel says. He wonders for a moment if his classmates are typing now too, or if they're all going to turn in a handwritten report with colorful illustrations at the top and his will stand out, but not in a good way. He knows he shouldn't compare. What he needs is more time to work on essays. What he needs is to type instead of print because writing by hand is very difficult for him. These accommodations are in place just for essays like this, the typing and the more time. So he might as well use them.

"Type," Ms. Dale says, like she can see the very thoughts piling up and up in Axel's head. Her eyes drop down to her own computer across the table from him, and she begins to type, so he may as well too.

His head bobs between the messy draft and the computer screen, one word at a time.

He starts with the fallen nest and Braviary's rescue. That part goes quickly.

But the rubric for the assignment asks for dialogue. Dialogue means that he has to type a whole conversation. It's hard to remember a whole conversation. Who can do that? And because technically there is no way to tell a true conversation without having one recorded, and because he technically can't think of one that he had during his break that wasn't a break, Axel decides to type up what he remembers from a talk that he had with Frank yesterday.

It's the best he can do, and besides, interrupting Ms. Dale to ask if it's okay to break the rules doesn't seem like something she would be interested in right now.

So he types about Frank at the house after his walk with Ray yesterday. The walk where they didn't see any birds, and it didn't feel magical at all to be out in the open in the clearing, the way it used to feel being under the canopy of trees, surrounded by green in all directions.

"I found this," Frank said, trying to hand Axel a feather. "You still collect them, don't you?" Frank asked.

"Turkey feathers?" Axel responded, noting its brown and tan stripes.

"Feathers," Frank said. "We couldn't walk two feet without you picking one up."

"Dr. Martin says that feathers should not be removed from nature unless for Indigenous or religious reasons." Frank passed the feather from one hand to the other. "I don't collect them," Axel clarified.

"Oh," Frank said, and then let the feather go. It didn't flutter to the ground the way you might expect a feather to do. The shaft was thick, the plume dense. It dropped. Straight to the ground.

Axel could feel the hurt coming off his father, so he said just what he thought might make it better. "Do you collect anything, Frank?"

Frank said something about fishing lures and then asked Axel to come fishing with him over the weekend.

"No," Axel said, because he doesn't like fishing.

It doesn't seem like a great conversation to put in the assignment, but it is all that Axel can remember. The turkey feather and how Frank asked about fishing, and didn't ask about going to the cabin to look for sandhill cranes. But that they both told the truth, Frank with his fishing lures and Axel with the feathers, and even though it wasn't a special conversation, it was good enough.

It takes more than one day for Axel to get the whole

conversation typed up into a document. He finishes just in time to play Uno with Ms. Dale before Friendship Club. When Daniel and the other kids arrive, Ms. Dale finds ice pops in her freezer and announces that it's free time Friday and they can talk about anything, as long as they are good listeners when another friend talks.

So Axel talks about branching.

Daniel acts out the jumping from branch to branch and makes his thin arms flap.

Ms. Dale doesn't yell at Daniel for being out of his seat or letting the ice pop melt on the table, because all she said was that they had to listen when their friends were talking, and Daniel is definitely listening.

Axel says hop, and Daniel hops.

He says fly, and Daniel flaps his wings.

It's like a party in Ms. Dale's office, and things feel like they are fluttering back to normal. Back to school. Back to Friendship Club. And back to time with Daniel, best of all.

After school, Emmett takes Axel to the Delaware Valley Raptor Sanctuary, then Emmett goes to his favorite grocer for ingredients. More things are falling back in place, like when Axel sees Braviary hop and flap, just like Daniel, from the swing to a stump. Not pretend like Daniel, but really do it. The eagle's body looks stuffed like a beanbag, not fluff and bones, like before. Like there is some shape to him.

When Emmett and Axel arrive home, Frank's in the driveway.

"It's almost ready," Frank says, pointing to the house, which looks wrapped like a present in white paper. He grabs a grocery bag from the back of Emmett's car.

Things are fluttering back to normal here too, Axel thinks.

"Want to go for a walk?" Axel asks.

"Sure," Frank says. "Let me load these into the house."

Ray comes barreling out, and Aunt Nancy waves from the porch. "How's that bird?" she calls.

Axel runs up the walkway, lets Ray give him a quick hello. "He's getting stronger every day."

CHAPTER THIRTY

Memories

From A. P. Brown's *Collection of North American Birds*, page 669

WINGSPAN: distance from one wingtip to the other when a bird's wings are outstretched and fully extended

BY THE FOLLOWING WEEK, the side of the house is closed up all the way.

Even the one space where once there was a window, the only window, is boarded up, and there's even more of the waxy white paper stuck to the house. Frank called it tech wrap and acted like this was one of the very last touches the house needed to be complete. Yet, with all the waxy paper, and the board over Axel's favorite thinking spot, Frank still shows up, day after day. Sometimes with his crew, in the early morning hours before Axel and Byrd drive off to school. Sometimes without his crew at all.

There are things that Axel likes about this: seeing his dad, hearing his voice. And the fact that Frank hasn't said one more thing about burning the nest. But there are things that make him worry, too. Like when Frank and Byrd go off and whisper words together, away from Axel, away from the rest of the family, like they still have so many secrets, like maybe Frank will forget that he promised to tell the truth.

And he did lie, just yesterday. He said that the house was

finished enough for Byrd and Axel to move back in. "Just cosmetic things," he said. Whatever that meant. He said he'd help carry their bags over to the house, help Byrd clean up the guest room at George and Emmett's. But he did not. At the last minute he said, "Not today."

From the back of Emmett's SUV, Axel has a clear picture of Byrd and Frank today. He can see them down at the picnic table by the creek. No work being done. Just talking. Somehow this view of his parents makes the lie from yesterday stick sharp in his side. Axel knows that he has to be brave. He knows he needs to find out from his parents what's really going on.

"I'll let Ray out," Emmett says as they exit the car. "Want me to carry your backpack up?"

Axel hears Emmett's words, but his heart is too focused on the picnic table and the smiles, and the way Byrd keeps laughing with her whole body. The way his parents don't look away from each other long enough to even notice that he's home.

Maybe he should just wait until they do?

Stand right here, right in the middle of the driveway until they look up from the creek, across the front yard, over Byrd's raised garden beds, over the fence and see him standing here.

"Anything good happening?" Aunt Nancy calls from the porch. Ray slipping from behind her out into the open air. If they hadn't looked before, they really should now, the way Ray is carrying on. Axel knows what's on Ray's mind—a *w-a-l-k*. But Axel has a great big mystery to solve first, and Ray will just have to wait.

"Nance," Emmett says, approaching his house. "What are you doing?"

"Getting off this porch to find out what's going on over there," Aunt Nancy says. Axel turns to see Aunt Nancy fling her rollator at Emmett. Emmett with his already full hands.

"Nance," Emmett warns again.

"Either get out of my way or give me a hand," Aunt Nancy says. "None of this 'Nance' crap."

"Where's George?" Emmett asks, like this will delay Aunt Nancy from doing whatever she wants.

"Napping under some book filled with fancy words . . . For Pete's sake, give me your hand," Aunt Nancy demands. Her thick white sneaker toddling on the first step.

This all happens between glances for Axel. An ear on Aunt Nancy's orders and eyes on the picnic table.

"They've been nestled up there for too long," Aunt Nancy says when she reaches Axel's side. "They're dodos, those two." She turns her rollator so that she can sit facing the scene by the creek. "Dodos," she says again.

"Turkeys," Axel says. "Everyone knows that turkey brains are the worst."

Right there, from her perch on her rollator, Aunt Nancy cups her wrinkled hands around her wrinkled mouth. "You have turkey brains," she hollers. And this, this has them turn from one another and scan the creek and the front yard and Byrd's raised garden beds and over the fence until their eyes finally land on Aunt Nancy and Axel.

And just in case Byrd and Frank weren't sure what the noise was, Aunt Nancy shouts again, longer and louder this time, "TUUUUUURRRRKEYYYYYY BRAAAAAAAIIINS!"

They smile back like being called a turkey brain is hilarious and they couldn't possibly be keeping secrets.

"You know what I could use?" Aunt Nancy asks in a softer voice. "I could use some intel. Think you could go down there and find out just what they're talking about? I think this is as far as my adventure will take me today, so it's up to you to find out more."

Axel wants to run straight down there, demand to be seen and told the truths that they are telling each other, but he isn't Aunt Nancy. Demands don't come as easily to him.

"Aw . . . Go on," Aunt Nancy says. "Take Ray with you. Maybe he'll get something out of them, too."

It's hard sometimes to just put one foot in front of the other, even in the place called home. Axel looks down at Ray. "Should we go?" he asks.

And the thing about dogs is that the word *go* is a magic word, so Ray takes off, and all Axel can do is follow.

"Give 'em heck," Aunt Nancy calls.

Ray reaches the picnic table first, practically crawls on top of Frank, slipping right in between where Byrd and Frank sit side by side.

"Hey, buddy," Frank says, scratching Ray behind the ear.

"His name is Ray," Axel says.

Frank and Byrd share a quick look, only long enough for

Axel to know that there is a longer story behind the look, one that they haven't told him. Just another secret between the two.

"You have to tell me," Axel says. "No secret jokes between the two of you. You promised to tell the truth."

"It isn't that great of a story," Byrd says. "It's just, of course your dad knows Ray's name. He named Ray."

"You did?" Axel asks. He slides into the bench across from his parents. Ray ducks under the table and rests a heavy head in Axel's lap.

"Let me see if I can remember," Frank says. "It was a long time ago. You wouldn't know it, but he had even more energy then. This little fur ball made George and Emmett so happy. Your mom and me, too. He was like a ray of light. A ray of sunshine."

"But he's not golden," Axel says, looking at Ray's sweet face.

"A ray of light can come in any color," Frank says. "And this guy made us smile. He had these huge ears and paws."

"He still has big ears."

"Right, and if you can imagine, those big ears on a little puppy. His ears are the same size now as when they brought him here, only his body was, like, half as big."

"More like ten percent as big," Byrd says. She holds her hands like she's holding a baby. "Remember?"

"That first weekend they brought him up. No name. They'd rescued him from a place near where they worked. I know we have a picture somewhere from that first visit with

Ray. He curled right up on your mom's belly. You were in there. He wasn't much bigger that day than you were when we brought you home a few weeks later. I bet we have a picture of that too." He turns to Byrd. "Remember that day?"

And now it makes sense, the way they were smiling before when Axel saw them from the driveway. Sharing memories like this brings on smiles.

"I'd like to see those pictures," Axel says.

"Well, let's go see if we can find them," Frank says.

"Where?" Axel asks.

"Inside," Frank says. He stands up and offers Byrd his hand, and she stands too.

"It's safe?" Axel asks.

"Today's the day," Frank says. "I think they're in the basement, those photos."

Axel enters his house after Byrd and after Frank, and even after Ray. It's his house so it shouldn't feel like anything but "home" but so much has changed.

And it smells funny inside.

Ray sniffs around too, especially over in the living room where all the furniture is missing and there are new floorboards.

"That's where he peed," Axel says.

At the same time, Byrd says, "Oh, no you don't."

At the same time, Frank says, "Ray," in a singsongy voice.

Ray looks up, tilts his head like the commands don't make sense altogether. Maybe they don't, but something about it does make sense.

And just like the smiles outside at the picnic table, all three Rastusaks laugh inside their home. Their laughter echoes in the empty space with no carpets or furniture or houseplants to dampen the sound.

Just like the smell, it's a different sound than Axel remembers in the house. The echo of them laughing. All three of them. All in on the same joke.

It's a different sound, yes, but one thing Axel knows for sure: it is a sound he loves to hear.

CHAPTER THIRTY-ONE

Pasta-palooza Take Two

What it is:

Elbow macaroni.
Gluten-free fettuccini.
Angel hair.
Rigatoni.
Fusilli.

Marinara.
Alfredo.
Butter.
Pesto.

Meatballs.

THERE'S SOMETHING ABOUT THE LAUGHTER in the house, and being brave enough to walk right up to Byrd and Frank and ask what they were talking about, and even knowing a story from long ago that once he didn't know about Ray and his name. There's something about all of this that swirls inside Axel's very head, and his heart too. Like the way it must feel to fly.

"We're celebrating," Emmett says when he places the last bowl of pasta on the table. It's elbows with extra butter and extra salt, and it is right in front of Axel.

The table is crowded again, because the sixth chair is squished next to Byrd again. But this time it's not that bad. After all, this time is a celebration, like Pasta-paloozas are supposed to be. Lots to celebrate.

"Cheers," George says, raising his water glass. The wineglasses are still missing, and if the clues are all true and in place, Axel knows exactly why the wine isn't part of tonight's celebration. And that's just fine; Axel doesn't drink the wine anyway.

Even Aunt Nancy raises her glass. It wobbles a little, but she touches it to Axel's without spilling. "You ready to celebrate?" she asks out the side of her mouth.

Axel nods.

"Well, then I am too," she says. "But I'm also ready to toss the table if needed."

Axel can't help himself, he laughs. The image in his brain of Aunt Nancy tossing a table is just too much. Ray would sure like it, the pasta all over the floor. A real feast for him. A dog celebration.

Too bad for Ray that isn't going to happen. Not tonight. Tonight isn't a dog celebration.

"To Frank for finishing the house in record time," George says, raising his glass in the air again.

Frank blushes a deep purple color. Axel does that too when the spotlight is on him. "I don't know about finished," Frank says. "But it's safe for Byrd and Axel to stay in tonight."

Axel's suddenly on his feet. His bedroom with its hawk eyes and books and ticking clock. Why hadn't he gone to look when he was inside the house with Frank and Byrd? When they'd gone for the pictures down into the damp basement? Now his whole body radiates: ROOM! ROOM! ROOM!

"Where do you think you're going?" Byrd asks.

The word pops out. "Room!"

Byrd reaches across the table and, as best she can, chimes

the side of Axel's glass with a spoon. Another nice sound. "I want to give a toast, too."

"I yield the floor to you," George says to Byrd. He sits, and then Axel does too. It seems like the right thing to do, even with his room and all his things waiting for him.

"I want to toast to Frank, but not for the house," Byrd says. She grips her water glass in both hands, pulls the glass close to her chest. "Thank you for coming back to us," she says. "Again," she adds, but barely, the word almost invisible.

Frank stands up, wraps Byrd into a thick hug. The kind of hug that swallows another person. The kind of hug that only feels good if you really, really want it to happen. And Byrd does. She and Frank stay like that for a little while. Everyone else at the table frozen, like maybe this wasn't something they were meant to see. Like maybe a secret has passed between Frank and Byrd, wrapped inside that hug.

A secret.

Like maybe Axel doesn't know the whole truth of the things that happened between Byrd and Frank, and maybe—no, definitely—he doesn't know what happens next. These mysteries are too hard to solve. Too big to fit into one hug, or one celebration, or one house, or one nest. These mysteries have slithering parts. Byrd should know this better than anyone, but she doesn't.

She's too busy wiping her eyes with the backs of her hands. Smiling and crying at the same time like her brain can't make up its mind any more than Axel can make out what's happening here.

"Coming back?" Axel asks. A simple question, really. Two words.

"To us?" Aunt Nancy asks. And for just a moment, Axel imagines that this is the time she throws the whole table. Elbows with butter and salt, meatballs, and red sauce. All of it thrust from their side of the table to Frank's side.

Why is it that each time he feels like he knows the truth, there is something else they've kept hidden? Why is it that when they were laughing in the house or smiling at the picnic table, that they couldn't tell him about this whole "coming back" business, whatever it means? So many more whys. Again.

It isn't his room calling this time, it is *ROOM*.

Room to think. Room to breathe. For the second time, at this round table, in this fine house, with all of Emmett's great pasta, Axel escapes. His chair once again knocking back onto the wooden floor. Ray jumping up, too. Ray racing out to the living room, through the door, to the porch, down the steps, and all the way out into the field.

The field with the bald acre of trees before it. Ugly and raw.

The nest starting to slope into the earth. Bent and broken.

His heart hammering in his chest. Again.

They have secrets. Again.

Always.

Byrd catches up to him the field, but this time she doesn't

hesitate, she wraps her arms around him, pulls him close. "This okay?" she asks. Axel lets her hold him. "It's a lot," she says. "It's a lot," she repeats.

This is beyond obvious.

"I don't like it when you leave me out. I don't like it when you don't tell me everything," Axel says, the bubble popping in his chest and all the words falling out at once. "Frank said he would tell me the truth. He promised."

"I know," Byrd says. "That's why I—"

"You're not doing it right," Axel says. "Before, you kept him away by keeping a secret. Now you say he's coming back to us as a surprise. I just want to know what's going on. No surprises. No secrets."

"Axel," Byrd says in her cooing voice. The one that makes it sound like she's talking to a baby. Axel isn't a baby. "Axel," she says again. "We have grown-up things to figure out, but we won't do anything big without talking to you, okay?"

"Grown-up things." *Caw.* Like what? Secrets and snow-storms and car wrecks? *Caw.* "Frank promised to tell me the truth. Don't you stop him this time."

"Me?"

Like he could mean anyone else. "Yes, you. You stopped him from coming before. You lied. You can't do that anymore," Axel says, bravery filling him from the inside out. "Just like Frank, you have to promise to tell me the truth, Byrd. Can you do that?"

This is not a simple request, especially not for Byrd. So,

Axel understands why she thinks for a little. Thinking time is important, especially with a big question. He turns from Byrd toward the big red barn. The tall trees lined behind it that weren't knocked away by the storm. The way the shadows climb all over the barn, and the swallows too, and the early evening hugging what's left of the sun.

Byrd takes one of her big, deep yoga breaths, lets her chest rise and fall.

"I promise," she says simply.

Axel holds on to this hope, like those eagle parents do when their baby falls from the nest. He holds on to Byrd's simple words, her promise.

Hope isn't light like feathers.

It isn't.

It's thick like that hug. Like the one that Frank gave Byrd at the dining room table, and like that hug by the muddy pond years ago.

It's tight.

But it's good because it's holding on to you and you're holding on to it. Hope.

Hope like that can't just float away.

Hope like this should make Axel feel warm inside, and it does, but there's something else, too.

"Should we go be buttervores now?" Byrd asks.

Axel nods. "We have something else to celebrate."

Byrd looks around the field, like maybe her son is talking

about nature again. Like maybe an eagle has come around to check on the nest or some other clue she missed.

"This," Axel says, pointing at his mother. "You, Byrd," he says.

"Me?" Byrd asks. "What on earth did I do?"

"You promised to tell the truth," Axel says simply. Something she has never once promised to do. Never once said out loud to him. And now she has. And Frank too. And Axel has told them that he expects it.

Byrd follows Axel inside, where their family is waiting, and the buttered noodles are already on his plate.

CHAPTER THIRTY-TWO

Touch

A person isn't made of
Air-filled bones.

He is sturdy.
He is whole.

He, of course,
Can take the weight of
Things when they lean
Against, push
Into him.

When they hold on to him
And he holds on to them
Equally.

When they don't let
Go and leave him
Alone to lift into the air.

Dear Axel,

Braviary is growing stronger each day. He's almost ready to return to the world. We'll release him where it all started. This Saturday at 8 a.m.

I'm going to switch the meet-and-greet to Friday since we'll be with you Saturday morning. I know that the meet-and-greet isn't your favorite activity, but come if you want to. You'll get to meet some other members.

Sincerely,
Dr. Taylor M. Martin
Delaware Valley Raptor Sanctuary
VMD-PhD

P.S. Have your neighbors lock up that dog on Saturday.
P.P.S. Lark wanted me to let you know that she is excited to see you on Saturday.

FROM: Axel Rastusak
TO: Dr. Taylor M. Martin
SUBJECT: Re: Re: Re: Re: Re: This is Axel

Dear Dr. Martin and Lark,

This is Axel.

That dog's name is Ray. He is a ray of light. (That's what my dad says, anyway.)

I will ask George and Emmett to keep Ray inside. Though, I know Ray would want to be there when we set Braviary free. Ray was with us when we found the baby.

I'll be there at 8 a.m.

When we let him go, will Braviary know how to find his family?

I hope so.

Sincerely,
Axel Rastusak

CHAPTER THIRTY-THREE

Dreaming

From A. P. Brown's *Collection of North American Birds*, page 104

". . . Good question. Scientists from the University of Chicago theorize that birds in fact do dream. Their work suggests the probability that birds dream in song patterns, as though they might be rehearsing for the day, or reliving the past. It should be noted that their sample size was small and limited to . . ."

AFTER BRUSHING HIS TEETH, and washing his face, and emailing Dr. Martin and Lark, and picking a book, Axel climbs into his very own bed for the first time in over three weeks.

"Miss me?" Byrd says, leaning against the doorframe of his room. She crosses the floor, climbs onto the end of Axel's bed.

"Don't mess the blankets," Axel warns. He has just gotten everything right. "I don't need you to tuck me in."

"I know, I know," Byrd says. She breathes in the room like somehow she missed it too, the four walls that hold all of Axel's most precious things. His bookshelves, the Delaware Valley Raptor Sanctuary calendar with Braviary's release circled in red marker, even the index card that he thinks she doesn't know he has.

The deep blue paint framing his twin bed. The ticking clock. The far wall, like her far wall, sloped to make the roof outside, and inside a perfect angle for his hawk eye stickers. So much wall, no windows.

"I wonder what Ray is doing?" Axel asks, bringing Byrd from his four walls to face him. "You know, with us gone."

"I bet your Ray is passed out on his back with one paw in the air and squirrels filling his sleepy mind."

Axel can picture that, too. "Dreaming of chasing squirrels through the forest. But not the clearing—our old forest, back the way we loved it."

"Dreaming of huge meatballs raining down from the sky as he runs after squirrels in your forest," Byrd says. She crosses her arms. "We may never know what Ray dreams, but I am sure he's already off to dreamland by now, even without us there."

"I hope he knows we'll be back tomorrow. You know? Like he didn't think we were all starting to live together or something and now he wonders where we are? I mean, he's a dog, so he doesn't understand the storm and needing to stay there until the house got fixed."

"I think he knows," Byrd says, pressing her hands against Axel's blanket-covered feet.

"I hope so," Axel repeats.

"Speaking of 'starting to live together,'" Byrd says, borrowing the phrase that Axel just used. Byrd looks back to the wall, like the rest of her sentence might be found splattered against it.

"It smells in here," Axel says, filling in Byrd's pause. "I don't like the smell of it."

"It's the paint," Byrd says. "There's still some finishing touches to make, and we'll leave the windows open so the paint smell dissipates."

"So Frank will be back?"

Byrd's mouth opens wide, her eyes too, like Axel has found the words she's been looking for, like he's solved the very mystery from before. She nods.

"He'll finish things up downstairs," Axel says, more of a question, but Byrd doesn't answer. "He'll get the furniture back in place? And what about my window? It's still all boarded up. Will he fix that, too?"

Byrd nods again. "Yes, Axel, Frank's coming back."

And here's the thing about truth, right here, right in this room with these four walls. Byrd says her truth about Frank's return, and Axel says his, but, just like guessing Ray's dreams, truth depends not only on who is telling it, but on whose mind is filled with the words and pictures.

Axel does worry about Ray, the whole night, actually. Even with his weighted blanket, the ticking clock, and the hawk's eyes. *Caw.*

When he can feel the sunrise, feel it in his bones, he slips out of his bed, down the stairs, out the front door, past Byrd's flower boxes, all six of them lined up and still filled with the mess of the storm. He goes through the gate, turning to close it quietly behind him. He isn't one toe on the gravel driveway—not one toe—when he hears Ray's bark.

George opens the front door, shoos Ray outside, doesn't even wipe the sleep out of his eyes to see that it's Axel. He knows, just like Ray knows, that it's time to think.

Time to walk. Time to be together.

They don't walk through the field or wander in the bare patch left by the storm and on out to the creek. No. Today they walk straight down the driveway.

"I didn't want you to think we left for good," Axel says to Ray.

Ray lets his tail wag at the idea, ears perk to the sound of his best friend's voice.

"We had to move back. That was the plan," Axel says. "But I will miss coming down the stairs to see you right away in the morning."

Ray picks up the scent of something new, his nose to the ground. Axel's been on the driveway to school and back. That one walk down the road when Byrd told him about Frank being reckless. But in those times before, he hadn't noticed the tree that had been cut in half. One of the tall sugar maples that turns bright orange in the fall. But this tree won't see the fall.

The bottom, thick, rough trunk, like an elephant's leg pulled to the right of the driveway, the top, green and lush, rolled to the left. How had Axel not seen this clue before? A tree like this that someone had to move in order for someone to get down the driveway. It was a part of the story from the night of the rescue. Part of the story that Axel hadn't known.

He knew about the storm. He knew about the tree in the house, and the nest in the field. He knew . . . Axel lets his own memories wash over that night with the rescue and the first sight of the baby eagle in the nest. He can almost reach out and touch that memory.

Ray stops to sniff the downed tree. There are so many of them to explore farther up on the property, but this one, this one might hold a secret. At least that's the way it seems with Ray sniffing at it from all sides.

"I guess I missed a few things that night," Axel says. This fallen tree not part of his truth from that day. He hadn't included it in the report he had to write in school, hadn't told Ms. Dale about it or Daniel. Because he didn't know it was there. All along, this tree was part of the destruction that the storm caused. And Axel didn't know.

"Somebody had to cut this in half. Somebody strong had to drag it onto the sides of the driveway, just so our road was passable," Axel says. He reaches out to the fallen tree, tugs at one of the leaves, which pulls away easily from its branch. A branch that would've been so far from Axel's reach before the storm is right under his palm now.

Is it possible that Axel missed more that night? The night of the storm? More than a tree being cleared from their driveway sometime between the storm and Dr. Martin coming? And what if he missed a few other clues between trees falling down and him touching a tree right now?

There isn't just one kind of missing. There's the missing that comes from being apart, like last night with Ray, or before with Frank. There's also the missing like this tree. That even though something was right in front of him. A clue. A truth. He still didn't see it.

Axel thinks about Byrd at the table with the toast for Frank, and the way she said in his bedroom last night, "Frank's coming back." He hopes that this isn't the other kind of miss. The kind that means he can't reach out and touch it, know that it's real.

Ray has finished with the mysteries of the tree. He whimpers, begging Axel to leave the chopped tree for a better adventure.

And, since Axel missed Ray last night, he decides to leave this maple to decompose now. Close this part of the story from the night of the rescue. Even though someone had chopped it down. Someone had made a path for his family to come and go. For Dr. Martin to get up the driveway to the nest. For Frank to come and fix the house. Whoever did it, Axel is grateful. Maybe that's enough.

"Come," Axel says then to Ray. "I bet I can beat you home."

CHAPTER THIRTY-FOUR

Ready?

Peregrine wonder,
a wandering hunter.

AT SCHOOL, Axel wishes he'd gotten a little more sleep the night before. His mind wanders, like it sometimes does, to images outside the walls of the school, even while his teachers are asking him to think about things inside the school.

It's Daniel that wakes him to the day. Axel sees him just ahead in the hallway.

"Daniel," Axel calls in a non-pigeon voice.

Daniel slows for his friend. "I asked my mom," he says. "And she says that she can't get me there by eight a.m."

"But Braviary," Axel says. "You won't get to meet him before he flies back to his family." Axel stops in the hallway. So Daniel stops too, but just a little farther ahead. Far enough that he needs to do one of his fancy backward walks to get to Axel. Has to raise his one eyebrow at his backward dance move and try to make his friend laugh. But this time, it doesn't work. Somehow the eyebrow trick, the one that gets a real-Axel-smile every single time, doesn't work.

"I'm sorry," Daniel says. "I tried, but no one can bring me, and she is not about to let me ride in anybody else's car besides family. That's a 'no way' from my mom."

"I want you to meet Braviary," Axel says.

"Well, imagine me there," Daniel says. "I'd say, 'Look at that bird soar' and 'That's one we don't *gotta catch*.'"

And this, this, the *gotta catch* from Axel's very favorite theme song, finally brings on the smile that Daniel'd been waiting to see. "Ha! There," he says. "My mom can bring me as soon as she gets home from work. You can tell me all about it before we have our epic day in the forest." Daniel starts down the hallway again, hoping his movement will bring his friend along. "I think we should focus on Legendaries this weekend. See what's been hiding in that forest, since we've missed the last few weeks."

"The forest is bald," Axel says. "They had to clear the fallen ones, and I'm not allowed where it's all knotty. Where the foresters haven't been able to clear." He stops walking again.

"Axel . . . there might be ice pops. And they're going to be melted before we get there if you go this slow." Daniel isn't raising eyebrows to this. He's serious.

"But what if we can't do it tomorrow? What if we never get to play Pokémon in the woods again?"

"What? That's not what I said," Daniel says.

"But the trees where we used to go are gone, logged, cut up. And the deeper parts of the forest are still too dangerous. And that only leaves the trees by my house, and maybe some right behind the barn."

Somehow Daniel knows it's time for something unexpected, not an eyebrow or a dance move, not a plan for what they *could* find in the woods, but a friendly dose of the truth. "Axel, it doesn't really matter where we are, by your house or right behind the barn, or even in that wide open field, what matters is our imagination. I could picture a Ho-Oh right over there by Mx. Desi's door. Can't you see the orange feathers poking out from their mailbox?"

Axel turns toward the music room door, tilts his head a little. Blinks to clear his eyes. "Right there," he says finally, conclusively. "Maybe we should let Mx. Desi know that there's a flying fire type outside their door?" Axel whispers.

"Naw, I think they know. Besides, if we tell one teacher, we'll have to tell them all. Look over there!" Daniel points across the hallway.

Sure enough, another Legendary. "I guess you're right," Axel says.

"Of course I am," Daniel says. "That's just a fact."

After school Axel and Ray take their second walk of the day. They head into the clear-cut path all the way down to the creek. Ray sniffs at the huge tire tracks left behind by the heavy machines that dug and pulled away the fallen trees. There are still clues, Axel supposes, but not like the ones in the deep woods. Not like the ones from under the canopy of green leaves, among the waving ferns.

These clues are tire tracks, a Diet Coke can where it doesn't belong, stumps and branches, and mud. And then Axel notices a print. Not a paw, like Ray's. Or a shoe, like his own. A print with lines like a thin sparrow, like an arrow pointing down.

"A turkey," Axel says, pointing. The prints line up like the bird was walking a tightrope, not through a muddy path. And then Axel sees another clue, a feather, like the one Frank brought him two weeks ago. When so much had already changed, and then changed again.

Axel looks beyond the cleared area into the space that runs behind his house where the wild turkey prints lead. It isn't a dense forest in that direction, spots of trees that dot along the creek, ferns and brush. But it looks like a place that he and Ray can start to explore, and maybe even Daniel too. He hopes it's a place where Braviary and his whole family might come to live. In one of those trees, in a new nest they've built, just along the twist of the creek. A place Axel could've seen from his perch in his favorite window. If only the window weren't boarded up.

Ray perks to something, a sound behind them.

Axel half expects to turn and see the turkey, but it's no turkey; it's George.

Ray races over to him, places muddy paws on George's chest. Kisses and kisses all over George's face.

"Are you finding 'pleasure in the pathless woods,' as Lord Byron would say?" George asks.

"This is one big path," Axel says. "Not pathless." He walks across the squishy ground to George.

"We could get brave and head that way," George says, pointing off beyond the big red barn.

Axel thinks that George is kidding, he does, but George doesn't smile or laugh at the idea. "We can't go that way," Axel says, just to be sure George knows the truth.

"I know," George says. "I made that rule. I was testing you." At this he smiles a bit.

Axel starts to make his way home. It isn't like before when he and Ray would get to the edge of the forest and their whole world would open back up, seeing the farmhouse and the fence, seeing Byrd's potting shed and his house for the first time when they'd cross from forest into clearing. It isn't like that now, because so much has been flattened, and even from the creek, he can see everything all at once. Everything about his home is *always* there. He doesn't have to search at all. He doesn't have to discover it new each time he leaves the forest.

Even today, he sees Byrd at her raised beds. Sees her in her baby blue shirt and big hat. Sees her from a spot that once was covered in pines, now open to his home.

"I'm going home," Axel calls.

He doesn't wait for George to say any of his fancy words because sometimes no words are needed.

CHAPTER THIRTY-FIVE

Or not?

From A. P. Brown's *Collection of North American Birds*, page 663

FLEDGE: ready, able to leave the nest; a nestling taking flight

BYRD IS ELBOWS-DEEP in a raised bed when Axel rounds the corner of the fence toward home.

"How was your walk?" she calls over the fence post.

In his mind, Axel's moved on from the walk with Ray already. He's moved on to the place he needs to do his reading, which is not the place he *wants* to do his reading. He wants to come from his walk with Ray, go into his house and grab a seat in the window that looks out over the creek. But that isn't possible. After all, that's a space that didn't get fixed in Frank's weeks of being at the house.

His bedroom will be just fine. He can take his second-favorite book, the one that wasn't completely swallowed by the tree in his living room after the storm. *Fly with Me* will be just right for today's reading time. He'll fill out his reading log, and Byrd will sign it. Then he'll do as he likes to do, keep reading.

This plan is laid out perfectly in his head as he walks from fence post to fence gate to stone pathway. The plan takes easy steps toward the front door, that is, until Byrd goes running, knocking into him. Screaming her head off, shaking her fists in the air.

Snake. Axel knows before the word even falls from Byrd's lips.

"You should favorite roadrunners," Axel says. Byrd turns at the front door to face him, composing herself with a deep yoga breath.

"I should," she says in a huff. "I should fill this yard with roadrunners. They'd have a feast."

"Actually, roadrunners couldn't survive here," Axel says. "Aunt Nancy could have had them in her yard out west, but not here."

Byrd shakes her head, not like she's doubting Axel's knowledge of roadrunner facts, like she's shaking the last images of the garter snake from her mind. Wiping it clean so she can start with a new image.

"Red-tailed hawks would like to eat those snakes. We have red-tailed hawks all over. Those white bellies sticking out all over the place," Axel says. "Frank likes red-tailed hawks, remember?" Axel remembers, anyway, sitting in the back of Frank's old truck, driving anywhere on any afternoon, and Frank counting the red-tailed hawks along the highway as they drove. "One, on the exit sign to Milford . . . Two, on that light post . . . Three, in that white pine . . ."

The memory is almost enough to derail Axel's quest for his quiet bedroom and a good book. Almost.

"Move," he says to Byrd.

"Hey," Byrd says, not shifting from the door. Well, maybe shifting a little. She crosses her arms, tries to make herself big in the space so that Axel can't get through without saying what she wants him to say.

Axel knows these clues inside and out. "Please move," he says.

"Just adding the word *please* doesn't change your tone," Byrd says.

Caw. There's nothing helpful in Byrd's words for Axel's case, so rather than continue to play her game at the door, Axel turns his body into the sleek shape of a peregrine falcon and dives past her hip, straight for the front door's knob.

"Wait," Byrd says, catching Axel in flight.

"I have a surprise," Byrd says. "Well, two."

Axel rocks back on his heels, just out of Byrd's reach. The idea of a surprise is good. After all, they almost always lead to something special; it's just that Axel would prefer a surprise either be something he gets to help plan, or he doesn't have to wait to find out.

"One surprise is just behind this door," Byrd says. "So we'll get right to that. The other is, well, the other is more me keeping a promise to you."

"That shouldn't be a surprise," Axel says. He narrows his gaze on the door, and what surprise might be behind it. Or maybe it's a who? That's the thing about surprises; you just never know what you are going to get.

Byrd relaxes in the doorframe, the doorknob within Axel's

sight. Maybe a pigeon would wait? Maybe a pigeon would let Byrd go on and on outside while it bobs its head from side to side? But not Axel.

He takes a second dive for the doorknob; this time he connects, and pushes past Byrd into the house.

From the time he left in the morning until this very moment, so much has changed. The smell still lingers. A sharp, chemical-filled smell.

But there's new light in the space. A new couch. A new rug.

And the wall of windows, returned but different. The smooth glass as wide as George and Emmett's table, wider, maybe, and tall too. Like before, it stretches all the way to the ceiling, the view uninterrupted by any frames it had before. It is one large wall of glass that ends now at a bench. A bench that lines the entire width of the window, with shelves underneath for books and treasures. For now, only one thick book, as thick as a brick, rests with its golden letters turned out to face the room: A. P. Brown's *Collection of North American Birds*. New and waiting for Axel.

On top of the bench, pillows. Red and blue. Axel's favorite color next to Byrd's. One right after the other.

"Your dad finished today. He wanted to be here when you got back, and I thought we had more time. I forgot that you didn't want to go to the meet-and-greet this afternoon. By the time I remembered, Frank had already gone."

"Is he coming back?"

"Yes, that's the other surprise. That's what I wanted to tell you," Byrd says. She steps farther into the room, grabs Axel by the hand, and brings him into the new space. She touches the bench like an invitation for them to sit in this new place together. So much new.

The new bench is good. It is sturdy and beautiful. It gives a clear view of the creek and those tall trees outside that dot its banks. Axel can see the picnic table from the window. The stump from the fallen white pine now holds one of Byrd's clay planters on top. Axel sees the patch of grass where Byrd likes to do her yoga is now safe for her to sway and breathe. The stump, the grass, the creek, he's seen them all before, all from right here, only now they are different. Different from this new window. Different after the storm.

What if Axel misses having the pillows on the floor and the wooden crosses that framed smaller sections to look through? What if the old A. P. Brown's *Collection of North American Birds* was the one with all the facts, and this new one is missing something? How will he know the difference?

"I'm going to read in my room," Axel says, without settling onto the bench.

Byrd rises. Like this is her chance before her son flies off, she lets go of the other surprise. "Your dad is coming back tonight. He wants to spend more time here. More time with you and with me. With us. This is a good thing." Byrd knocks the wooden bench. One, two, three knocks. Is it Byrd's wish for good luck? Or just the end of surprises? Axel doesn't know.

"Oh," Axel says.

"This is what you want," Byrd says, like maybe she doesn't know Axel at all.

"I want . . . I want . . . I know what I don't want," Axel says. "I don't want him to smash up his truck. I don't want him to be reckless. I don't want you to treat me like a baby. I don't want you to break promises. I want a plan for what happens next, not surprises." This should be enough. He's said his words now, and she's said hers.

Axel walks across the new rug that is too puffy, and too bright.

He reaches the first step before Byrd says, "The plan is we spend more time together."

But that's not a plan at all. A plan is sturdier than that. It gives a clear view. It's an open window, steps on a stone path. "Spending more time together" is just an idea. Too big an idea, really. Like something could blow in at any moment and swirl it away. Like the tornado on Byrd's flower beds. Like the high winds in the woods. Like the fallen eagles' nest.

"I don't like change," Axel says, even though it is the most obvious thing in the world. Even though Byrd should know this. Even though this is at the very heart of his mind. At the very being of who he is!

"I know that you don't like change, Axel. But sometimes change is the only way we can move forward," Byrd says. She doesn't leave the window. Doesn't come to him. Doesn't ask, "This okay?"

Axel pulls his arms tightly around himself and drops down on the step that he wanted to walk up. He squeezes his own arms into his own sides, like he's giving himself the hug that Byrd forgot to give. The hug she forgot to give when she forgot to say, "I know you don't like change, so that's why we're going to take things very slowly. We'll start back with every other week, then every week. Until your dad shows up for every day of our lives."

Instead Byrd says, "Things are going to change." She doesn't knock on the wood of the bench, and she doesn't say it with a laugh. The words come softly. Slowly.

And in that moment, with all of the new things in the house, and the sharp, bitter smell in the air, and Byrd's soft words about a hard thing, Axel realizes two things. One, of course, is that Byrd is right. Things are going to change. And the second comes as no surprise, either.

He isn't ready.

CHAPTER THIRTY-SIX

Cracked Eggs

From A. P. Brown's *Collection of North American Birds*, page 667

OUTER CUTICLE: the outside layer of egg's shell, must be
tough enough to protect embryo as it grows, fragile
enough to break during hatch

AXEL MAKES IT TO HIS ROOM without any other surprises from Byrd. He doesn't get right to reading, like he had wished; instead he checks his email for any surprises from Dr. Martin about the release. There aren't any. Of course.

The date, tomorrow, the first Saturday in June, is circled in red on Axel's Delaware Valley Raptor Sanctuary calendar. They planned this date for the release, and the release will happen.

If he had gone to the sanctuary today, he would have come home to Frank here, and the surprises would still be in place from Byrd. But, if he had gone to the sanctuary, he'd know even more about the release tomorrow. Even more about the plan. He sends a quick email to Dr. Martin and asks one simple question. Then Axel curls up in his bed with his book. He brings the heavy blanket over his legs, his chest. And then, without warning or a plan at all, Axel's eyes close, shutting out the four walls of his bedroom and putting to bed the entire day.

It's no surprise when he wakes early to a new smell coming

from downstairs. Overnight someone must have removed his shoes and socks. But aside from that, he's still in his clothes from the day before. Axel leaps from bed. It's 6:55 a.m., his ticking clock tells him. The only thing worse than falling asleep the way he did would be missing the release today. For a moment, he lets his brain hope that if the time were ticking near the release, Byrd would have come to wake him.

She would have.

He thinks.

Instead, he doesn't have to wonder on that thought too long, because it is about an hour until the release, and Byrd is cooking something in the kitchen. Axel slips on his Crocs and follows the smell down the stairs to find another surprise.

"Scrambled?" Frank asks as he stands at the stove top, like this is a normal way to start the day. Like scrambled isn't the way Axel feels seeing him here this morning.

"I don't eat eggs," Axel says. He walks to the kitchen island to get a closer look at the clues he missed while he slept last night.

"They used to be your favorite," Frank says. Frank, who isn't in his baseball hat and dirty work clothes. Frank, who is in pajama pants and a white T-shirt. "Bread with butter?" he asks.

"I'll get my own breakfast," Axel says. He walks into the small pantry just off the kitchen where the washing machine rumbles and canned goods that never get eaten line the shelves. Axel grabs his loaf of bread. He holds it against his chest, then shuffles back out of the pantry to find Byrd in the kitchen. She touches the back of Frank's neck. Stands so close to him, even though there is plenty of space at the island. Plenty of space in the living room.

This too scrambles Axel's insides.

"Big day," Byrd says. "I didn't even wake you for dinner last night. Figured you needed the sleep." She leans over Frank's shoulder, looks at the cracked eggs in the hot pan.

Axel takes all of his energy to focus on spreading soft butter on every square inch of white bread. No corner left uncovered.

"Do we know what time Dr. Martin is coming?" Frank asks, pushing against the eggs with his spatula.

"We?" Axel whispers.

"Eight," Byrd says. She steps back, just an inch, from Frank's side, turns to her son. "Your dad and I are so proud of how you helped with this rescue."

Axel crushes his buttered bread into a butter-bread-ball and eats it like an apple. Big bite after big bite, while the two of them return to staring at dead birds in a frying pan.

"So what's the plan?" Frank asks, sprinkling salt over the yellow muck.

"That's what I want to know," Axel says, but this time, there is no whisper left in his voice. This time he says just what he means.

At this they both turn, Frank from the stove top and Byrd with a look on her face like it all just dawned on her, everything all at once. The epic mess, the second epic mess about Frank, but the first time, the very first time that she broke her promise.

Because this is not telling the truth. This is placing a cold, hard stone at Axel's feet and then stepping away to see if it explodes. This is not the work of an osprey mom, who protects her baby no matter what.

This is the behavior of a snake.

CHAPTER THIRTY-SEVEN

Deep

Rapid heart.
Trembling muscles.

Stay and fight?
Flee and flight?

AXEL FLIES. Emmett and George's woods beyond the barn are crisscrossed, leaning, too big to go over, too scary to stay in one place for too long, so Axel races deeper and deeper, under and through. Under and through.

Axel promised not to go here. Not to go too deep into the woods behind the barn. The woods that the foresters said couldn't be cleared yet. Too dangerous for their big machines. Too much for those claw arm trucks, and tires that leave deep gashes in the earth.

Yes, Axel promised not to go here. But Byrd made promises too, that she didn't keep.

A branch snaps behind Axel.

Byrd?

Frank?

No.

It's Ray who has followed him. Of course it's Ray. He walks toward Axel with his head low, eyes lower, like he's asking permission to go on this adventure, like this might be one of those trips George reads poems about. Things a person must do on their own. In silence. In the deep.

"You can come, Ray," Axel says, because maybe, just maybe, he needs some company for this next part of the journey.

Ray takes the last two steps to be at Axel's side. "Which way do we go?" Axel asks, looking out over the woods before them, woods that look more like one of Emmett's bowls of spaghetti than any forest. Stringy, where once mighty oaks and sturdy pines stood.

If this morning's view in the kitchen filled him with anger and disappointment, then this view now fills him with something too. His insides flame with fear. Fear that maybe they've gone too far. Gone too deep into the woods that aren't quite woods. George was wrong yesterday in the clearing: Those were not the pathless woods; these are. And to answer his question, no. No, Axel does not think he can find himself in pathless woods. Not at all.

But Ray has other plans.

His pointer nose, then pointer eyes, then pointer stance locks on a squirrel up ahead. If ahead is what you can call a place that twists and turns in each direction. The twitchy squirrel looks like he too might feel a fear.

So the squirrel does what a squirrel's instincts tell it to do in the bull's-eye focus of a dog like Ray; it leaps.

Root. Root.

Branch. Branch.

Bush. Ground.

Under. Through.

Ray can't help himself either. Instincts.

"Ray!" Axel shouts. "Come!"

The chase begins, squirrel and dog and boy. Under and through. Until an entrance opens, like a cave, but really just mangled trees and roots in a massive pile. Stacked higher than where that nest used to rest in that tree that used to stand by the creek that flows by Axel's house. A house that feels gone for good.

Ray doesn't turn back. He doesn't come.

Ray enters the mangled maze.

But Axel stops, holds himself at the same spot that Ray ran through. Squints for any light, and movement where his friend might be. But there's nothing.

Nothing until, something.

A crack. A fall. A cry.

It's Ray.

Root. Root.

Branch. Branch.

Axel is called to help his friend, no matter how hard it is to see. Each step he takes, he promises his mind that it is a step closer to Ray. But this promise, like others, mists into a lie, because how can Axel tell if the steps he takes are moving toward anything? It is gray all around him, a hazy darkness before, around, over, and under him that makes right turns feel like they are behind him, and left turns feel like nothing at all.

So Axel stops. He stops the promises in his head and lets the thumping of his heart take over all sounds. It's panic, not just for Ray, but for everything. There's cracking branches, sweat piling on his skin, and no one here to save them. No one to rescue them the way they rescued Braviary.

But Axel is too far into his worry now about Ray to even think about Braviary's rescue, or the fact that Braviary will be set to the sky this morning. Because to Axel, how could he be sure it is still morning at all? Or that there is sky at all? In the mangled maze of dead trees, he can't feel those things.

How long it takes for a new image, a change to flutter into his mind, he does not know, but it does. Even with all of the fear, and with all of the time passing, somehow, a new image floats into his very heavy mind.

A pigeon flying above the maze.

A pigeon can always find its way home. After fires, and under fog, and even during storms. It follows its instincts.

Axel crawls backward. Rises tall when he can.

He uncurls the tangled mystery of this maze. Looks for clues, the best he can, until, he's back at the entrance, which is now an exit. He won't leave this place forever—he can't. But he will find his way home.

"I'm going for help," Axel calls back into the maze. There

isn't a bark in return, no cry, but Axel must hope that Ray can hear him. He must hope that Ray knows he will come back, no matter what. When it matters most, Axel will always come back.

CHAPTER THIRTY-EIGHT

Song

Every bird has a song.
Long and short.
Clipped and metered.

A way to connect.
A way to find what's most important.

Safety and food and comfort and
Home.

AXEL DOESN'T MAKE IT TO HIS HOUSE, not even back to the big red barn, but places aren't always what is needed to feel home. He makes it to a clearing, just one, that is in front of another. One with sunlight from the morning, higher in the sky, lighting a man's back as he turns from one direction to the other but never fully around.

Axel catches him from behind. Pulls Frank tight against him, the way hope is meant to be held. Axel reaches up on the tops of his toes as his dad's head drops down to meet his own. Axel lets no air between his dad's ear and Axel's words. The words he sings from that song long ago. Back when Axel needed to hear them. And now Frank gets to hear them too.

Words about a bird in the night who learns to fly.

If this were enough to feel home, Axel would know. It would be like soaring, like that sweet and open feeling he had known before. But he's only partway to that, because he made a promise. A promise to come back for Ray.

"Ray," Axel says.

"He's here. He's here," Frank calls.

And Axel breaks from his dad to see his best friend. But that isn't what's happening at all. Frank isn't talking about Ray; he's talking to Byrd and Dr. Martin and George. All in their boots and stomping in the woods.

"Ray," Axel says again. This time he demands the word.

Finally, Byrd—who is still in her pajamas, the green ones with pink polka dots, and her muck boots—says, "Where's Ray?"

"He ran," Axel says. "He followed me into the woods and chased a squirrel, and—"

"What?" George says. Then he yells, "Ray! Come!"

"No, he can't," Axel says. "There was a crack, and I heard Ray's cry. I could hear him, but I couldn't see him. I think he's trapped."

George by now is off. He's far ahead.

And Dr. Martin says, "You go tell Emmett and Nance and Lark that we found him." She says this to Byrd and Frank, and then to Axel, she says, "Take me to him. If he's hurt, I can help."

And that's it. They don't wait for questions from Frank or worry from Byrd; they are gone. Dr. Martin and Axel are off. Under and through, until they catch up to George, who somehow manages to move faster than Axel has ever seen him move before.

"This way?" Dr. Martin asks, like Axel may know the secrets of these pathless woods better than anyone else. He doesn't, and this is why getting back to Ray takes a long, long time.

But then Axel does see the entrance. The tangle of trees, fallen in such a memorable way. He can picture the last sight of Ray's tail before the darkness swallowed him up.

George and Dr. Martin have phone lights, and this helps, but not like it makes it clear, more like it shows ways not to go and leaves the choices up to them. George taps things before going under. Presses against things before stepping over. They keep asking, "This way?" But Axel doesn't know. He wishes he did, but he doesn't know.

Could it be that they've come back and Ray isn't here at all?

There really is only one way to know. "Ray," Axel calls, hands cupped around his mouth. "Ray!"

George joins the song. "Ray!"

And Dr. Martin too, because of course they need to let Ray know that they've come back for him. And if he's conserved his energy, like that eagle might conserve for a hunt, this is the time to let it fly. This is the time for Ray to sing out too, so that they can find him. So that they can bring him home.

Only, it isn't his song, his cry, his instinct, that brings Ray back to them. It is perseverance.

Axel, Dr. Martin, and George turn over branches and search under the debris until a paw brings them all to their knees.

There, pinned to the earth, under a thick branch, is a brown dog with a white patch on his chest. With golden eyes that they cannot see, because his eyes are closed.

"Ray," George whispers.

Ray.

CHAPTER THIRTY-NINE

Rescue II

Careful.
Careful.
Careful.

      Dr. Martin.

Slow.
Careful.
Let
me.

      George.

It's
all
my
fault.

      Axel.

GEORGE CRADLES RAY IN HIS ARMS. Carries him out of the maze like a path has been laid before him to the exit.

He lowers Ray to the ground in the first patch of bareness he sees. Dr. Martin bends down, runs a hand over his snout. Turns her ear to his chest. And it is in that moment, with the prayers coming from George's lips and the care coming from Dr. Martin's hands, that Axel sees the unmistakable rise and fall of Ray's barrel of a chest.

"He's breathing," Axel says. George kneels on the ground next to his best friend and stroking his soft ear and whispering his words, finally looks at Ray's chest too. Rising up and dropping down.

Dr. Taylor M. Martin lifts Ray's lip. "We need to get him warm," she says. "Shock," she says. "Can you carry him?" she says.

And George is already pulling off his shirt, ripping it away from his body, and Axel is taking his off too. "Let's go skin to skin," Dr. Martin says to George.

George picks Ray up again and Dr. Martin tucks the shirts around Ray's body. Axel can hardly believe his eyes. The sight of George holding Ray in his arms. Ray, who weighs almost as much as Axel himself, sheltered in George's old-man arms. He wouldn't have believed it was possible. Like Daniel saying that his mom could lift that car.

And now Axel knows that to be true. These are the things we do for family. We are stronger than we might appear. Braver too.

The three of them walk-run as best they can the whole way back, over those roots and branches, until they are home. As soon as Axel sees the big red barn, he charges ahead and shouts for help. Frank hears the call and comes running.

Dr. Martin shouts for blankets.

When Axel's dad arrives at George, ready to take Ray into his own arms, George can't let go.

He won't.

So Frank keeps at his side, keeps step with him. His arms under George's arms, trying his best to give as much support as he can.

And they load up, like this was the plan all along, in Dr. Martin's truck, which is last in line in the driveway. Frank and George in the back seat, with Ray and Dr. Martin up front.

The dust pushes toward the sky as the truck rolls away from the others, Axel out in the driveway all alone. He hears the chatter from the porch, the wishes and prayers. But he has to watch the truck as far as he can as it speeds down the driveway. Has to watch until it disappears.

"You don't have a shirt on," Lark says, suddenly at his side.

After the truck is gone, Axel replies, "Ray needed it."

"He's a dog," Lark says. "Dogs don't wear shirts."

But Axel doesn't clarify. He doesn't say, "He's not just a dog." Even though maybe Lark would understand.

She doesn't ask for more words anyway; she stays at his side and looks down the long driveway. Right next to Axel while the dust scrambles its way to the sky.

It isn't until much later in the day, after Byrd asks Axel to "please drink something." And he ignores her. And Emmett asks Axel to "please eat something." And he ignores him. And Lark wants to go for a walk down the driveway, and play Pokémon, and talk about Braviary's release, which he missed. And Axel tries his best to ignore her. That Aunt Nancy finally snaps. "Leave the darn kid alone. For Pete's sake, haven't you all just ever wanted to be left alone?" She accentuates this with a stomp of her rollator on the front porch.

A moment later she adds, "Feel free to feed me, though. I'm as hungry as an old lady who hasn't even been offered breakfast!"

All but Axel head inside for food. It isn't until Emmett waves from the porch later, his phone in his outstretched hand, that Axel drops from the fence and joins the others.

Emmett stands in the middle of the living room, right at the center of the braided rug's swirl. "Uh-huh," he says.

"Put it on speaker," Aunt Nancy says. She isn't about to get up from the table. Byrd and Lark do come to greet Emmett on the phone in the living room. Axel stays in the doorway, one foot inside and one still on the outside.

Emmett fumbles with the phone then, and suddenly, inside and out, the space is filled with George's voice. "He's banged up . . . Three broken ribs . . . It could've been worse . . . Dr. Martin got us here, and Frank carried him in . . . He's still out . . ." Somehow he holds back bitter words like *hurt* and *anger*, even though Axel knows he must feel them. Axel feels them. He's the one who took Ray into the woods.

Byrd says, "Thank goodness you got him there in time."

And Aunt Nancy says, "You tell that good boy I've got a pile of meatballs here for him when he gets home."

And Emmett says, "I love you. It's going to be okay."

Lark is busy clapping her hands and twirling around the living room. No words needed.

But then Emmett turns to Axel. "Do you want to tell him anything?" In this moment, Axel wants to tell him everything. That he's sorry Ray was hurt, and he's sorry he said Ray could come, and he's sorry he broke his promise about not going into the woods behind the big red barn.

Axel swallows, tries to remember what it felt like to be brave enough to say the things he needed to say before. But this time, those words just won't come.

"Hey," Aunt Nancy calls from the table. "We just want you all to come home safe and sound. That's all. Got that?"

George lets out a breath on the other end of the line. "Got it. I love you," he says before Emmett clicks the call away.

The room goes back to silence with George not there to say all the words, without the sound of Ray's collar jingling.

"I'm going back to the fence," Axel says, and he's not quite sure why he does. It doesn't really matter, does it? Where they sit and think? It just won't matter until Ray's back home.

CHAPTER FORTY

Forgiveness

In a world full of
rough and rowdy, rage and wrong,
nothing's more powerful
than a single
word.

IT'S BYRD THAT FOLLOWS AXEL out to the fence. Byrd that says, "Bones mend."

Axel climbs up onto the fence. Looks away from Byrd and out over the field, out toward the big red barn. The way it hides everything that happened behind it earlier.

"We have to open our hearts up to the miracles around us, Axel. You found Ray. He made it to the clinic in time. He's going to heal." Axel can't quite think about miracles right now. But the real things that Byrd says make sense; only he wasn't the one who found Ray. He was the one who let Ray get lost.

"I hurt my best friend," Axel finally says, turning from the big red barn to Byrd.

She runs her hands down her pajamas. Still in them from the morning that feels forever ago. She shakes her head, not to say, *No, Axel, you're wrong*—more like the words he said have never felt truer to her. Like these were the words she'd been looking to say. "I know just how you feel," she says. "I hurt you, even though it is the absolute last thing on earth I ever, ever want to do. I hurt you." She grabs hold of the fence then with both hands, feels the prick of the rough wood under her skin. "I'm sorry, Axel," she says. "It isn't enough, but it's all I can say."

Axel takes his hand, slides it on top of his mother's; as tightly as she grips the wood, he grips her. They stay like that, holding on longer than Axel would have thought possible, but they do.

It isn't until a truck comes rumbling up the driveway, throwing dust all over, that Axel hops off the fence and Byrd lets go too.

"Mommy," Lark calls, running from the porch and down the steps. She's just as surprised as Axel when they see that it isn't Dr. Martin who hops out of the cab. It's Frank.

"Frank," Byrd says. She throws her arms around him. Even though it is just the two of them, somehow Axel feels this hug too.

"He's okay," Frank says. "What a fighter. And Dr. Martin, she's amazing."

"That's my mom," Lark says, interrupting. "But where is she?"

"I'm going to go back with a car for George and me, and then we'll take the truck back to your mom. She's with Ray."

"I'm ready," Lark says, then promptly climbs into the back seat of her truck, not waiting for any other plans or explanations. She knows what she wants, and she isn't shy about saying it.

"Why don't you follow me, Emmett?" Frank says. "I'll take this back to Dr. Martin. You can follow and then we can see what George wants to do."

"I'll grab my keys," Emmett says. "And maybe a sweater for George."

"He got his shirt back," Frank calls, but Emmett's already inside the house. "Here's your shirt," Frank says, handing Axel the T-shirt that now smells just like Ray. "And George wanted me to give this to you, too." A red collar with three tags hanging from a silver loop.

Axel shakes it before pulling it to his chest, just to hear the sound of Ray.

"Do you want to come?" Frank asks Byrd. "Or I can just call if I need a ride."

"Okay," Byrd says. "We'll stay with Nance."

And that should be enough. Frank asked. Byrd answered. But for some reason, Frank turns to Axel. "Do you want to come?" Like Byrd's answer wasn't for both. Like Axel gets a say in what he wants to do.

He can't imagine staying here when there's a chance to see Ray.

"I want to go," he says.

Emmett's down the stairs now, across the driveway. Car started.

"I'll ride with you," Axel adds. He climbs into the back of Dr. Martin's red truck, in the seat behind the driver. There are blankets in the back seat, and a black bag that must have been used in Braviary's release. It smells a little like Ray inside, and a little like Dr. Martin, and a little like Frank.

"Can we go now?" Lark asks. "Come on." She kicks her feet at the back of the seat in front of her.

"Ready?" Frank says, and even though he doesn't need a reply, Axel gives one anyway, because this time there is no doubt whether he is ready or not.

This time, Axel says, "Yes."

CHAPTER FORTY-ONE

Thank You

FROM: Axel Rastusak
TO: Dr. Taylor M. Martin
SUBJECT: Re: Re: Re: Re: Re: Re: This is Axel

Dear Dr. Martin,

This is Axel.

Byrd said that Ray's rescue was a miracle and it didn't seem like that was quite right. Until I saw you tonight at the emergency clinic. Reading us Ray's chart. Telling us what all of the things meant. Showing me where I could touch Ray to let him know I was with him.

I think sometimes about what it means for you to be so good at your job. To help animals like Braviary and Ray and even the golden eagle Maxwell. Do you remember him? Animals that don't have a way to say what they are feeling. That can't tell you where they hurt or how they feel. Your instincts are so good.

Thank you for helping Ray, and all the animals.
Thank you for helping me.

Sincerely,
Axel Rastusak

Dear Axel,

Sorry for the delay. It was a long night.

It takes many people to rescue an animal. Think about our Braviary. You had to care enough to make the call. We—you and me and Lark and George and Byrd—had to move Braviary from the fallen nest. At the Sanctuary, we all had to work on his care. Me and the vet techs and the volunteers. All of us.

Not to mention, Braviary. He had to fight to get better. It wasn't a miracle. It was many people coming together to help one bird. And one bird deciding he was going to fight to survive.

But if Byrd sees it as a miracle, that's okay, too. Whatever it takes to make people want to care about rescuing animals. And Ray, well, that dog's a fighter too.

His rescue took you coming back for help, and George bringing him from the woods, and getting to the emergency vet quickly. It took their whole team to set Ray's bones. I wasn't his vet. I was a part of the rescue, like you and George and your dad.

Lark and I stopped to see him this morning before church. Sounds like he'll be released in the next day or two. I bet he's eager to get home. He's lucky to come home to a friend like you.

Sincerely,
Dr. Taylor M. Martin
Delaware Valley Raptor Sanctuary
VMD-PhD

CHAPTER FORTY-TWO

Miracles

From A. P. Brown's *Collection of North American Birds*, page 660

AERIE: raptor home constructed in high places, returned to again and again; see also nest

RAY WEARS A SPECIAL T-SHIRT when he comes home. He has a cone around his neck. He sleeps more than he's awake.

Axel reminds everyone that Ray needs to conserve his energy. That's what his body is telling him to do.

Axel tells Ray about everything else. About the foresters bringing more rigs out to clear more trees, the enormous flatbeds that rolled across the field empty and returned with logs piled higher than the barn's roof. He tells him about the squirrel that Aunt Nancy shooed off the porch in his honor, and the fact that bird activity in the yard and near the creek is pathetic on account of those big rigs making so much noise. *Caw.*

He tells Ray that he hasn't seen a bald eagle the entire week that Ray's been resting here at home and that, no, he hasn't seen Braviary. Braviary wouldn't yet look like his bald eagle mom or dad. He'd be dark brown, almost black, his feathers with a shine to them. His feet sunflower yellow, like the color of the ones that grow in Byrd's garden, and each dotted with a black talon. And even though Axel can picture the way he would look in his mind, he hasn't seen Braviary, or any juveniles at all.

And even though Ray's sleepy, and it takes all of his energy to lift his head, each time he hears Axel's voice, he comes out of the place where his dreams fill his own dog mind with squirrels and meatballs, and he greets his friend.

Axel reports today's findings and then lets his friend rest, finds his dad outside watching the trucks with the logs.

"Want these?" Frank says, pointing to his earmuffs. But it's too noisy outside to hear even this simple question, so Frank points to the house. Their house, the cottage next to the creek.

They walk through the gate and down the stone path, through the front door, and into the living room.

"That's some operation," Frank says, placing his earmuffs on the kitchen island. "Want something to eat?"

"No," Axel says. "I just want to think." He walks over the new rug that's still too fluffy and pulls his book from the shelf under the bench that his dad made.

"Mind if I sit?" Frank says.

Axel pulls to one side of the bench, lets his back rest against the wall, his feet toward the center of the bench, still plenty of room for Frank to sit.

"Ray doing okay today?" he asks.

"I guess," Axel says. He runs his fingers over the paper edges of his book. There is something more he wants to say.

Something he hasn't reported to Ray or told Byrd. He hasn't even said anything to Ms. Dale or Daniel in these last days at school.

"He'll be ready for a walk before you know it," Frank says.

But this isn't the thing he wants to talk to Frank about. It is about the one thing that Axel wishes he could fix. And, no, it's not Braviary's release, because that already happened and he missed it and there's nothing he can do about that now. And, no, it's not fixing Frank, because that's something that Axel can't fix. He knows that's something that will take time. Every day that Frank shows up makes the next day even better. It's not even fixing Ray, because he is getting better. Every day.

Axel looks out the window, where Byrd isn't in her garden; she's doing something she hasn't done in a very, very long time. She's reaching way up to the sky with two hands, breathing in, and out, bringing prayer hands to her chest. Byrd is in the yard doing yoga. And he can see her clearly from this seat that his dad built.

The next time Byrd breathes way in, Axel does too. And when she lets all the air out, he lets his out too.

"I wish I could fix George's anger," Axel says.

"George? George isn't angry," Frank says.

"I know." This is obvious.

"Then what's the problem?" Frank asks.

"He should be," Axel says. He pulls his legs to his chest now, squeezes his book between thighs and ribs. It isn't comfortable, and that's okay, because that's just how Axel wants it to feel.

"Why?" Frank asks, like he just can't imagine the ways these clues could ever line up in the right order. That this mystery makes no sense at all.

"He should be angry at me," Axel says.

And that's when his dad closes the space between them, puts both hands on Axel's bent knees. "George knows that it wasn't your fault."

But that's not quite right, is it? "I told Ray he could come. We went too far," Axel says.

"Axel," Frank says. "It was an accident."

"An accident I caused," Axel says. He pulls his book out, drops it on the floor, and brings his knees closer in to himself.

"You're a pretty logical guy, so let's think logically about this," Frank says. "Dogs run after squirrels. That's instincts. You know that. Right?"

Axel nods, because yes, obviously he knows that dogs run after squirrels, especially Ray. He knows that. What he doesn't know is bigger than that. "Then why can't I get rid of the feeling inside me when I see George?"

"Emotions can get all jumbled up, like those trees behind the barn. Like sometimes when I drive up this driveway I feel guilty and happy all at the same time. Guilty I missed so much, but so happy that we're spending more time together. Both of those emotions stuck right here," Frank says, pointing at the center of his chest. "Do you know what I mean?"

Guilty, happy. Hopeful, sad. Everything all at once. "But why can't it just be easy?" Axel asks. "If George were angry, then I could apologize. If he were mad, I could try to make him happy."

"That's the big question, isn't it? Sometimes, things just aren't easy," Frank says, and he takes one of those big yoga breaths, like maybe Byrd's had him practice it too.

It's quiet then. A good time for thinking. Thinking about what Frank said. Things getting jumbled up. Axel tries to lay the facts flat inside his head. There was the storm that led to the tree that led to Frank fixing the house that led to the bench that led to them here. That seems simple enough, but it misses out on all the things that crisscrossed it, like the eagles, and the secrets, and Ray's injuries. No matter how flat Axel tries to lay down the clues in his mind, they just keep curling up at the ends.

What do people do when the ends don't lie flat? Ms. Dale might try to unpack it. Byrd might try to put it in the ground, see if something else could grow in its place. Daniel might use his imagination. George would use his poems. Aunt Nancy might take a shovel to it, and not in the way that Byrd would use the shovel.

Axel likes to think that his dad would try to look at it from all directions. Sketch out a plan like he does for houses or barns. See what fixes can be made.

Maybe there are lots of ways to solve a mystery? And maybe some mysteries never get solved?

The front door opens, and Byrd steps into the room. She washes her hands at the kitchen sink, wipes a towel across her neck. She crosses the too puffy rug in her bare feet.

"Got room on this bench for one more?" she asks. She's sweaty and smells like her yoga mat. But Axel makes a little room, and Frank makes a little room too. All three of them on the new bench.

"You can see almost all the way up the creek now," Byrd says, facing toward the window.

"That was the plan," Frank says. "It curves out slightly, see?" He points at the trim holding the window in place. "Like a bubble."

The window really is a magnificent thing. Maybe the plan all along was to get the whole family gathered right here, right in this spot, to look out on the beauty outside their window?

It would take one of Byrd's miracles for Braviary to fly past the window just now, as the three of them look at the sky and the trees and the creek.

Only, maybe it isn't what's outside that's the miracle at all, maybe Byrd and Frank and Axel being right here, inside this place right now, is miracle enough.

CHAPTER FORTY-THREE

Changes

FROM: Axel Rastusak
TO: Dr. Taylor M. Martin
SUBJECT: Re: Re: Re: Re: Re: Re: Re: Re: This is Axel

Dear Dr. Martin,

This is Axel.

I haven't seen Braviary. Not once. And now that school's out, I have all day to look. And nothing.

Do you think he survived? I'm trying to have HOPE.

I hope he knows that even though I missed his release I still care what happens to him.

Do you think he knows that?

You should come and visit Ray. Come on a Saturday so that Lark can play Pokémon with me and my friend Daniel. She doesn't need cards. Just her imagination.

And, I have an idea about the fallen nest. I will wait to tell you until you visit, but come soon because the forester keeps saying he can "clear it." And you know what that means!

Sincerely,
Axel Rastusak

FROM: Dr. Taylor M. Martin
TO: Axel Rastusak
SUBJECT: Re: Re: Re: Re: Re: Re: Re: Re: Re: This is Axel

Dear Axel,

Sorry for the delay. Lots happening here.

We picked up a saw-whet owl on Wednesday. A landscaper found her in a tree trunk. She was struck by their tree trimmer. She's here now. Lark's named her Saw-weetie.

We'll be over next Saturday. I've messaged your mom, too.

Am looking forward to hearing about your plan for the nest. I have something to share with you too.

Sincerely,
Dr. Taylor M. Martin
Delaware Valley Raptor Sanctuary
VMD-PhD

EPST, A E 5567

Saturday, March 12, 2022

CHAPTER FORTY-FOUR

Found

Dusk gathers red barn,
potting shed, porch swing,
brightens my path home.

OF COURSE DANIEL AND LARK GET ALONG. And they are both excellent in battles.

Daniel is right about the bald spaces still holding plenty of Pokémon. Lark thinks of a way to add a whole new dimension to the game. The three of them flying back to the red barn each time a new Pokémon is captured so that they can make a pretend record of their battle.

The game is more fun than Axel can ever remember, but Daniel's mom calls for Daniel too soon.

"Should we run that way instead?" Lark asks, pointing to the clearing made by the big rigs. Pointing away from where Daniel's mom is calling for him. From where Byrd and Dr. Martin and Ms. Berrios stand with hands on hips.

"That's a negative," Daniel says. "We have to go back. But we always have next time."

After Daniel leaves, Axel and Lark go to visit Ray, who is out on the porch, curled up on the love seat. Aunt Nancy is on her rollator, shaking a finger at Frank. "Get down from there," she says.

"I'm almost done, Nance," Frank calls. He's balanced on the porch railing. His screw gun above his head.

"Your dad's going to make my heart stop," Aunt Nancy says. "How will you feel then, Frank? An old lady's heart . . . Pow!"

"I'm done . . . I'm done," he says, hopping from the railing to the ground. "We need to get the swing up so we can enjoy it this summer."

"I'll give you a swing," Aunt Nancy says. Frank smiles before jogging across the walkway toward his truck.

"Where's your mom?" Aunt Nancy asks, turning her attention from Frank to Axel.

Only, Lark answers first. "They went to set the table."

"We're very fancy here," Aunt Nancy says. "You'll learn this about us, Lark."

When Frank returns, he's balancing a swing on his head. And not like the one Braviary practiced on at the sanctuary, a swing as wide as the love seat that Axel and Lark and Ray are on.

"For Pete's sake, get some help," Aunt Nancy says, like that's all there is to it.

"George'll help when he's done out back."

"Busy, busy, busy," Aunt Nancy says. "Everyone's acting like we're in some big race. Get the swing up. Make food. Set the table. Mow the lawn. At least you two know how to have a good time," Aunt Nancy says.

"Us three," Lark says, petting Ray.

"Be careful," Axel says. "That's where he had stitches." He

doesn't say it mean, just to clarify, and Lark's okay with it. She doesn't want to hurt Ray, after all.

Emmett comes out onto the porch then with a drink for Aunt Nancy. "Can I get you anything?" he asks. But Lark and Axel are perfectly content with Ray, on the love seat. And Frank's putting chains on the porch swing. So he shakes his head.

"Thanks anyway," Frank says.

"We'll take two of whatever," Byrd says, walking up, Dr. Martin just behind her with an empty basket.

"We're ready?" Emmett says. "The table?"

Byrd nods, and Emmett no longer wants to talk drinks; all he cares about now is pasta. Mountains of it. Each person responsible for something. "Byrd, you take the gluten-free," Emmett says. "Can you carry the salad and garlic bread?" he asks Dr. Martin. "Nance, can you put the dressings in your basket?"

George comes from the back. "We're ready," Emmett cheers. "Pasta-palooza by the creek!"

George carries Ray, one step at a time, down to the creek, because naturally Ray needs to be there too. And Axel helps Aunt Nancy, just down the steps. She doesn't need his help after that.

Lark tries not to drop the pitcher of water while she walks, but it's no use. She's soaked, and Byrd refills the pitcher while Lark holds it as still as she can at the hose.

And when Emmett brings the last bowl of pasta out to the picnic table, there's a round of applause. George raises his glass and says, "Three cheers for the chef." Then he plants a kiss on Emmett's pink cheek.

The elbows with butter and salt are extra buttery tonight, just the way Axel likes them. Frank must like them too, because he takes a second scoop.

"So tell me about this idea for the nest," Dr. Martin says.

"What's this?" Byrd asks. She doesn't know, no one does but Ray and Axel. Axel's made the plan, and Ray knows how to keep a good secret.

Axel sets down his spoon. Takes a big breath. "I think we should take the nest to the educational room at the sanctuary. Frank can get us one of those claw machines from work, and we can put the nest in the back of his truck, and we can bring it to the sanctuary."

Byrd taps the side of her glass. "Hear, hear!" she says.

"I love it," Dr. Martin says. "We could—"

But Dr. Martin's words aren't quick enough, and Lark interrupts. "We could make a plaque. *For our Braviary*, it could say . . ." She says it like she's known the plan all along.

"We could tell people about the rescue and about our rescue team," Axel says. "And about what to do if an injured bird is found."

George raises his glass again. "To Axel!"

This doesn't feel quite right to Axel. It isn't "to him." Yes, he came up with the plan, but it isn't about that. It is about working together to take the nest to the right spot. To give the nest a home. To give Braviary's nest a place to land.

"To all of us," Axel says instead, raising his own glass. He taps his glass to Lark's and then to Aunt Nancy's. And other glasses ting along too, like a song. They have other toasts, and more words from George.

Then after Dr. Martin twirls her last forkful of fettuccini, she too has something to share during the celebration.

"I finished setting up the tracking app for Braviary," she says. "We tag all of our eagles when we set them to the sky." She pulls an iPad from her bag. "We can find Braviary with this."

Lark and Axel huddle over the screen while Dr. Martin opens tabs. Suddenly a map appears. There's a few blue lines, like waterways, and one glowing green dot, no bigger than a seed. It moves on the screen in a line. Then pauses, glowing in one place. They watch and watch. It's Braviary.

"Is he close?" Lark asks her mom.

"No," Dr. Martin replies simply before leaving Lark and Axel to watch on their own. Axel knows something that maybe Lark doesn't know. Axel knows that eagles can travel great distances in a day. A hundred miles or more. So even though the blinking dot is not in this yard, or even in George and Emmett's field, that doesn't mean that Braviary couldn't come by. Couldn't fly overhead on a day like today.

"Do you think he found his family?" Lark whispers , twirling her finger at the hem of her shirt.

Axel wants to believe that he found them, so he says, "I hope so."

"Me too," Lark says. Her eyes never leave the blinking

green dot, but Axel's eyes go to the sky. His eyes go to the trees, and to Byrd's garden, young shoots just starting to pop through soil. He looks beyond her garden to the nest out in the field, barely able to see its shape from this far away, but he imagines it already in the educational room at the sanctuary.

His eyes fall like the low sunshine against the picnic table, Emmett reaching for more food, Frank and George making plans to secure the porch swing. Nancy shaking her finger at the two of them, telling them not to climb on that railing.

He sees Byrd and Dr. Martin, too. Busy talking. Ray curled up at his mom's feet, just waiting for a meatball to drop.

He could go back to the screen with Lark, or go sit with anyone at the table, really. Listen to the talk of swings, or other things. Instead he wants to think. Right here is just about as great a thinking spot as anywhere.

There are mysteries in this world like Braviary and his family. If Axel just went by the clues, the facts—what he knows about birds—that might not be enough to solve this mystery. Because the facts would say that not all birds find their way back to family. That not all birds survive.

So Axel has to add his own piece, the most important thing, really, hope. He has to imagine a world where Braviary found his family in the sky. And that they're happy. They're as happy as any bird family can be, as happy as Axel is here in this special place with his own family.

AUTHOR'S NOTE

Dear Reader,

This is Alison. I am not the kind of person who lets everyone "in" and maybe that's why the theme of inside and outside kept coming up in the book? I think it is okay to be private and keep some parts of yourself for yourself and for those whom you choose to let in.

Though this book is a work of fiction, so much of it comes from personal places and spaces in my life. Questions surrounding Frank and his alcoholism are questions that I still process decades after being Axel's age.

Along with Frank and Axel, I can reach into my mind and touch all the other characters, each place, each moment of the book and know just how they came to be. As fictional as the characters are, real people inspired them. Real companions inspired Ray. Real heroes inspired Ms. Dale.

Ms. Dale is based on a counselor at our local school who makes space in the world for all kids. She hosts a Friendship Club. (I don't know if she has played Pokémon in the hallways, or throws popsicle parties, but she's the kind of caring educator who would.) Along with this counselor, Ms. Dale is also based on my son's second-grade teacher, who not only works to know all students, but creates moments to empower them.

I hope you have teachers or counselors like this in your life, who see you and make space for you. I want you to know that I see you. I want you to know that your instincts matter. There is space in the world for all that you are and all that you want to be. I know that you will soar.

About the soaring . . . We like birds in our house. (Maybe *more* than like them!) I think the first seed of this book came when my son told me one afternoon, "You should favorite roadrunners." Something he liked to do, match people with a favorite bird. The roadrunner is not my favorite bird, but he is especially attuned to my fear of snakes and made this recommendation. It was my son's love of birds that prompted us to seek out places for learning, like the Delaware Valley Raptor Center.

We enjoy the DVRC educational programs. We followed the DVRC social media when caring professionals took in four displaced eaglets after a storm ripped through our area in 2018. We were there when they set three of the eagles back to the sky. And the fourth bird? We were there at that eagle's first educational program. I am in awe, like Axel, of the way that good people give of themselves to care for creatures big and small. For you bird-loving friends, I've added some notes below related to what was "bird fact" and what was "bird fiction" in Axel's story. (No surprise, it's mostly fact!)

Axel is the heart of this story. While his character is a work of fiction, he is inspired by many people in my life—my son, my husband, students I've taught, friends, and Axel is part of me, and of course, all his own. He is one character who walks through one fictional world. As my husband said, "He is one in infinite." Each person is unique, and in this book I tried to honor Axel's one view in this one world.

The family in this book is likely the most tangible of all things I created. My whole life I have been lucky to have family from DNA and an overwhelming amount of found family. My editor noted in a very early conversation, "I haven't seen family shown quite this way before." Maybe he was talking about calling Aunt Nancy "aunt" when that isn't how it would be mapped on a family tree? My family tree is chaotic to say the least. Maybe a garden is a more accurate picture, people growing up around one another, filling in the spaces that have been left behind. Maybe your family is a little like that, too. Having family that grows up around you, fills in the special places in your life, is one of the greatest blessings I know.

For me, the world is truly filled with mysteries, just as Axel says. It is full, and round, and sometimes messy. The best we can do is be true to ourselves and let in people who make us feel whole. Thank you for letting in Axel, Byrd, and all of the characters from this make-believe world.

Thank you for making space for this book.

Alison

BIRD FACT/BIRD FICTION

I had some truly excellent professional and expert readers for *A Bird Will Soar*. I worked with a falconer, read stacks and stack of books, enjoyed many educational trips to nature preserves and raptor centers, and went birding as often as possible to observe birds and nests in nature. Here are a few places that my favorite bird facts blurred with the fictional world of the story:

EAGLE REGULATIONS AND REHABILITATION

There are many, many moments of pure fiction when it comes to Braviary's rescue and rehabilitation. The rescue itself was different from the way a real eaglet rescue would take place. For one, I made up the need for the pot and spoon and the teacup sheet. I wanted each family member, especially Lark and Axel, to have a special job in the rescue.

A real rescue of a bird of prey should always start with contacting an expert. Most towns have raptor rehabilitation resources. If you are unsure of whom to contact, you can call a local vet or the game commission in your area. If you do find an injured bird of prey, try not to disturb the animal without the help of a professional. They will know how to move the bird without causing further injury and they'll have strategies for keeping the bird calm and warm.

In most places, caring for a bird of prey in a private residence is against the law, even if your plan is to set it free when it is better. Specifically, there are laws and regulations protecting bald and golden eagles, including the handling of their eggs and young. You've probably already guessed, along with not being able to be as active in the rescue, that Axel and Lark would not have been able to hold Braviary, even with Dr. Martin supervising. It is important to note that Indigenous rights to eagles and their feathers are protected. There are special regulations for religious and educational handling of eagles and feathers as well.

BIRD EMOTIONS

In many of the poems I walked the line with bird emotions between fact and fiction. Bird emotions have been studied, as you can imagine, from the outside. Meaning that the most used method of study is observation. In birds, we can observe acts of aggression and affection, but can we observe hope or wonder?

I received a comment from an expert reader that said, "HOPE . . . This is quite a stretch." He was referring to Dr. Taylor M. Martin's email to Axel that the eagle parents had hope that Braviary had figured out a way to survive. More so that when all baby birds leave the nest, the parents have hope that the birds will soar.

I do not know for sure if all birds have hope that their babies will soar. It is not a fact. But I certainly love considering it and believing that Dr. Martin would share the idea of HOPE with Axel for many, many reasons. I want to believe that HOPE permeates through all living things.

FIGHT AND FLIGHT AND INSTINCT

In the book, I took the definition of instinct as: actions that occur automatically and in response to some kind of stimuli. I had a few early readers suggest that what I was referring to here wasn't "instinct" as much as it is "intuition" or "trusting your gut," like Ms. Dale says.

What I really wanted to explore in the book was the way we make space or understanding for some to have their own instincts (or intuition), and ways that others are not encouraged to embrace their instincts or intuition.

There must be room for us to navigate our own intuition and instincts, to not conform to one standard of operating that, frankly, doesn't make all of us feel safe or respected. In the book, the terms *intuition*, *trusting your gut*, and *instincts* are used interchangeably, though scientifically there are separate definitions and needs for all.

CAW

Another wonderful expert reader asked me why I included "caw" as an interjection throughout the book when that isn't a sound associated with birds of prey. This is true and I am grateful to this reader for pointing it out because maybe you wondered this, too!

While "caw" isn't a bird of prey sound, it is a bird utterance, and I wanted a short bird utterance to be part of the family's vocabulary. In our house, we have an utterance that conveys a world of things, known by the people in our four walls. So, "caw" might mean "really?" or "nope!" or "obviously!" or "not today" or "figures" or "I know!!!" or "caw." Do you have words like that in your family? Or maybe with a best friend? There's a poem in the book that explores other bird sounds. Would any of those sounds work for you?

PIGEONS

We actually love pigeons. (That is all.)

ACKNOWLEDGMENTS

This book was a joy and a challenge to write. I had something to say, but, as with many things, needed the help of so many people to get the words in the right order and have the courage to put the whole thing to the page. Without Linda Epstein's support I would have given up writing before this book ever came to be. Thank you for your support, Linda, in all things big and small.

Early readers of the book helped me open to Axel's voice. Thank you, friends, writers, educators: Meera Trehan, Jenny Herrera, Jennifer Kiesendahl, Bill and Beth Johnson, Kathy Erskine and Fiona, Katharine Brown and Anna, Bobbie Combs and Keane, Caitlin Benson Schmidt, Pat Cummings, Laura Parnum, and Maricka Armstrong. A special thanks to Heather Hogan and James Spencer for their child-centered insights, and to Jack Hubley, Christi Nelson-Epstein, and Sarah Kapit for their most important feedback.

Great thanks as well to those who believed in me and the book, even when I couldn't: George, Parker, Sarah, Heidi, Donna, Kim, Leah, Padma, Meg, Traci, Alex, Rona, Dahlia, Dwight, Nat, Julie, Karen, Greg, Cassie, and all of my friends at the Pennsylvania Writing Project, SCBWI, and my family and home at the Highlights Foundation. To former students and schools, thank you for sharing words with me and letting me share mine with you!

Jennifer Rofé, Kayla Cichello, and the team at Andrea Brown Literary, thank you for your care and support. Jen, thank you for finding a home for Axel. I owe you a million great owl books, and then some!

To the team at Dutton—Julie Strauss-Gabel, Andrew Karre, Melissa Faulner, Natalie Vielkind, Rob Farren, and Anne Heausler—thank you. To Anna Booth, Madeline Kloepper, and Samira Iravani, thank you for creating a beautiful book, inside and out. Andrew, my favorite call was the one about Emmett's shopping habits in a small town and an inner tube floating on a lake. Those two images cracked open a whole new part of Axel's world. Thank you so much for seeing something in this book and seeing it again when it changed from one form to another. (And thank you for lovingly considering all the times I wanted to use Mary Oliver, and then gently requesting that I find balance!)

Thank you, Dad, Jeannie, Maureen, Moya, Maria, Kurt, Caitlin, Cleary, Greta, and Nelly for being my messy garden of family. To the Pastusaks, thank you for giving me a place to land when I needed it most. The Browns, Chengs, Irwins, and Murrays, you are my home. To my many other found families, I love you for always making room for me.

And to Garry and Will, how lucky are we to be on this planet together? To walk the same woods? To snuggle the same pups? To share the same name? You are everything all at once, and I wouldn't have it any other way.

Letters from the West;
or a Caution to Emigrants

John Stillman Wright

READEX MICROPRINT

Foreword

Letters From The West; Or A Caution To Emigrants, written by John S. Wright and published in 1819, presents the impressions of the author about opportunities for settlement in the Ohio Valley. Having just completed a six months trip there, where he had gone "as a plain practical farmer, to judge for myself, of the merits of a country so highly extolled," Wright came back profoundly disillusioned. He believed his own experience demonstrated that before any man removed his family to a distant country, he ought first to visit it and judge of it himself. Wright's collection of letters serves as a forceful reminder that not everyone found the West to his liking.

Wright had followed a trade in the East before purchasing a farm in the Saratoga area of New York State. However, after six years of farming there, he was caught up in the "Ohio mania," which, he said, had for the past few years been "so generally prevalent in the east." Full of enthusiasm and hope, Wright journeyed into the Ohio Valley to find the best site to which to bring his family. His letters, written from various stops along the way, reveal a growing disappointment. When he saw good farm land, he learned that land speculators had already purchased it and that they would sell it only at an

TO THE PUBLIC.

THE undersigned, having perused the whole or a part of some manuscript letters, written, from various places in the western section of the United States, by Mr. JOHN S. WRIGHT, to his friends in this village, unite in opinion, that they are interesting and useful. From several years acquaintance with the author, we have full confidence in his veracity, and can assure others that they may rely implicitly on the correctness of his statement of facts. Believing that his letters contain information very much wanted, and very beneficial to a numerous class of citizens in the eastern and northern States, we advise their publication, and recommend them to general patronage.

ISRAEL WILLIAMS,
JAMES S. TIFFT,
MOSES COWAN,
CORNELIUS HOLMES,
JOHN GALE,
SIMON STEVENS,
WILLIAM MOWRY,
LEWIS SHEARER,
SIMEON TAYLOR,
OTIS WHIPPLE,
JOHN C. WALKER.

Union-Village, Washington Co. N. Y.
July 28, 1819.

PREFACE.

AS some account of the writer of these letters, and his motives for publishing them, may not, perhaps, be unacceptable, I shall endeavour to present the one, and explain the other, in as few words as possible. I was bred a mechanic, and followed my business assiduously until about six years since, when I purchased a farm in Northumberland, Saratoga county; and being better pleased with agricultural pursuits than the business I was bred to, I concluded to give my whole attention that way, as soon as I could obtain a situation to suit me. The *Ohio mania*, which has, for a few years past, been so generally prevalent in the east, at length infected my neighbourhood, and I did not escape the contagion. Unwilling, however, to rest my faith on common report, I made close inquiries, of every person I met with, who had seen either the country itself, or those who had visited it. I read the glowing descriptions given of it, in private letters and in the public prints; I procured and read every work on the subject I could hear of; I compared the different accounts, and left no means within my reach untried, to obtain correct

information. The result was a full con-
viction of the superiority of the south-western country, over the section we inhabit ;
and I determined, if permitted, to remove
thither. The severe winters, cold and dry
summers, and short crops, we had lately ex-
perienced, had their full weight and influence on my mind, in forming these conclu-
sions. Thus resolved, I sold my farm, and
returned to this village to complete my preparations for the journey : and so confident
did I feel of being suited with the country,
that I intended taking on my family at once,
thinking, that a previous journey, to look
at a country, with which I thought myself
already so perfectly acquainted, would be
only a sacrifice of time and money. Some
disappointments which I met with, in con-
verting my little property into cash, I found
would occasion a delay of six or eight
months, and I then concluded, to employ
this interval in visiting the country, and se-
lecting a spot for my future residence.

The reader, will now, readily perceive,
that my motives in visiting the south-western regions, differed widely from those of
thousands who have preceded me. I went
—not like the speculator—to purchase immense tracts of land with a view to future
profit by the monopoly ;—not like the traveller for amusement, who loves to *astonish*
his friends at home, with "something of the
marvellous ;"—not like the scientific enthu-
siast—to invade the secret recesses of na-

ture, to crawl through the tangled brake, dig into the ancient tumuli, roam the dark forest, and explore the hideous cavern by torch light, in order to enrich the "cabinets of the curious" with decayed bones, horned toads, skins of birds and dried leaves;— not like the philosophic Volney, who crossed the Atlantic, and scaled the Allegany, to "see which way the wind blew in the great Ohio valley;" no—nor yet, like the lovers of romance, poetry and fiction,— to store my mind with images of stupendous mountains, majestic rivers, immense prairies, magnificent cities, and empty visions of the future grandeur and glory of the great Empire of the West.—These objects, however pleasing, curious or useful, they may be, were not within the circle of my inquiries: nor did I go as an enemy, to "spy out the nakedness" or "bring up an "evil report of the good land;" for I have already informed the reader that my prepossessions were directly the reverse. But, I went as a plain practical farmer, to judge for myself, of the merits of a country so highly extolled; to examine the soil, the water and productions; to inquire into the state and profits of agriculture and domestic manufactures; to find the present prices of produce, and the prospects of a future market; to know the prices of the necessary foreign articles; and in short to satisfy myself respecting the salubriousness of the climate; the manners, customs and moral character of the inhabitants ; and the state and prospects of their literary and religious institutions. Several friends, in this village and its vicinity, previous to my departure, requested me to write as often as convenient, while on my journey. I complied with their request, and I likewise kept a journal in which I noted facts and observations, as they occurred. From that journal and those letters, I have made the compilation which is now offered to the public. In doing this, I am principally actuated by a sense of duty ; and the few friends I consulted, advised, or perhaps, it would be more modest to say, *consented,* to the measure ; not because they, any more than myself, expected that I would receive any pecuniary benefit, but because they believed it might be useful. For the truth of the statements I have made, I consider my character staked ; and I have given my name and place of residence.—Perhaps some may infer from the favorable description I have given of Chatauque, that I am governed by some interested motive, in so highly recommending that county ; I would only reply, that I have said nothing more than I believe to be true, and, that I own no more land there, than I intend, if permitted, to occupy. Should the county continue to settle rapidly, the value of the farm, and what improvements I may make on it, would be somewhat enhanced ; but I wish no person to rely on my description, and hazard a loss ;

on the contrary, I take this opportunity to repeat the warning I have given in the work, " *let no man, on any condition, or under any* " *circumstances, whatever, be induced to re-* " *move his family to a distant country, until* " *he has seen, examined and judged of it for* " *himself.*" Should this warning be the means of saving one family, from the cruel disappointment and vain regret, which so many thousands are now enduring, the work which I intrude on the public will not have been written in vain. I am not vain enough to suppose, that this small publication will arrest the great tide of emigration, or even produce any very sensible effect. Should it be the means of rendering people more cautious in taking steps which cannot be retraced—should it induce them to " look " before they leap," my highest hopes will be realized. To the criticks I would make my best bow, and beg of them to consider me entirely beneath their notice. I am a plain unlettered mechanic : I aspire not to the honor of *amusing :* my highest ambition is to be *useful.*

J. S. WRIGHT.

Union-Village, August, 1819.

LETTERS FROM THE WEST.

LETTER I.

Hamilton, N. Y. (Formerly called Olean.) Nov. 1, 1818.

MY DEAR SIR,

THIS day at noon I arrived here, somewhat fatigued, I confess, but not discouraged; on the contrary, I think my ardor rather increases to pursue my original design: that of exploring, examining and judging for myself of the highly extolled south-western country. This village is pleasantly situated at the head of the Allegany, at the junction of Olean and Oil Creeks: it contains, perhaps, an hundred buildings; some of which have a neat appearance, the rest are mere cabins, erected for the temporary residence of the eastern emigrants, while procuring boats and making other preparations for their voyage down the river. It is estimated, that there are now in this village and its vicinity, three hundred families, besides single travellers, amounting in all to fifteen hundred souls, waiting for a rise of the water to embark for "the promised land." I have just returned from taking a view of this *inland flotilla*, as they lie hauled up along the shore. These boats (or *arks* as they might very aptly be called) are quite conveniently constructed, for the accommodation of families and passengers: they are from thirty five to seventy five feet in length, and from eight to twelve in width; having the sides closed up, a door in each end, and an arched roof of thin boards, they contain a fire place, a cupboard, and decent births. They have two plying oars, and usually, two for steering: on the whole, a family on board, are tolerably well accommodated. I have engaged a passage to Cincinnati, in one which will leave here to-morrow. We are all very sanguine in our expectations (from the accounts we continually hear) of finding a country below which will afford the necessaries of life in profusion, and relieve us from the necessity of perpetual labor, for the support of our families and cattle. Such expectations induce the hardy, enterprising sons of the north and east, to abandon those frozen regions, brave the toil and perils of a long journey, and, by one vigorous effort, place their families (so far as depends on human exertion) beyond the reach of grinding poverty.

Yours, &c.

J. S. W.

LETTER II.

Pittsburgh, Penn. Dec. 3d, 1818.

My Friend,

Our voyage hither was rather slow and dangerous, owing to the shallowness of the water:—the frequency of rapids and shoals renders a pilot indispensable. The country we have passed is rather mountainous; affording very little bottom land, and that little not well managed. There are four or five villages, of some little consequence, scattered along the banks of the Allegany, which afford the mind a temporary relief from the gloominess imparted by the rude and barren scenery, which almost continually presents itself. These towns, however, afford but a scanty and dear supply, for the numerous wants of the passing emigrants. I saw, on my route, the 20 *cents per acre* land in Pennsylvania, so much talked of among our neighbours; but as I do not like it myself, I cannot recommend it to others. This place fully equals, and perhaps exceeds, the description generally given of it. The approach to it on the river is delightful: you are surrounded by rugged hills and finely cultivated vallies, decorated with neat cottages and elegant mansions. An immense column of dusky smoke, which is seen ascending, spreading in vast wreaths among the clouds, marks the site of Pittsburgh. The bold features of the surrounding country, lend to the town an air of grandeur and magnificence, such as we seldom meet with : nor is the voyager entirely mistaken; the town, on his entrance, presents him with numerous marks of activity, enterprise and wealth. Nature has been uncommonly bountiful in her gifts, but an indolent population could have received no benefit from them; she has provided an inexhaustible supply of stone-coal, iron ore of the first quality, numerous quarries of freestone, timber of ever kind necessary for the country, together with the finest of clay for brick, and sand for glass:—nor have these advantages been neglected; great quantities of glass are manufactured, of a superior quality; coal constitutes the principal article of their fuel, is exported in great quantities to the towns below, and is made use of in their steam boats, and in all their great manufactories, which are propelled by steam; among which are a grist and saw mill, a rolling and slitting mill; a paper mill, and a cotton and woollen manufactory.

This town is situated on a point of land, formed by the junction of the Allegany and Monongahela, at the head of the Ohio river, in the state of Pennsylvania. A bridge has been erected this season, over the Monongahela, consisting of seven arches, supported by stone piers and abutments, of masterly workmanship; another is now building over the Allegany of equal strength and elegance. The market here is well supplied, and tolerably cheap : the beef and pork of an excellent quality. Here I believe I have seen some of the largest and most powerful horses, that our country can produce : should I relate what I have actually seen them perform, you would be likely to tell me, I was making use of the traveller's licence, before I had earned it. There are several regular streets, with buildings of two or three stories ; and several churches, belonging to different denominations, which are neat buildings, and appear to be kept in good order : but the cloud of smoke in which the town is enveloped, gives a smutty appearance to every thing. A person after walking the streets a few hours, finds his linen badly soiled ; the sulphurous smell, too, emitted from the burning coal, will be quite disagreeable until he has become somewhat accustomed to it. The town would have been far pleasanter, had their steam machinery been erected at some little distance from it.

At one o'clock, this day, I attended the funeral obsequies, of the brave and lamented Commodore Barney. While in this town, on a tour to the south, he was seized with a violent fever, which, added to some old complaints, with which he was afflicted, terminated his valuable life yesterday, about three o'clock. The funeral procession formed at the Hotel, and moved with the remains, preceded by a military band playing a solemn dirge, to the Presbyterian

Church, in the cemetery of which, they were interred in Masonic order. It was a dignified and solemn scene ; decency, propriety and good order prevailed throughout, and the whole proceedings, reflected honor, as well on the living as the dead.—To-morrow we start down the river : our prospects brighten.

Adieu.

J. S. W.

LETTER III.

Cincinnati, Dec. 29th, 1818.

DEAR SIR,

I arrived here about the middle of the present month. It had not rained since we left Hamilton, until two or three days after we embarked from Pittsburgh. The sudden rise of the water was to me really astonishing : the waters of the Ohio were so uncommonly low, that our boat, though drawing only ten inches, actually grounded several times. It began to rain about noon, and continued steadily until night, at which time we found the water beginning to swell ; the next morning, it appeared, on an exact admeasurement, to have risen seven feet, three inches, perpendicularly. From this time our passage was more easy and expeditious. The scenery along the Ohio does not entirely meet my expectations : the bottom lands, indeed, are very extensive, but they are not in a very high state of cultivation; the buildings on the plantations, are not such as I expected to have seen—generally, log-cabins; and scarcely an instance of a framed barn, or any thing else which bore the appearance of taste, elegance or improvement. To the rude and slovenly state of the country, the towns present a striking and agreeable contrast: many of these have a neat and flourishing appearance. Among those entitled to notice, are Wheeling, in Virginia; Steubenville, in Ohio; Marietta, at the mouth of Muskingum, in the same state; and Mayville, at the mouth of the Limestone, in Kentucky. We had occasion to buy provisions at several of these towns, and, to our extreme surprise, found them scarce, and as dear as in New-York. Many of these places suffer by frequent inundations; Marietta, perhaps, more than others, for although it stands on a bank, at least thirty feet above the present surface of the stream, yet I actually saw high-water marks on the second stories of many buildings. Since my first arrival here, I have taken two tours into the adjoining country and returned to this place: the first led me through what is called the White-water country, in Indiana, and through a small part of Kentucky; in my second, I traversed much of the Miami country, in Ohio. But before I attempt to describe the country I have been viewing, let me pay a little attention to the town from whence I am writing.

Cincinnati is pleasantly situated on the north bank of the Ohio : the greater part of the town is on the second elevation, which secures it from the annual floods. It is said to cover a section and two quarter sections, or, in other words, nearly a thousand acres of ground : several of the streets are really elegant ; shewing extensive rows of superb brick buildings. Main street would suffer but little, by a comparison with the best in many of the eastern cities. There are four or five churches, two markets and other public edifices ; a grist mill, several cotton and woollen manufactories, all propelled by steam ; a saw mill driven by the force, or rather *weight,* of oxen or horses ; with numerous other buildings, for manufacturing and mechanical purposes.

The building of steam-boats is here carried on largely : four or five are now on the stocks, some of which are nearly ready to launch. Glass-making, is also pursued extensively. The inhabitants, or at least a great part of them, appear genteel in their dress, and easy and polite in their manners : but here let me make a remark, which applies to all the large towns in this country, as well as to this.—Here is the residence of the great capitalists ; here the speculators are assembled ; from these central points, the men of *cent per cent* calculation, carry on their monopolizing enterprises ;—let not this remark be forgotten.

I have frequently attended the markets, and you will doubtless be surprised, if not incredulous, at my account of them. We have always looked toward this, as a "land "flowing with milk and honey ;" or, at least, as abounding in bread, beef and butter :— no such thing. You shall judge—take the prices of the day—not a fabricated " price "current," but actual sales which I have witnessed myself :—wheat flour 3 to 4 cents per lb.—buck-wheat meal the same—corn meal, 50 cents per bushel—-pork from 5 to 8 cents per lb.—beef from 5 to 9 cents— cheese 25 cents—butter 25 to 31 cents— turkeys from 75 to 150 cents each—-fowls 18 to 25 cents—ducks 25 cents—geese 38 to 50 cents—quails 1 dollar per dozen— eggs 25 cents per doz.—beans 6 cents per quart—potatoes 1 dollar per bush. poor, and very scarce—hay from 12 to 25 dollars per ton—salt 4 dollars for 50 lbs, which is here considered a bushel—no fish in market.— A plentiful country truly ! These prices are not in consequence of any uncommon scarcity, or failure of crops, but as far as I have been able to learn, are about as usual. The beef and pork are miserable : an eastern farmer would scarcely think it in good store or working order.

Travellers experience much inconvenience from the circulating medium. The bills of the country banks are in low credit ;

specie is scarcely seen, for every purse in this country is drained of its metalic contents, to enable the trader to make his remittances to the Atlantic cities, from whence almost all the goods are brought, over land to Pittsburgh, thence down the river by water. From these causes, there arises a continual call on the eastern emigrants and travellers, for an exchange of paper, frequently offering a premium of ten per cent for eastern bills.

Most kinds of mechanical business have been very good here, though rather dull at present; partly owing to the general depression of business, and partly to the great influx of mechanics. Hence wages have become low; and many, not finding employment as mechanics, have hired rooms, and made use of what capital they possessed, in setting up little groceries:—of these, several in this town, appear to be doing very good business.

Having already mentioned the price of salt, 8 dollars for 100 lbs. I will now give the result of an estimate, which I have thought well calculated to place the profits of the Ohio farmer in a light very different from that in which we have been in the habit of viewing them. Suppose a farmer living thirty miles, by land, from this town, to bring here corn enough to pay for a barrel of salt, (if he allow himself the same for transportation that he would be obliged to pay to another,) it will, when landed at his

door, stand him in over one hundred bushels of corn. You may think this calculation erroneous, but I assure you it is correct.
I have spun this letter out to such a length,
that I must defer my account of the countries I have lately explored, until my next.

Yours, &c.

J. S. W.

LETTER IV.

Cincinnati, Jan. 6. 1819.

My Dear Friend,

THE countries I have lately been
exploring, on the Miami and White-water rivers, do certainly contain large
bodies of excellent land, beautifully undulating, and chequered with streams of whitish water, generally impregnated with lime.
The inhabitants however are, mostly, of indolent slovenly habits, devoting the chief
part of their time to hunting, and drinking
whiskey, (the only liquor in use,) and appear to be a meagre, sickly, spiritless and
unenterprising race : contented to live in
log-cabins, containing only one room, with
the chimney on the outside, and five or six
lusty dogs within. Very rarely is a school
house or church to be seen, and scarcely a
bridge of thirty feet in length. The improvement of public roads is entirely neglected ; and so negligent are they in man-
aging the concerns of their farms, that I dai-

ly see even large fields of corn not yet har-
vested ; for, it seems, they gather it no faster than their wants require. From the best
information I can obtain, their average crops
are, of corn, per acre, forty bushels ; wheat,
twenty five ; oats, thirty ; and potatoes, a-
bout forty. They raise very little rye, and
generally cut about one ton of hay to the
acre.—The people, in fact, appear too indolent to raise much grain : they do not usually clear more than thirty or forty acres to a
farm; leaving the rest in the state of nature,
for the benefit of "*mast** and *range*," as they
express it. In the spring, they plough their
land once, and plant the corn ; after which,
they give it no further attention, than what
is necessary to keep down the weeds: in
September; they sow their wheat among
the corn, and perhaps plough or harrow it
in, and in the winter, cut down their corn-
stalks and carry them out of the field.
Their hogs run at large in the woods, where
they keep in tolerably thriving order, and
from thence they are taken and killed, as
occasion requires, without further feeding.
The living, or food, of the country people,
is extremely unpleasant to an eastern stomach, it consists (to use their own language)
of " *hog, homminy, and hoe cake.*" Their
cattle are small, compared to ours, and
their cows do not yield so well ; it is thought

*By *mast* is meant acorns, beech nuts &c. which afford food
for swine.

a good one, that gives from five to six quarts at a milking ; and a hog that weighs 200 lbs. is over the usual size.

In certain parts of this country, there are poisonous roots or weeds, which frequently kill the cattle that eat much of any of them : and should a hog, dog or wolf, make a feast of the carcase, it inevitably proves his last. Poisoned milk, too, is quite common, of which, if people eat they sicken immediately, and will need medical aid before they are restored to health. Another of the evils of this " garden of the world," is what is termed *sick wheat :* this is most frequently found on the rich bottom lands, and is supposed to be owing to the fogs, which often prevail there. It is only to be distinguished, while growing, by the fuzzy end of the berry containing a small red speck : in all other respects, it appears like healthy wheat: it is said to be certain death to any creature that eats of it : consequently, whenever a crop is found to be infected, the whole must be destroyed. While on the subject of poisons, I will mention snakes, which are rather numerous ; especially the copper-head and rattle snake, which annoy the happy inhabitants of this *terrestrial paradise.* I have seen five or six persons who had been bitten : fortunately for them, however, the country furnishes an antidote, or rather remedy, in a certain plant, which counteracts the poison, when it can be procured in season.

Great numbers of people from New-Jersey, New-York and farther east, have settled in those parts of the country of which I am speaking ; but they are generally disappointed in their expectations, and dissatisfied with the country : many of them declared to me, that they would return if they possessed the means. They admit, that the country is not natural to grass ; nor can it ever become so, in consequence of the general growth of a certain kind of wild grass, by some called *blue joint*, by others *nimble Will*, which chokes out the English grass, and at the same time is not good itself ; for as soon as it springs up to the height of five or six inches, it becomes so hard and tough, that cattle cannot eat it. Flax, they assert, does *well*, and sheep tolerably : in one flock which I saw last week, I counted fifty lambs, which appeared sprightly and vigorous, but this flock was five times as large as any other I have seen. There are a few orchards of apple and peach trees in the Miami country, which appeared so thrifty and promising, that I am induced to think, that by attention and good culture, they could not fail to yield fruit in abundance.

Wherever, in my tours, I saw a situation that was desirable, I was naturally led to inquire for the owner : the answer was almost invariably the same : it is the property of the capitalist, the speculator, the resident of some adjacent village or large town, and cannot be had at a fair price : if there is even a lot of wild land worthy the attention of the farmer, depend upon it the speculator has his clutch upon it, and you cannot buy it short of, perhaps, three times the government price. This is so universally the case, that I consider the only chance now, for the emigrant to obtain public land, at the established price, is on some rugged hill or in some dismal hole, where the eagle-eyed speculator himself, can see no prospect of profit.

Thus far you will readily perceive, my hopes are not realized, but I am not yet disheartened. I shall endeavour, in my future progress, to let a reasonable assurance animate my exertions, " for he that despairs of success will not succeed ; and to him that believes every thing impossible despondency shall render it so ; but he that persevereth shall overcome all difficulties." I shall continue to pursue my first object, until I find a country to suit me better than any I have yet set my foot on ; or I will return to my native land and endeavor to be satisfied with the situation in which a wise Providence has placed me ; for truly says the precept, " the cup of felicity, pure and unmixed, is by no means a draught for the lips of mortals."

Yours, &c.

J. S. W.

LETTER V.

Vincennes, (Indiana,) Feb. 6, 1819.

DEAR FRIEND,

We had a quick passage down the river from Cincinnati, in a skiff which we navigated ourselves. We passed several towns along the river; among those that deserve mention, is Rising-Sun, about thirty miles below Cincinnati, which contains about a hundred houses, pleasantly situated on a lofty bank, above high-water mark: it appears to be declining; the country around it is quite hilly and broken. Vevay, a Swiss settlement, forty-six miles below Cincinnati, contains but few houses, and is only remarkable from the vineyards in its vicinity. These are situated below the town on the bottom land, and afford a delightful prospect. The vines are planted in rows, about six feet apart; are supported by stakes and bars, to which they are bound with straw; and are hoed and cultivated like Indian corn. Port-William, at the mouth of the Kentucky river, a small town subject to inundation; the country in its rear very pleasant, distance below Cincinnati seventy miles.— Madison, in Jefferson county, Indiana, ninety-two miles below Cincinnati, contains about a hundred houses, situated above high-water mark: a flourishing town, surrounded by lofty knobs, which give the landscape a very singular and picturesque appearance.

At the falls of Ohio, are six towns, viz
Jeffersonville, Clarksville and New-Albany,
on the Indiana side; and Louisville, Shipping-
port and Portland, on the Kentucky side.
Louisville, at the head of the falls, is a town
at least two thirds as large as Cincinnati;
contains several regular streets, with elegant
three story brick buildings: but, unfortunately, its situation is unhealthful, being surrounded by swamps and stagnant waters.
The tavern charges, here, are the most extravagant I ever paid. Fifty cents for a
common meal, twenty-five for lodging, twenty-five for a gill of spirits, and seventy-five
for horse keeping: I may venture to assert
without fear of contradiction that travelling
is more expensive, considering the quality
of food, in this boasted *land of plenty*, than
in any part of the northern states. We passed a number of other towns, but there is
so little variety in their appearance, or that
of the country about them, I will not fatigue
you, or myself, by an attempt to describe
them. I shall, therefore, only mention Evensville, where we landed. It is situated
just above the mouth of the big Pigeon-
creek three hundred miles below Cincinnati, in Vandenburgh county, Indiana. It
was first settled as a town about three years
ago. It now contains perhaps fifty houses,
and judging from its local situation, must
eventually, rank high in the scale of western
cities. It is the nearest point of the Ohio,
to Vincennes, (fifty-five miles,) and in con-

sequence of the difficulty of navigating the Wabash, a great part of the year, in all probability, the supplies of merchandise for a large extent of country north, will be carried by land from Evensville ; provided a sufficient degree of spirit ever exist in the country to render the roads passable. Here I first saw the reed cane ; it is an evergreen, and appeared to great advantage among the leafless trees of the forest. Between Evensville and this place, is some land which may be called good, the soil a gravelly loam, with a smaller proportion of clay than is usual. There is a great variety of timber, and the face of the country is agreeably undulating ; but the inhabitants, buildings, roads, improvements, (or rather the want of them,) are of just the same character, with those described in my last letter. There are some fine looking bottom lands on the Petoka and White rivers, which we crossed, but good farming lands are here, as elsewhere, in the hands of the great landholders ; and consequently, are exorbitantly high, every thing considered.

Vincennes is situated on a prairie, of some thousand acres in extent, bounded on the west by the Wabash, and by the uplands in all other directions. On the borders of this vast plain, are some three or four of those ancient mounds or tumuli, which have so often been the subject of deep interest, laborious research and profound investigation. The base of one covers, at least, an acre of ground, in a circu-

lar form : the summit towers to the height
of a hundred feet. They are composed
of earth, scooped out of the bank on each
side, and must have been a work of immense
toil and fatigue ; especially, if, as is generally supposed, they were erected by the te-
dious process of manual labor. Vincennes
contains about two hundred houses, scattered irregularly over an extent of two hundred acres: the greater part are of logs, or
rails laid up in the manner of logs, bedaub-
ed with clay, and destitute of every appearance of order or cleanliness : but the owner of the mansion appears, dressed in skins,
or linsey-woolsey of family make ; he comes
out, but whether to labor in the field, or to
display his mental and bodily powers, in training his dogs or his horse, the effect, on the
traveller possessed of feeling and information, is the same ; his emotions of pity are
mingled with contempt, and could he forbear
laughing he might possibly find in his heart
to weep at such an exhibition of ignorance,
stupidity and self-conceit. Lately, however,
some eastern people, have fixed themselves
among these semi-barbarians, and have commenced the era of improvement by building some decent houses. This course, will
eventually dislodge the ancient half-French,
half-Indian horde, that have so long disgra-
ced these beautiful plains ; for nothing in
nature is so opposite to their notions of
comfort, as " yankies," civilization and improvement, The Wabash, is here, about

two hundred yards wide, and is said to be navigable for boats (part of the season) seventy miles higher, to fort Harrison. The surrounding country, is timbered chiefly with white oak: the soil of the upland is composed of clay and sand; sometimes with an admixture of gravel: the bottom lands are a deep, vegetable mould, and are, really, as rich as can well be imagined; though not quite so superlatively productive, as we have been led to believe. From the best information I have been enabled to obtain, I believe, notwithstanding the boast of an hundred to the acre, I hazard nothing in saying, that forty bushels of corn is an average crop. The vile, disgraceful and inhuman practice of kidnapping, is not only carried on, but even countenanced here. The unfeeling, avaricious monsters, with brutal ferocity, seize the ignorant, unprotected African, and, deaf to his cries and supplications for mercy and liberty, bind him hand and foot, drag him from his weeping helpless family, hurry him away to the southern states, and barbarously sell their fellow-mortal, to drag out a miserable existence in slavery, doomed to suffer all that avarice can command or unrestrained cruelty inflict. O christian humanity! how are thy benign and heavenly precepts disregarded, where the most wicked and attrocious traffic in human flesh, is esteemed a mere matter of business—a common and innocent speculation!—I will give you one, of many instances I might relate. About three months ago, five free blacks were seized by these, worse than savages, in this place and its vicinity, and hurried off toward the south for market. Two days had elapsed before the outrage came to the knowledge of the few New-England people here; they spent but few moments in deliberation, having but little confidence in the arm of the law; knowing its effect was tardy and uncertain, they seized *their own arms*, and pursued the ruffians eighty miles on the route to St. Louis: where overtaking them, they fought, and freed the captives. The brutal captors they took back, and delivered to the civil authority at Vencennes. This glaringly outrageous act, was laid before the grand jury since my arrival here: but corruption had been early at work; the presiding judge, and three fourths of the men who composed the jury, were interested in this, or some other kidnapping concern; consequently, although the friends of humanity did all in their power; although the case was clear and undisputed, yet so was the thing managed, that no bill was found; and the vile band of marauders escaped unpunished.

Yours truly,

J. S. W.

LETTER VI.

Vincennes, February 18th, 1819.

DEAR SIR,

SINCE my last, I have taken a tour into Illinois, and I most sincerely wish I could say, that the change of scene had produced a change of prospects; but a regard to truth, and a desire to give you correct information, forbid me to say so. I must either cease to write, or I must spread before you, my opinions and feelings, just as they spring, warm from the head and the heart; yet, perhaps you may think me too much influenced by fancy or the whim of the moment: with respect to unsubstantial things, I will not deny that I am "even as others." But fancy or whim, my dear friend, can neither produce or destroy a *fact* :—Fancy and whim cannot level mountains or elevate vallies, elicit springs in the sunburnt prairie, nor change a quagmire to arable land: no; nor alter the habits of the western planters, nor fill their paper banks with a specie capital. *Facts*, then, are the solid foundation on which my opinions rest : *facts*, the knowledge of which, I have acquired, either from the evidence of my own senses, or the testimony of others that appeared entitled to credit ; not an idle tale from an idle individual, but the aggregate of what could be learned from all, examined, compared, and tested by each other, and by my own actual observation. To return from this digression, wherever I have been since I wrote last, the general face and state of things seem to be the same: wherever there is a situation favorable for water machinery; wherever there is a spot, that, from local circumstances, exhibits a prospect for a little town; or wherever there is even a tolerable farming tract, the result, on inquiry, is still invariably the same :— they are held in the iron grasp of the insatiate land-jobber; and the industrious, the needy emigrant, must submit to *his* terms or flee to the wilderness, far beyond the precincts, of even such society as exists here. I have, I believe, made the same or similar remarks in my former letters, but these things in a manner force themselves upon me: they meet me at every turn—the *sameness* of every thing throughout such an extent of country astonishes me.

On entering Illinois I beheld a vast, and almost boundless body of land, stretching before and around me: equal, or nearly so, in point of fertility, to the boasted swales of the western parts of New-York: every thing seemed to invite me to select a spot, begin my improvements, and enjoy my happy fate. But ah! like the enjoyment of forbidden pleasure, there is a sting behind. Not only is an exhorbitant price demanded, but the *inhabitants*, the people among whom I must spend my days; with whom my intimacies, my friendships are to be formed : to whom I must look for all those delicate attentions which spread a charm over socie-

ty ; for an interchange of all those kind and
endearing offices, so indispensably necessary in the hour of trouble and sickness : the
inhabitants I repeat, are sufficient to dispel
the gay vision : it is impossible to dream
long in a land of such palpable realities.
They are a motly assemblage of Pennsylva-
nians, Virginians, Carolinians and Kentucky-
ans with a few yankies intermixed, scattered over the face of the country, at the distance of from two to eight or ten miles
apart, in order, as they say, to have sufficient range for their cattle, and *mast* for
their hogs. At this distance they wish to
keep ; and they look with a malicious, scow-
ling eye, on the New-England men who
settle among them, and begin a course
of improvement by clearing their lands. I
have now come to a question, which I free-
ly acknowledge myself unable to solve : but
first let me state the *fact* which gives rise to
it. It is a *fact*, for the truth of which I consider my character pledged, that the northern emigrants, (with some few honorable
exceptions,) who remove to this country,
and settle as farmers, among the people
from the southern states, *do degenerate.* The
question then recurs, what is the cause ?
Many reasons may be offered, though none
are to me entirely satisfactory. It may
arise from a wish to avoid giving offence to
the people among whom they live, and with
whom they must associate and form con-
nexions : a love of ease may induce the
abandonment of those habits of industry.

which the methods of farming pursued by
the southern settlers, and the modes of living which prevail among them, do not require: intermarriages, too, may have their
effect, or, lastly, there may exist a deterio-
rating principle in the very climate, which
enfeebles the mental, as it *actually does*, the
bodily powers; and, added to the force of
example and the causes assigned above, may
produce the lamentable effect. It might be
adduced as a proof of the debilitating nature of the climate, that a race of people
did certainly once inhabit these regions,
who were much farther advanced in civilization, than the natives were at the discovery
of America, or than their descendants who
inhabit the wilderness are at the present
day. What has become of this people? Are
they extinct? This is possible; but even
in case of utter extermination, we might
reasonably have expected that some tradi-
tion of a people, so far superior in the arts
to themselves, would have remained among
the posterity of their ruthless conquerors.
Did they remove? The extent of country
over which the stupendous monuments of
their existence are scattered, seems almost
a sufficient negative to that idea; but should
the affirmative be admitted, a question, quite
as difficult to answer, presents itself; where
did they settle? They certainly are not now
to be found: wherever these mounds are
discovered, they uniformly bear one distin-
guishing mark—*antiquity*. The question

may, lastly, be viewed in the light which was first suggested: and here you have *my hypothesis:* that the ancestors of the natives of this part of the country, emigrated from the north of Asia, and gradually spread themselves south and east: that they were somewhat advanced in civil arts, but had no knowledge of letters; of course some other method must be adopted, to perpetuate the memory of remarkable events and distinguished persons: that the building or heaping up piles of earth were the means resorted to; and their different forms and sizes no doubt had their peculiar meanings: that from the enervating influence of the climate, this more active race sunk gradually to a level with the more savage tribe who surrounded them: that as their habits of sloth and apathy gained ground, what few arts they possessed, fell into disuse and were forgotten: that as ambition decayed, the motives to great actions were lost; and none being performed, of course no monuments were necessary to record them: and that in the lapse of a few ages, the purposes of their erection were alike disregarded and forgotten: the monuments alone remaining, sole history of themselves, to brave the fury of the elements, and puzzle the brains of Philosophers.

The prairies of this country, so highly extolled, are nothing more or less than large tracts of untimbered land; generally level or nearly so: some are of vast ex-

tent, stretching before the eye until bounded by the horizon; while others are of
quite diminutive size. Many different
theories have been woven to account for
the absence of trees, but I shall not repeat
them: the only beneficial inquiry is, are
they to be considered as advantageous to
the country, or otherwise? On one side it
may be urged, that they are ready cleared
to the hand of the settler, which, to him, is
an entire saving of time and labor: and that
what he does not wish to enclose and culti-
vate, affords pasturage for as many cattle
as he chooses to keep: others will say that
the want of timber for building, fencing and
fuel, and the want of water and shade, are
disadvantages, that more than counterbal-
ance all these benefits: all this is said, on
the supposition that they are uniformly fertile; this, however, is very remote from the
truth. The *low* prairies, are fertile indeed,
but most certainly unhealthful: the *high*, or
at least, a great proportion of them, are
merely *oak barrens*; of a clayey or sandy
soil; the grass they produce, is a tall wild
kind different from that before described;
it affords a nourishing luxuriant pasturage
while springing up, but soon becomes so
hardened that cattle cannot eat it.

I have seen and conversed with many
people, men of understanding, who have
travelled extensively to the west and south
of this place, particularly a missionary from
New-Connecticut: however much they dif-

fered in opinion on many particulars, they all agreed in this, that from what I *have* seen I may fairly judge of what I have *not* seen: that the like sameness prevails in lands and water, habits of the people, and foresight of the speculators. In consequence of these representations, and the disappointments I have every where met with, I have concluded to proceed no farther, but to face about, and, returning by a different route, explore at my leisure the northern parts of this state and Ohio. I contemplate taking a north-easterly direction, as my main course, deviating to the right or left, as fancy or the information I receive, may prompt. As I purpose making some little stay at Cleveland, my next will probably be dated there.

Yours sincerely,

J. S. W.

LETTER VII.

Zanesville, Muskingum Co. Ohio, March 2d, 1819.

My Dear Friend,

I did not expect to address you again until I reached Cleveland, but I have become so fatigued with "marching and counter marching" through this wilderness of mud, that I have thought prudent to make a halt for a few days and rest my weary limbs; but a state of positive idleness is more fatigueing to me than severe exercise; and as

nothing better offers at present, I again
point my pen towards Union-Village.——
Were bodily weariness all that debilitated
my frame, I might even here obtain the rest
required; but my living (nay, dont laugh)
has in this "granary of the world" been so,
I will not say absolutely bad, but rather so
unvaried, morning, noon, and night; there
has been in it so much of that confounded
sameness of which I have so often complain-
ed, that my spirits are beginning to flag:
only think, my dear Sir, for a moment, think
of my fare, and thank your kind stars, that
prevented you from accompanying me; be
thankful, I say, while I assure you, that for
twenty days past, I have not eaten a mouth-
ful of beef steak, oven bread, pudding, pie,
sauce or cheese; nothing in short but one
everlasting dish—"hog, homminy and hoe-
cake." If to this be added, the continual
necessity of wading, half-leg deep, in mud
and water, exposed to the inclemency of
the weather through the day, and at night,
sent to lodge in a half finished room, where,
for lack of mud between the logs, and sometimes for lack of a door, the unwholesome
damps of the night, always considered dele-
terious in this country, were fanning my
broken slumbers; when these things are
told, will you wonder when I assure you,
that my spirits lose their wonted elasticity,
that my strength decays, that my flesh is
wasted, in short that I am reduced to a mere

travelling mummy, or full length figure of an Arab of the desert.

The number of my weary steps has, in all my rambles, been much augmented by the difficulty of keeping the direct road: this difficulty, sufficiently perplexing in the inhabited country, is painfully increased in the woods, where, if a tree happens to fall across the road, no one thinks of disturbing it: new paths are opened, and these, winding about to shun sloughs, underwood, hillocks, windfalls and other obstructions, cross each other in all directions, and involve the "way-worn traveller" in successive labyrinths. To add to his distress, he cannot find one person in five who can direct him three miles from their own doors; nay, more, I have met with numbers, who could not tell me the name of the county or town they lived in, or even that of the Governor of the state. While I am in this desultory mode of writing, I will mention some detached circumstances, and observations that have been neglected in their proper places. We are frequently shocked with unpleasant incidents, which naturally happen where domestic slavery is permitted; but of the horrors of such a state of things, we can have no conception from viewing it in the mild form it assumes in New-York: to be made fully acquainted with the shocking aggregate of torture and contumely, which the wretched children of Africa are doomed to undergo, one must travel south. The picture of slavery, among the Arabs of the desert, as drawn by the masterly hand of a Riley, is *only* a *picture,* a faint imperfect sketch, of the horror-breathing original, as it stalks over the lovely plains of Virginia and Kentucky: I could tell what my eyes have witnessed, but my soul recoils with horror from the recollection, and I gladly drop the subject.

I have conversed with many people, who have removed from the north and east, to this country, who appear dissatisfied with their exchange, and heartily wish themselves reinstated in their former condition: but this being beyond the extent of their means, and feeling restless and uneasy where they were, many had determined to go further. Although the fair goddess of the terrestrial Elysium, would not unveil her beauties in Ohio or Indiana, they still hope to pay their homage at her shrine, in some more favored groves: some expect to find her on the vine-fringed banks of the Arkansaw; some, amid the fragrant meads of the Red River or the Obine; while others, less sanguine, do not expect to overtake her short of the falls of St. Anthony, whither, they think, she has winged her flight, to bless the *infant* colony of the infant Bishop P*****

Speaking of these restless, disappointed wanderers, reminds me of a young gentleman I accidentally became acquainted with. His countenance and deportment interested me, although his dress (as the world goes) added nothing in his favor. I afterwards learned his short history. He was from the east, Boston or its vicinity : his father was in easy circumstances, able to assist his children, whom he wished to keep about him : this young gentleman unhappily was seized with symptoms of the epidemic, with which our eastern friends have been lately visited: I mean the *Ohio fever*. His tender parent did all in his power for his relief, but in vain : nothing but a change of climate seemed likely to effect a cure : he received, as an out-fit, a horse, saddle, bridle, portmanteaus well crammed with clothing, a watch, and six hundred dollars in cash. Thus equipped, he bade his friends adieu, and with spirits buoyed aloft, by the most sanguine hopes of sudden wealth and future greatness, he bounded gaily and rapidly along. The remainder of the tale is soon told ; disappointment crossed his path, and sickness stopped his course : when I saw him he was employed as a common laborer at fifty cents per day : but he was five hundred miles on his journey home : his heart much humbler, and his head much wiser than when, like a prodigal, he left it, like a prodigal to return.

Horses that are driven to this country from the east, must inevitably undergo a seasoning, as it is called, as well as their drivers : the roads are so bad, and their feed so different from what they have been accustomed to, that they soon pine away, and continue in a feeble, sickly state, until they become, in a measure, inured to a different diet. Corn in the ear, and corn blades, are almost the only horse-feed attainable on the road, and a comfortable stable is a rarity.— Corn, indeed, is the principal article of food for man and beast: for while the hogs, horses and cattle are masticating it without doors, the family and dogs are feasting on hoe-cake and homminy within. Cattle are very subject to the slobbers, and in the hot season, the flies torment them, and gorge their blood to such a degree, that they grow thin in the very season when they should thrive best. The article of salt, has ever been, and still is, very high: but people are now in hopes that this evil will be remedied; partially at least. A great number of wealthy men are now engaged in boring in various places: some have already succeeded in obtaining salt water, at the depth of many hundred feet, from which they make salt to great advantage.

I have more than once mentioned the ancient mounds, but neglected to describe one, which is entitled to particular notice. Circleville, a town on the Sciota, Pickaway Co. Ohio, is enclosed with two circular walls of earth, about sixteen feet apart, perhaps twenty feet at the base and ten in height: the open space contains about four acres of ground: there is no appearance of the earth having been removed, within or without the walls; But between them it is somewhat depressed; a circular mound once stood in the centre which is now removed, and a Court-house erected on the spot. Adjoining the circle on the east, is what might be termed a fort; it is square, larger than the circle, with gateways at each corner, and two mounds within the square on the east side: the whole bears marks of design and skill.

Yours as ever,

J. S. W.

LETTER VIII.

Cleveland, March 10th, 1819.

DEAR SIR,

I am here, and my wanderings I hope are at an end. I have explored, to the extent of my wishes, the countries below, embracing a great portion of Ohio and Indiana, and parts of Virginia, Kentucky and Illinois. I have given you my observations and remarks on what I saw in my travels, just as they occurred to my mind, together with all the information (to be relied on) which I have been able to draw from others. It only remains that I should endeavour to collect my scattered ideas, examine my memorandums, and, after comparing, collating and revising, try to present to your view, the countries I have explored, with their advantages and disadvantages; in a more condensed form, and with all the candour and honesty I am possessed of. In doing this, however, I must be allowed to take my own way. I am too little accustomed to writing, to treat this subject methodically; all I promise on that point is, that I will be as clear and concise as possible.

There is in this country a certain class of men who are, undoubtedly, in the possession of great advantages; I have adverted to them before, they are the land-jobbers, the speculators, the rich capitalists, the men who were wealthy when they came here—who were able to purchase large tracts and retail them out, reserving, however, every valuable privilege to themselves; men who were able to build mills, machinery and even towns; they were likewise able to obtain the right of propelling boats by steam, and in their hands, almost exclusively, the great advantages of the steam-boat business center. These men, as I before observed, reside in the towns along the river, they are at the head of all great business, they build elegant mansions, live in style, and diffuse an air of business, life and activity all around them. These circumstances give to the river towns an appearance of wealth and business, which has been the means of deceiving thousands. The conclusion, that where a large flourishing town exists, a fertile and populous country must lie in its rear, is so natural, that it can create no surprise that so many have believed it to be so. These appearances are, however, in a great degree fallacious; it is not the produce of the land, but the profit, drawn by the speculator, from the retail purchaser, which gives such a flourishing aspect to the towns. When we consider the immense sums which have been carried from the east, all of which have been paid in that country for lands and improvements; when we consider too, how much is paid out there yearly, by the multitudes who are continually traversing the country, in all directions, and who never eat a meal without paying for it; when these things are duly considered, we might naturally expect a country to flourish. If a farmer can sell all his surplus produce in his own house, at twenty-five cents a meal, and with no expense or trouble but that of cooking it, what should hinder him from growing rich? and with these advantages some of them have actually done so, but their numbers are comparatively small.*

* From what is here stated, and from what is said in page 19 respecting the prices of various articles of produce, in the Cincinnati market; the unwary reader may be led into a mistake, in estimating the profits of the farmer of that country. In a Cincinnati paper, now in my possession, dated Feb. 2, 1819, are two advertisements, one dated August 25th, 1818, offering 87½ cents per bushel, for good wheat; the other dated January 11th, 1819, offering $1. In Albany, at the same period, it sold for at least $1 75, this fact speaks volumes; and it is hardly necessary to add, what, however, is strictly true, that, owing to the bad state of the roads in that country, the transportation of produce to market, by land, is twice as expensive, as here; and the demand must always be limited, as it will seldom pay freight to New-Orleans. Farmers do, and will continue to sell much of their produce in their own houses, so long as eastern people continue rambling through that country; but that source of profit must be exhausted, sooner or later. Foreign goods, groceries, particularly, are and I believe ever will be very high, on account

The banking establishments are in the hands of the same class of men I have mentioned : a class who own almost every thing worth owning. For a time they were extremely profitable. During the war they made great advances to the officers of government ; and it is often boasted that the army must have been disbanded, had not the Miami Company, furnished Gen. Harrison with funds for its maintainance, at a period of peculiar danger and difficulty. These banks had, during the war, the advantage of receiving as deposits, most of the immense sums, which were profusely poured into this part of the country, for the support and payment of the army and militia ; and for the building and equipment of the naval force on Lake Erie. In their vaults too, have been deposited all the money which has been paid for public lands. While government thus furnished the capital, and was at the same time the best customer, the affairs of the banks went on " in the full tide of successful" operation ; their paper circulated widely, was in good credit ; every thing wore a smiling appearance ; and strangers, nay the people, and even the bankers themselves were deceived. The United States Bank was incorporated, and branches

of the expense of transportation. In January last, brown sugar, was selling in Cincinnati, at 25 cents, coffee 56, hyson skin tea $2 50. Molasses, I never saw while in that country ; the cost of transporting a hogshead of that article, from New-Orleans to Cincinnati, could not, at the steam boat price, amount to less than *forty-eight dollars.*

were established in every state. Do you not recollect reading the newspaper account that the western legislatures were attempting to levy a tax on these branches? At that time I could not conjecture the cause of this hostility; but I now find the reason very obvious; the United States branches were in future to be the places of deposit for all monies belonging to the government, thus at a blow, depriving the state banks of their capital. The stockholders raged and swore, the legislatures blustered and enacted laws; the judges of the supreme court of the United States declared these laws unconstitutional, and the states must submit. In the mean time, the branch agents receive the state notes in payment for stock, and then call on the banks for specie; this measure almost drove the bankers to despair; but a blow still more serious awaited them, the branches having drawn the specie from the state banks, into their own vaults, commenced business and as a home thrust, issued an order "that nothing should be received from the people in payment of their debts to the general government, but United States paper or specie." This unexpected blow laid the whole state banking interest prostrate, and rendered their paper, as was waggishly observed, "the substance of things *hoped for*, the evidence of things *not seen*." The effect of these measures was not confined to the rich; the trader, the manufacturer, the farmer, the mechanic, in short, every class of people felt the shock; their debts must be paid, or their land forfeited ; every newspaper was filled with the advertisements of brokers, offering great premiums for United States bills, or eastern paper, (which was equivalent.) Every mouth in community was calling to the passing yankee, (while every hand laid hold on his button,) " have you got any eastern bills—twelve, fifteen, twenty per cent for eastern bills—eastern bills—eastern bills." Knaves tried to take advantage of the avidity of the people, and thousands of dollars in *spurious* eastern bills were thrown into circulation. The people who were thus imposed on, however, comforted themselves with the reflection, that the rogues had gained little by the exchange.

I have frequently spoken of the soil and qualities of the land in the places through which I have passed ; and as these are the principal points which engage the attention of most people, I will venture a few more remarks on the subject, although I am sensible they must appear to be mere repetitions. These countries, collectively, have been long and loudly extolled, as exceeding all others, in point of soil and natural productions, and in a limited sense, perhaps, the boast is not altogether false ; for if any reliance can be placed in my judgment, many, very many thousand acres of river bottom land, equal, if not surpass, the best lands in the state of New-York. These bottoms, in their natural state send forth an astonishing growth of vegetation; and when cultivated as they should be, generously repay the hand that tills them. The natural growth of timber on these lands, are sycamore, black-walnut, honey-locust, buck-eye, black-gum and pawpaw: this last bears a fruit resembling a cucumber, which some people are quite fond of. Many of these different kinds of trees grow to an enormous size. Grape vines too, of surprising luxuriance, entwine themselves around at least every fifth tree; and weeds and wild plants of an enormous growth fill up every vacancy. Some tracts of upland too may safely be pronounced good; but on an average, I think, they are not of the first quality. The timber of the uplands (remember I am speaking in general terms) is principally white-oak; with here and there a mixture of hickory, and what we call white-wood, here called poplar. Beech and maple are very rare. The soil of the upland, is almost every where the same, consisting of a whitish clay mixed sometimes with gravel, though usually with sand, insomuch, that when brick are wanted, they generally find the materials as completely mixed as the most skilful brickmaker could desire. This mixture, however, is very inconvenient to the farmer; if the season is a little too wet his lands are a bed of mortar, if too dry it is so baked as to be almost impenetrable. These countries are not so level as is generally thought;

they differ little in that respect from New York, and I verily believe, that a tract of country, cannot be produced in the Ohio valley, of an extent equal to the state of New-York, which contains as great a proportion of good farming land. Travellers are frequently deceived by false appearances ; they pass through this country in the growing season, when corn stalks, wheat-straw and weeds, exhibit such a wonderfully luxuriant growth : surely, surely, they exclaim, this is the most fertile country on earth. These hasty opinions have given to the country are putation, which I sincerely think it does not deserve ; the question of comparative fertility should never be decided until after harvest ; in *that day* New-York will never blush at a comparison with her younger sisters.

Farewell.

J. S. W

LETTER IX.

Cleveland, March 13th, 1819

My Friend,

I shall continue the subjects commenced in my last. The country, its advantages and disadvantages were under consideration. The water of a country is one of its most important articles ; where the water is good we usually find the people healthy, and *vice versa.* If this will hold good as a

general rule, and none I believe will dispute
it, what must we think of the country we
are speaking of? Its waters are almost universally impregnated with lime, more or
less; its taste is extremely unpleasant, and
its effects are almost always felt by the new
settlers, especially among the little ones; it
usually produces a dysentery which sweeps
away the poor innocents by hundreds, before they have been a year in the country.
But its ill effects are not confined to infants;
adults must undergo a seasoning, which to
many constitutions is too hard a trial. I
witnessed a scene at Cincinnati which will
ever be impressed on my memory; a family was landing from a boat in circumstances
of peculiar affliction : a widow, who had the
day before, buried her husband thirty miles
up the river, where he had died on their
passage, now arrived with her three beautiful, interesting children. If ever, my dear
friend, I felt the genuine glow of sympathy,
if ever a tear of sacred pity decorated my
cheek, it was on this occasion; a wretched
mother, bereft of her husband, her fatherless
children clinging around her, far, far from
all friends, thrown as it were among strangers, destitute of the means of obtaining
support or even a shelter from the weather;
borne down with grief, but not a solitary
being to whom she might unburden her heart,
from whom she could expect either counsel
or relief. But however affecting the situation of this poor forlorn wanderer was to

me, I soon found that her case was by no
means a singular one ; instances of this kind
frequently occur among the emigrants ;
some of which have been within my own
knowledge. One man whom I left sick at
Hamilton, died before his family had got
in readiness to embark. Another died at
Cincinnati during my stay there, who had
seven children with him ; some of them however were of age : no attention was paid to
this family during the sickness of the father,
the funeral charges cost them thirteen dollars. The last season was said to have been
uncommonly sickly. At fort Harrison and
its vicinity, it is said, one fourth part of the
inhabitants died in the short space of three
months : Harmony Society on the Wabash
lost a great number of its members of the
same fever : in the burying ground at Vincennes I counted about fifty graves which
appeared to have been made within a year ;
speaking of this, brings to recollection a circumstance that nothing but my sincere in-
tention of representing facts and objects
just as they exist, could induce me to mention. The church-yard belonging to the
largest religious society at Cincinnati, pre-
sented a most disgraceful instance of a total
indifference to the sanctity of the sepulchre,
and repose of the dead ; it is entirely unen-
closed, lying open to the streets, with wag-
on roads over the graves, and many of the
headstones broken down ; and in this situation, it has, I am informed, remained for se-

veral years: the subject, I was pleased to
find, had at length attracted attention, several severe remarks have appeared in the
public prints, and I hope for the honor of
human nature this foul stain may shortly be
wiped away. But to return to my subject,
I was speaking of the water of the country,
but, I scarcely know how, got to descant-
ing on very different topics. I asserted that
the waters were almost universally impregnated with lime and tasted extremely unpleasant; I now add, that *generally*, where
the land is best, there the water is worst.
—The rich bottom lands are intersected
by bayaus, or inlets, which receive water
from the rivers at their rise, and retain them
to stagnate, and putrify, during the exces-
sive heat of the summer; a season that the
most hardy anticipate with unpleasant ap-
prehensions. One of the bad effects, perhaps the most pernicious, of the insalubrity
of the water, is, that it forms an apology for
drinking ardent spirits, commonly whiskey;
such quantities of this vile liquid are consu-
med in the country, that distilling may be
considered the safest and most profitable
business that is carried on; the demand for
it is so steady that if a person wants only
half a barrel he must bespeak it some time
before it is called for, and it is a common
thing, to see the jugs of the customers, stand
waiting their turn to receive the poisonous
drug as it runs from the still. The distiller
pays twenty-five cents per bushel for corn,

and usually gets seventy-five, per gallon, for the whiskey: hence you may judge the profits of the business, and of the state of society, where it is thus supported. These distilleries are the curse of the country; more deadly in their effects than the tree of Java, they are fatal not only to the animal life, but to the moral and intellectual. The Bohon Upas destroys only the body; while it is greatly to be feared, the baleful influence of whiskey endangers the soul.

In speaking of the soil of this country, there is one circumstance I have hitherto omitted, but is too important to be neglected: it is incapable of withstanding the effects of a long drought. The rains here fall so heavily that the surface of the earth becomes, as it were, a bed of mortar, and is so filled with water, that notwithstanding the great proportion of clay, it seems to be incapable of retaining it, but suffers it to leak off so rapidly that subterranean streams are formed, which, no doubt, cause those great sinks in the land, which are so frequently to be seen, and occasion, by their under-drains, the springs to become dry, almost as soon as the rivers. Hence arises, that standing apology for the negligent culture of the land. It is a favorite maxim that the less the ground is stired, the longer it will retain its moisture—hence they never plough, and seldom hoe their corn; hence it is that seeding with English grass is much neglected: it cannot withstand the extreme ter meal than I had tasted for a month previous. I shall probably write you again before I leave this place.

Yours,

J. S. W.

<hr>

LETTER X.

Cleveland, March 16th, 1819.

MY DEAR SIR,

I expect you feel an anxiety to hear something of this place and its neighbourhood, and I would joyfully attempt to gratify you : but we must both be patient. I have many fine things yet to say about the lower countries and until I have said them, I can talk on no other subject. We have been discussing the advantages and disadvantages of the country below at large : if I have said more about the latter than the former, I have at least two weighty and cogent reasons for so doing ; the first is, because these advantages are few in number ; the second, because they are all engrossed. I have stated, and I now repeat, that there are many wealthy people, who reside, almost to a man, in the large towns ; they are engaged in, and control, almost all the profitable business of the country, and every man of capital, that removes there, from the east or north, uniformly invests his property in the same or similar schemes. Their business may continue profitable some time longer, but eventually, must decline. The spirit of rivalship will soon destroy the profits of the manufacturers, and land-jobbing has already become dull in the section of country we are considering: in the rage of speculating, many men bought in at extravagant rates and must sell at a loss. Those who now expect to make a profit by the rise of land, must resort to the Obine, Missouri and Arkansas. From what I have said you will perceive the truth of these remarks, that to the poor man every avenue to wealth is sealed up—that the advantages of the country are engrossed by (comparatively speaking) a few men, and that this body of citizens pay no attention to the great source of all profit, the cultivation of the earth :— the agricultural interests being left to the management of the indolent, loitering, tipling race of mortals, I have so often spoken of, and, I think, by this time, you have some idea of their skill and assiduity. I have frequently had occasion to mention the *sameness* or want of variety, which overspreads these regions : it prevails indeed to a degree that I believe to be unparalelled on the face of the *civilized* earth : I speak in general terms, and exceptions are always supposed : with this proviso, a description of one tract of country, one river bottom, one bayau, one body of upland, one country town, one plantation, one family, and one pack of dogs, would, with a little addition of light or shade, (as the case might be) afford a tolerably correct representation of any, or every other object of the same denomination, which would be seen in a course of two months travelling. I will give you a specimen. A log house, containing one room—chimney out side—chinks of the logs filled with mud—one or more windows—the sash filled with old hats, cradle-blankets, petticoats, paper or glass, according to the taste, fortune or whim of the owner—a log barn with an open threshing-floor—the grain stacked out—a corn crib or two of poles—a little corn in each—a log stable, and a log spring house, when they are so fortunate as to have a spring. The family who inhabit this splendid mansion, are clothed in linsey-woolsey. The men and boys wear hunting shirts and leggins; you will excuse me from attempting to describe the costume of the ladies, as, with all my veneration for the fair sex, I am quite unequal to the task. I would only remark that stripe seemed to be the favorite material. When an eastern traveller passes, he is usually complimented with an enlivening peal of vocal musick, from a full choir of canine performers, who keep time and chord most admirably, except now and then, for a few moments, when they just stop to bite a little: should the traveller return this piece of civility, by gently tapping their heads with his cudgel (just to let them know he understands beating time,) and by this means break up the

concert, his ears will probably be greeted
by the enchanting sound of a female voice,
sweetly pronouncing accents like these "see!
there goes a yankey, only do but see how
he looks—all dressed up, in a cloth coat,
and cloth jacket, and cloth trousers."
Should the traveller turn his eye toward the
house, at this interesting and critical moment, he would, probably, be blessed with
a glimpse of the fair damsel, whose curiosity he had excited, as she modestly peeps,
like John Rogers' wife in the primer, from
behind a dozen half-naked smiling cherubs,
who fill up the door-way : and happy, indeed, twice happy, should that yankey
think himself, who escapes without losing
his heart, or a slice from the calf of his leg.
One may travel here an hundred miles
without finding a bridge : a school-house is
rarely to be seen ; a church more seldom
still.* The little attention paid to educa-
tion, and to even the outward forms of religion, affords to the reflecting mind, a very
melancholy view, in regard to the morals
and character, of the rising generation.

* It cannot be amiss, in this place, to present the reader with
the following extract from the last Annual Report of the Direc-
tors of the " *Washington County Bible Society, N. Y.*" which shews
that the want of bibles in this section of the United States is no
less deplorable than the scarcity of churches.

" By missionaries, who have explored the western parts of the
United States and estimated their wants, it is reported, that in
Tennessee there were 10,000 families, in Louisiana 8,000, in the
Mississippi Territory 5,000, in Missouri, Illinois and Indiana,
12,000, in Ohio 13,000, and in the state of Kentucky 30,000 fami-
lies without a copy of the Word of life."

Perhaps it would be profitable for an unbeliever in divine revelation (if a man of this stamp can be found who is otherwise a man of sense) to take a tour through this country. He might here see, what so many of them have pretended a desire to see—*society without religion:* with minds free and unshackled : not a particle of traditional prejudice to warp their understandings; their reason left free and unbiased, and no human impediments to prevent them from " choosing the good and refusing the evil." *Yes, such a state of society exists,* and an infidel would be appalled at a view of it. A glance would be sufficient; he would see the long black catalogue of proofs that our nature is depraved, sunk as it were, in a sea of moral polution, to a depth that human assistance cannot reach, from whence divine power alone can *save :* where love divine only would *look.* Yes, I repeat it, *such a state of society exists,* and the proofs of it are open, palpable, undeniable and undenied. Although every county has its *seat of justice,* as they are termed, yet people, most frequently, depend on their own personal powers, for the redress of their real or imaginary grievances ; and the most powerful arm generally wins the cause ; except when, as has sometimes happened, the knife or dirk of one of the combatants ends the awful conflict. This heathenish mode of deciding controversies is so frequently resorted to, that the sight of persons disfigured by having an eye gouged out, or a nose, lip, ear, or finger bit off, is too common to excite surprise or disgust, after a person has been a short time in the country.

From the absence of religious impressions, arises, no doubt, the frequency of breaches and dissolutions of the matrimonial contract, and the numerous instances of people who have left families in the eastern States, being permitted to live here in a state of open, undisguised adultery. To the same cause too, may be fairly attributed, the inordinate avarice and desire of over-reaching, which is so prominent a trait in the character of this people, from the great landholder who persuades you to purchase a farm at triple its value, who recommends, as salubrious, a situation where the settler would lose half his family the first year, who would induce you to buy a town lot, at an exhorbitant price, on a spot where three log cabins will never be found within gun-shot, or try to sell you a mill-seat, on a stream that would not drive a grindstone, three months of the twelve—down, through every humbler grade of paltry *take-ins*, to the lazy, avaricious clown, who will not assist the traveller to cross the swollen brook, or even guide his steps the shortest distance, without demanding an extortionate recompence for his services:—from the pompous Nabob who will defraud you of a thousand dollars, with all imaginable politeness, down to the profane, quarrelsome, whiskey-blotch-

ed boatman, who will tell twenty lies, or
swear twenty oaths, to cheat, or bully you
out of sixpence. I am weary of the subject
and hasten to conclude though I have by no
means exhausted it: after reviewing every
circumstance on both sides of the question,
I have no hesitation in saying, that I would
rather have a conveniently situated farm in
one of the New-England states, or in New-
York, than almost any that could be offered in the south western country: and, I
sometimes could wish it was possible, to ex-
tend a warning voice to every family in the
east: to bid them beware, how they suffer
themselves to be seduced from their comfortable homes, and transport themselves
to a country, which, to the poorer class at
least, is a "bourn, from whence *few families* return:"—and that they never, on any
conditions, or under any circumstances, remove their families, until they have first
seen and judged for themselves. That country has been highly extolled for its fertility,
the mildness of its climate, the facility of
getting a living, and the wealth of the inhabitants: on the first point, I have already
expressed my opinion decidedly; on the
second, I remark, that I prefer snow to
mud :* on the third, I answer, that if a fami-

---

*When speaking in this way of mud, I would not be under-
stood to say that it does not freeze there; on the contrary, I can
assure the reader, that it not only freezes intensely, but that the
changes from heat to cold, and vice versa, during the winter, are
frequent, and very sudden. The effect on the constitution, of
such violent and unlooked-for changes may be duly estimated

ly in the east, would content themselves with just such living as the western people enjoy, they may remain where they are and a very moderate share of labor will be sufficient to acquire it: on the fourth, that (speculators &c. excepted) if the people of that country are *really wealthy,* they possess the art of hiding their riches, in a greater degree than any people I ever saw or read of; for, I believe it is the last thing of which a traveller would accuse or suspect them.

But however others may judge of the country, for myself, I will close with saying, that I shall never cease to be grateful to the wise and kind Disposer of all events; that my disappointments prevented me from removing my family at once, as I had originally intended. You will probably hear from me again, as I propose taking a view of the Holland Purchase before I return home.

Yours, &c.

J. S. W.

LETTER XI.

Fredonia, Chatauque Co. N. Y. April 15th, 1819.

My Dear Sir,

In my last from Cleveland, I suggested the probability of my writing again:

by every person of reflection. While on this subject, it is, perhaps, proper to repeat, that the damp evening air of this country, is extremely prejudicial to health; to northern constitutions, exposures to it are peculiarly dangerous, after the fatigue and perspiration, of a hot summer's day.

I had however little idea, at that time, of taking the tour I have since performed. I proceeded as far as Batavia on my way home, and took a pretty extensive view of the eastern part of the Holland Purchase; but not being perfectly satisfied, and hearing a certain situation highly extolled in Portage county, Ohio, forty miles south of Cleveland, I was induced to return and examine it. In doing this and including the distance from Cleveland to Batavia, I have travelled five hundred miles, since I left the former place. The particular object that drew me back, did not exactly meet my wishes; but the Connecticut Reserve (in which it is situated) is in general, a fine body of land for farming: the water is tolerably good; but the immense number of marshes, ponds and small lakes, which are spread over the country, are certainly an inconvenience, and one would naturally suppose might be injurious to health: the inhabitants, however, say otherwise, and their florid looks give a pleasing assurance of the truth of their assertions.—There is a tract of land running parallel with the Lake, from three to five miles in width, on which the Lake road runs. The soil is a mixture of gravel and loam, and it appears as pleasant and productive as could be wished. The timber is chiefly oak and chestnut, with some other kinds intermixed of a really heavy growth. Further back the country is handsomely rolling and well watered, the timber chiefly beech and maple, though white oak is quite frequent; the soil is generally a dark loam with sometimes a mixture of gravel. There are many handsome and well cultivated farms, with large and convenient houses : the barns well filled and the cattle looking thrifty. The inhabitants are principally from Connecticut : an industrious, enterprising people ; and the difference between industry and indolence, was never more strikingly displayed than in the two sections of Ohio I have lately been exploring; for the north is by far the best cultivated, and the people appear to be thriving in full proportion to their assiduity. The beautiful rolling make of the land, the ever varying scenery, the extensive improvements, the elegant, painted houses, the lofty spires of the village churches, and even the sportive groups of decently clothed, well-behaved children, going to, or returning from school, form so strong a contrast with the dull uniformity of the land, mean habitations, slovenly apparel and coarse manners, of the people of the lower country, that the traveller is almost led to believe himself transported to a land inhabited by a different order of beings. The charm is complete, when the easy manners, refined conversation and open, cheerful countenances of the people, assure him a welcome reception in every house he enters. This tract (Connecticut Reserve) in point of soil and fertility is equal, perhaps, to the best parts of New-York, and was it within the limits of that state, I could certainly recommend it, to those who are determined to emigrate: but, my friend, it is within the jurisdiction of Ohio, and that circumstance, alone, is sufficient, in my estimation to reduce its value, at least fifteen per cent. This opinion, may, perhaps, appear somewhat fastidious and romantic: but I am serious in it, and were you as well acquainted with the government, laws and institutions of that state as I believe myself to be, I should entertain no doubts of your hearty concurrence in my opinion.

The town of Cleveland is situated on lake Erie, two hundred miles, west by south, from Buffalo, at the mouth of the Cayuhoga river within the Connecticut reserve. It is a pleasant, flourishing place, and being the first town of eastern people I had entered, after leaving Hamilton, I felt myself quite at home, although at so great a distance, and passed the time I was by business detained there so agreeably, that I was soon perfectly restored to my usual health and spirits. It was the endearing society of the east, and I felt the powerful ties by which nature attaches us to the objects of our early affections.

Chatauque is the most western county of New-York; it is bounded on the east by Catteraugus, south and west by Pennsylvania, and by lake Erie on the north. It contains large tracts of excellent land cov

ered with a fine growth of every kind of
timber natural to the climate, the surface
gently undulating, the soil, in general, a
dark loam mixed with gravel; and water is
plenty and of the best quality. The soil
seems perfectly natural to the best kinds of
grain, fruit and grass; and the streams are
stored with a variety of excellent fish. Its
situation, with respect to markets, is truly
admirable, the farmer may choose between
the Canada, the New-York and the Ohio
markets; at the latter, his butter and cheese,
will always command the highest price, having the preference to their own, which is,
not unfrequently, tainted by the noxious
plants I have mentioned. This county is
included in the Holland Purchase: the a-
gent Mr. W. Peacock, lives in Maysville,
at the head of Chautaugue lake, seven miles
from the lake Erie road. Lands sell from
three to five dollars; eight years credit;
two without interest. This, I think, is the
best chance for obtaining good land, I have
yet met with. Early frosts have never injured corn here, since the first settlement,
nor have droughts ever seriously affected
the crops of any kind.

The north west township, called Ripley,
I think the pleasantest part of the tract; in
that town, about five miles south of the lake
road, excellent lots may be had at five dollars per acre, on the usual credit. The
land insensibly rises from the lake towards
the land in question, perhaps two hundred

feet ; it is a beautiful rolling tract of country, covered with beech, maple, ash, elm, lyme and other timber, chequered with numerous limpid streams, meandering in every direction ; the land generally inclining to the south and west. Here, my dear sir, I have found a situation, far more agreeable to my mind, than any place I have seen in my six months' wanderings ; a situation which nearly answers (if the thing be possible) the exalted notions I had entertained of the south western country. If every person who has imbibed the same high opinion of Indiana, Illinois, &c. would first take a view of Chatauque he might perhaps avoid the life of corroding reflection and bitter regret, that so many, within my knowledge, are now leading. There are many families here, who have been over the whole ground, but finding no situation to their mind, and having the means in their possession, returned, and at length, settled here, declaring themselves perfectly satisfied, in the election they have made. It would be unpardonable not to mention, that wherever I have been, the men of talents, information and enlarged views, speak of the state of New-York, in terms of high encomium. It seems generally to be considered, the first state in the Union, and its laws, courts, institutions and usages are quoted as the highest authority. The grand canal, in particular, is at this time the leading subject of inquiry, and its progress is viewed with deep interest, and in-

creasing admiration. I felt, I must acknowledge, some little degree of state pride, to
hear a Virginian of some eminence, declare,
that none but Yorkers could originate the
bold conception of uniting lake Erie with
the Atlantic, and that New-York alone was e-
qual to the task of completing a project, which
the general government very modestly de-
clined. Many merchants on the Ohio, men
of business and practical knowledge, gave
it as their opinion, that when the canal is
finished, goods may be transported from the
city of New-York, on that route, as low
down as St. Louis, cheaper than from New-
Orleans. The steam-boat proprietors of the
Ohio, of course, look with some degree of ap-
prehension, at the rapid progress of the work;
it may possibly interrupt the march of their
monopolies; the time may come when they
will no longer think it prudent, to charge
five dollars per hundred for the transportation of goods from New-Orleans to the falls
of Ohio, and one hundred dollars for a pas-
senger the same distance; but the owners,
and consumers of goods, will be benefited;
and they rejoice in the prospect of a comple-
tion of the stupendous undertaking. "New-
York and Cincinnati, say they, will be, by
this means, brought within two hundred
miles of each other, and the east and west
will be united, in the powerful bond of mu-
tual interest and reciprocal advantages."
I was happy to find by the papers I saw in
Batavia, that all parties in our state are at

length united in support of this grand undertaking ; it will open an inland water communication, such as no country on earth can equal. When completed, the Michigan territory will present a wide field for the surplus population of the east ; there an active, industrious and moral people, may transplant their excellent institutions. The soil, I am informed, is of a superior quality, and the climate more congenial to northern constitutions, than the sultry swamps or scorched prairies, of the lower countries. As I expect to set out on my return in a few days, your patience will no longer be taxed with the dull detail of my wanderings.

Adieu.

JOHN S. WRIGHT.